PRICELESS

Amato Brothers Book Three

WINTER RENSHAW

PRICELESS

WINTER RENSHAW

COVER DESIGN: Louisa Maggio

COVER MODEL: Joseph Cannata

EDITING: The Passionate Proofreader

PRICELESS

DEDICATION

For my husband. Ours is the most priceless adventure of all.

xoxo

Winter

PRICELESS

DESCRIPTION

It was New Year's Eve, and I should've been ringing in the night with cheap champagne and bad decisions at home in New York. Instead I found myself holed up in some hotel room in southern California.

But I wasn't alone.

I was in the company of a fellow stranded traveler by the name of Cristiano. We spent one night together – forced into the same hotel room by the snowstorm that cancelled our flights and changed our lives.

His dimpled smile, panty-melting kisses, and charming wit were a temporary distraction from the chaos of the day . . . or the past year. But as soon as morning broke, I set my sights on getting home. I rented a car, mapped out my 2,749 mile journey, and packed my bags.

Only Cristiano insisted on joining me. He needed to get home, too. His best friend was getting married on Saturday. And he refused to let me go it alone. It wasn't safe, he said.

Trekking across country with an alluring stranger was certainly one of the more adventurous moments of my life. Falling for him was certainly one of the most daring. But uncovering his secrets? That was the most challenging. And the truth I learned . . . would shatter us both.

PRICELESS

Chapter One

Daphne

I'm pretty sure wine is the only thing that is going to save me today.

Or one of those tiny bottles of vodka they give you on the plane.

And at this point, I'm willing to save a little time and drink it straight: no mixer, no chaser.

Checking my watch, I mentally calculate that I'll be on my flight in less than an hour, biting my nails until we take off and the in-flight beverage service comes by.

Shoulder to shoulder with grouchy holiday travelers on New Year's Eve in a small, southern California airport isn't ideal, but my twin sister, Delilah, called me this morning, frantic and telling me the doctor thinks she's going to go into labor any day now despite the fact that she's not due for two more weeks. She was spouting off a bunch of things about centimeters and contractions, all the while sounding like a crazy person. I tuned out the part where she discussed the current state of her cervix in great detail and tuned back in just in time to hear the panic in her voice when she realized there was a good chance I might not make it home in time.

"I'll be there," I promised her at the time. *"No matter what. I'll move heaven and earth. I won't miss it. Don't worry. Just keep your legs squeezed together really, really tight."*

She laughed at the time, but I still heard the worry in her voice. Our oldest sister, Demi, will be there, and obviously Delilah's husband, Zane, but being twins, we've always done everything together. We're impossibly close. And it would *break my heart* not to be there.

Glancing around the crowded airport, I scan the length of the line before me. At least eight people wait ahead, and the woman currently congesting this process seems to have her shit strewn out on the tile floor, rearranging items and shoving her giant hair dryer and moving several hardcover Stephen King books from her checked bag to her carry-on.

Sighing in commiseration with my fellow travelers, I watch as she zips her bag and hoists it back onto the scale. The face of the Jet Stream airways attendant says it all, and the woman begrudgingly yanks her bag away and attempts to reconfigure her baggage situation once more.

It's safe to say we're going to be here a while.

Out of pure boredom, I take another gander at the folks in line behind me. It appears I'm in the company of predominantly baby boomers and parents with young children who aren't having any part of this travel stuff. I'm guessing all the people my age are wisely out living it up, ringing in the new year with cheap champagne and bad decisions.

God, I was hoping I'd get a chance to make a bad decision tonight.

Guess there's always next year . . .

Two years ago, I rang in the new year in Paris with my Parisian lover who turned out to be a royal scumbag.

Last year, I rang in the new year at home with my family, quietly nursing a recent breakup with a professional football player named Weston. He was still madly in love with his ex but kept his feet planted in denial until I finally showed him the writing on the wall. And that was the end of something that could've been pretty freaking amazing.

A job interview at a small, private fine arts college landed me here this week, and I was planning to meet up with some old college friends in Vegas tonight, but Delilah's cervix thinned, or whatever, and now here I am.

I'm seconds from facing forward again to reassess the state of this slow moving line when my eye catches a tall man, approximately my age, with messy dark hair and a laser sharp stare pointed directly at me. My heart skips for a second, and I face the front of the line. I'm not sure it's possible to physically feel someone staring at me, but my entire backside is tingling and warm. Not the front. Just the back. My ass, if I want to get specific.

I'm half flattered, half annoyed, and one-hundred percent determined to ignore his shameless behavior when all of a sudden a loud chime plays above the chatter and drone of anxious travelers.

"Attention passengers," a woman's muffled, muddled voice comes over the intercom at Seaview International Airport. "Flight 802 with nonstop service from Seaview to Dulles International Airport in Washington, D.C. has been canceled. Please report to your nearest Red Jet Airways desk for further information."

I lift a brow, release a breath, and silently sympathize for the hundred-plus passengers whose hopes of ringing in the new year in another part of the country have suddenly been dashed.

The line moves ahead, and I grip the handle of my wheel-y

bag and move ahead an entire eighteen inches.

Yay, progress.

A man in front of me wears a frown as he checks his phone.

"They're saying almost two feet of snow in some parts," I hear him tell his wife. "And even more tomorrow."

His wife covers her mouth with her hand, her eyes holding worry. "I was hoping we'd be able to get back before the storm hit. You think they'll cancel ours next?"

The man shrugs, dragging his thumb down the screen of his phone as he reads. "Possibly. The storm's moving north now. Parts of Maryland are without power already. All of Baltimore is covered in a sheet of ice."

She clasps a palm at her chest, twisting a gold cross necklace between her fingers, the corners of her mouth pulled down. "Surely they'd have said something by now. Our plane boards in an hour."

"You're right, Margaret," he says, slipping his phone in his pocket and putting his arm around his wife's shoulders. "We have nothing to worry about. They'd have canceled by now."

The line moves ahead once more, and I check the time before scanning the area behind me again. Tucking a strand of white-blonde hair behind my ear, I peek from the corner of my eye and accidentally meet *his* gaze again.

The dark-haired guy.

He's *still* staring at me.

Whipping my attention toward the front of the line, I realize there's a good three-foot gap between me and the couple ahead. That's what I get for paying more attention to the Greek Adonis behind me and not watching the line.

Clearing my throat, I pick my bruised ego off the floor and pull my bag ahead. The lady with the overweight bag appears to be long gone, which explains why the line's finally moving.

Dragging in a long breath, I dig my hand into the front pocket of my jeans to retrieve my ID. I stuck it in there before I got in line because I hate to be that person standing at the desk, dumping out their ridiculously overstuffed purse in search of their license because they failed to prepare for their turn.

I'm a bit of a budding world traveler. I love to fly. I love to jet-set across oceans and continents, countries and states. I've flown dozens of times in the last few years alone. Preparation is my middle name.

My heart jolts a little when the tips of my fingers feel nothing but the cotton lining of my pocket. I check the other side, my blood running cold with panic. The line moves again. I'm next. Sitting my purse down, I shove both my hands down the front and then back pockets of my jeans, digging deep and coming up with nothing but lint. I'm sure I look like a crazy person, but I'm dead set on finding my ID.

It's in here.

I *know* it is.

My mind functions in warp speed, replaying my earlier steps and wondering if there was any possible way I somehow *thought* I put my ID in my pocket but actually forgot. Mentally retracing my steps, I think back to my hotel room. My bag was packed. My purse was lying on a table by the door. I checked out. Hailed a cab . . .

My mind runs blank.

I could've sworn I grabbed my ID from my wallet after I paid the cab driver.

Yes.

I was standing on the sidewalk of the drop off lane.

I *know* I did.

There's a quick tap on my shoulder and a shadowed presence behind me. My body freezes as I'm startled out of my own thoughts, and I turn to face this person that dares to interrupt me at this horribly inopportune moment.

"You dropped this . . . *Daphne*." The handsome stranger wears a half smirk and flicks my driver's license between two fingers before handing it over.

"Oh, God." I swipe it from his grasp. "Thank you."

"Sorry for staring," he says, his eyes almost smiling, as if he's not *truly* sorry. "I wanted to make sure this was you. You should be more careful. This gets in the wrong hands and you never know what could happen."

My words catch in my throat as my brows meet. I'm appreciative of his good deed but not in the mood for a lecture.

"Next," the woman behind the desk calls out.

His gaze flicks over my head, and I turn around to see that I'm, in fact, next.

"That's me," I say. Turning back, I start to tell him, "Thanks for . . ."

But he's already returned to his place in line.

I check my baggage, get my boarding pass scanned, and make a mad dash toward security. The waiting area just outside security is packed like sardines in a can, and squeezing myself through the thick crowd proves to be a bit of a challenge, but I make it to the escalator and breathe a sigh of relief when I see the actual security line isn't half as long as I thought it would be. I'm sure a lot of that has to do with stranded travelers, and I can't help but feel for them.

I'd hate to be in their shoes.

I'd probably cry.

By the time I make it past the initial checkpoint, I'm yanking off my shoes and shoving all of my things into a gray bin. Checking my jeans pockets, I'm doubly relieved to feel the hard plastic of my ID in the left front pouch.

As much traveling as I've done over the last couple of years, I should be a pro at this. This *so* isn't me. I'm not this disorganized. I'm not so easily rattled.

"Next," the security guard calls. We make eye contact and he motions me forward, his front two fingers bent and his lips holding a flat line.

I step forward, let them scan my body, and immediately receive a green light. Glancing back, I watch for my gray bin to come down the conveyor and unintentionally spot the tall, dark, and mysteriously fetching stranger readying to come through. Wearing fitted indigo jeans and a simple gray t-shirt that clings to the curves and muscled bulges that make up his torso, he motions for the guard to step closer, and then he says something. The guard then turns to another and makes some kind of hand signal. A third guard appears from out of nowhere and pulls the stranger aside to begin a patdown.

Weird.

My bin finally comes through, and I grab my purse and leather Oxfords, locating a nearby bench so I can get these things back on. They're easy to pull off and impossible to put back on. I should've known better than to travel in these, but at least I won't have to take them off again. This is a non-stop, direct flight from Seaview, California to JFK International in New York.

Tugging and pulling, I wriggle my heel into my left shoe and prepare to begin again with the right.

"You don't have to do that, you know," a man's voice says from my right.

I glance up.

It's *him*. Again.

"You don't have to go through the x-ray machine," he clarifies. His brows meet when he glances up at it. "It's invasive. I don't like it. You can request a patdown."

I snort. "Because having someone's hands all over you is somehow *less* invasive?"

"I'm fine with someone professionally touching the outside of my clothes," he says. "I'm not fine with someone checking me out naked because the government tells them it's okay."

I shove my right heel into my shoe and stand up to jam it in a little better, bracing myself on a nearby window ledge. Outside it's sunny and these Californian skies are baby blue and cloudless. It's hard to imagine there's a snowpocalypse sweeping the northeast as we speak.

"Good to know," I say with a mild smile, politely pretending to be appreciative of his second round of unsolicited advice. I could give a rat's ass if someone sees me naked. I've modeled nude in enough art classes that taking off my clothes is a bit of a pastime at this point.

Glancing at my phone, I realize I'm boarding in fifteen minutes, and I still need to grab a book and some coffee for the plane.

"Have a good flight." I sling my purse over my shoulder and trek toward the coffee cart halfway down Terminal A. Perusing the menu, I decide on a half-caf soy latte with cinnamon and sugar-free vanilla syrup because just thinking about the snowflakes I'll be feeling on my face in a mere five hours and some change makes me crave something warm and comforting in my belly.

I place my order and slip the cashier a five-dollar bill and exact change.

"Thank you," I say to the cashier, re-adjusting my purse strap on my shoulder and tightening my grip on the coffee. The paper cup is comfortably warm in my palm, and I can already practically taste the rich, bold flavor on my tongue.

Turning on my heels, I find myself face to face with *him* again. He's right up on me. His deliciously clean scent invades my airspace, and I could probably calculate the distance between our faces in mere inches. But the sheer unexpectedness of his proximity to me causes me to stop hard in my tracks, which then proceeds to cause the scalding coffee in my cup to splash up over the lid, dribbling molten brown liquid all over my shoes.

"Wonderful," I sigh, lifting my cup and moving out of the way.

His hand reaches for me, gently gripping my forearm. "I'm so sorry."

He sounds genuine. This time. It's not like earlier, when he was "apologizing" for staring at me. This time his eyes are softer and his expression is void of any kind of ornery glint or smiling eyes.

"I was looking at the menu. I didn't mean to stand so close . . ." he says, exhaling.

There's a small stand to our left that holds straws and cream and sugar, and I watch him yank half a dozen paper napkins from a dispenser before lowering himself to my feet and dabs, pointlessly, in an attempt to salvage my Oxfords.

"It's okay," I say. Even though it's not.

I know it was an accident.

I know I should be gracious and giggle and pretend this is some kind of romantic comedy, but these shoes weren't cheap.

And they're my favorites.

And they're ruined.

And my others are currently sitting in my suitcase in the belly of my plane.

And I'm going to have to smell stale, sticky coffee wafting off my shoes for the next five hours.

I'm sure there's a gift shop around here that sells flip-flips, but I'm not exactly heading into flip-flop friendly weather.

"No," he says, rising to a standing position and holding out his hand. He's got height, this one. And his shoulders are so broad. Distractingly broad. And so round they fill out his clingy t-shirt. I try not to stare at the centered veins running down his biceps. There's no good explanation as to why I'm focusing on these things right now, but I am. "It's not okay. I'm so sorry. Take them off. I'll go rinse them off in the bathroom."

"It's fine," I say, eyeing the terminal up ahead. "My flight's boarding soon, I need to go."

"Which flight are you on?"

"Five-twelve," I say, brows scrunched because I'm not sure why it matters.

"Me too." He flashes a half-smile, and I momentarily lose myself in the golden flash of his irises because apparently I'm running low on self-control today.

I bet this works for him.

I bet this is his shtick.

He messes up in life, flashes his pearly, dimpled smile, winks his honey-brown eyes, flexes his biceps, and all is right again. I bet he gets off the hook for everything because he's obnoxiously good-looking and knows how to charm his way out of any situation.

Too bad for him, I don't have time for *this*.

"Do you ever shut it off?" I ask.

His expression fades into confusion. "Um, what?"

"This," I say, waving my hand up and down his length.

"I have no idea what you're talking about," he says, eyes searching mine.

Groaning, I feel the burn of word vomit as it rises from my core. I'm not sure if it's the holiday travelers, the packed airport, the fact that I'm running late, or the fear of not getting home in time to be with my sister, but I couldn't be in a worse mood than I am right now and this guy has the audacity to try and be all cute and charismatic?

"The smile," I say. "The eyes. The staring. The following me around and trying to be all charming and helpful. You think I don't know what you're doing, but I know. But I'm trying to get home, and listen, I'm not going to buy whatever it is you're selling, so please, leave me alone."

I chuck what's left of my spilt coffee into a nearby trash can and push past him.

I swear I'm not normally this big of a bitch.

I'm just having an off day.

A really, really, *really* off day.

The second I storm off, I instantly regret not being kinder to him . . .

. . . especially when I remember we're going to be on the same flight for the next five hours.

Oops.

Nothing I can do at this point but pray we're in completely different sections of the aircraft.

Gate C1 lies ahead, and I see the sign indicating we'll be boarding soon. I find a seat next to a phone charging station and juice up while I have the chance.

When a text from Delilah appears on my screen, asking if I made it to the airport okay, I quickly respond, letting her know I'll see her in time for dinner. When I ask her how she's feeling, she immediately replies that she feels like she could burst at any moment. Delilah's not hyperbolic or dramatic. I know she's not trying to be some cutesy, nine-month-pregnant lady. She could literally go into labor at any moment, and that does very little to quell the anxiety I'm feeling right now.

Seats fill all around me, everyone sitting around with their noses buried in their phones. To my left, a mother rocks her baby, humming what sounds to me like *Bad Romance* by Lady Gaga, and I chuckle, because I would probably be doing the same thing. Screw *Brahm's Lullaby*. Give me something with a real melody I can get down with.

I'm not a baby person at all. I mean, I'll love any and all nieces and nephews thrown my way, but as far as having a kid of my own, it's never really been something I've fantasized about.

Maybe one.

Maybe when I'm pushing forty and that fertility window of opportunity is closing down on me and I've got some long-term boyfriend begging for me to carry his child before it's too late and I feel that deep tug on my heartstrings when I see a pudgy faced kid smiling at me in line at the grocery store. *Then* and only *then* will I get knocked up. But until that time comes? I'm soaking up my freedom and independence because I've only got this one life.

Checking my phone, I see my battery has gone up a whopping two percent since I've sat down. I note the time and feel a tiny leap in my chest when I realize we're going to be boarding any minute now. I just want to hear the high-pitched whir of the jet engines and feel the G-force pressing my chest as we begin our ascension because that means I'll be that much closer to my little bottle of airplane vodka.

"Attention passengers," a muffled, muddled voice comes over the intercom a moment later. I glance up to see the lady behind the flight attendant's desk at our gate holding the mouthpiece of a phone up to her moving lips. "Flight 512 with nonstop service from Seaview to JFK International Airport in New York City has been canceled. Please report to your nearest Jet Stream Airways desk or the counter at gate C1 for further information."

My jaw falls in tandem with the sinking of my heart in my chest.

No . . .

No, no, no, no, no.

Chapter Two

Daphne

"I'm a passenger with Jet Stream Airways." I slide my hotel voucher across the front desk at the Blue Star Hotel across from the airport, feeling like the pregnant Virgin Mary desperately trying to find an inn for the night. "They said you might have a room available."

I cross my fingers, and my toes, because the last three hotels I stopped by were at full occupancy being that it's New Year's Eve and one of their busiest days of the year. Seaview, California is one of those towns you could blink and miss, and because of that, their hotel situation is severely lacking.

The front desk clerk tucks her dyed purple hair behind her ear before pushing her thick-rimmed glasses up the bridge of her nose. She looks like one of those cool moms, the kind that let their kids get tattoos on their eighteenth birthday and probably competes in air guitar competitions nationally. Biting the corner of her pierced lip, she focuses on her computer monitor.

"I'm sure going to try, doll," she says, her voice not holding the amount of certainty I'd like to hear in this type of situation. "An hour ago we were full, but I think there may have been a recent cancellation."

Her long, electric-blue nails click against the keys and her expression lightens a moment later.

"Oh, thank goodness," she says, exhaling. "The Diamond suite is available tonight."

"Suite?"

"It's all we have, unfortunately." Her head tilts. "And it's really nice. King bed. Mini bar. Jacuzzi. Your voucher will cover it."

"Let me stop you there," I cut her off when I remember none of this is coming out of my pocket. "I'll take it."

She smiles. "Sure thing. It won't be ready for a little while, but feel free to wait in the lobby. We also have a bar down the left hall and past the pool."

I slide her my ID so she can grab my name and sign off on a few liability waivers. Gathering my bags, I wheel myself to a nearby chair in the lobby and retrieve my phone so I can update Delilah. I'm not looking forward to this call, but there's nothing I can do at this point.

"Hey," Delilah answers her phone with apprehension in her voice. "Why are you calling? Why aren't you on your plane?"

"Have you looked outside lately?" I ask.

"Yeah," she says. "It's snowing, but that's normal. It's December in Rixton Falls."

"There's apparently a huge snowstorm moving north. It's right outside New York City right now. Don't you ever watch the news?"

Delilah exhales, and I picture her plopping into her favorite chair. "I try not to. Too depressing, and everything makes me cry right now."

"Yeah, well, they're calling it one of the biggest snowstorms of the last decade," I say.

"Lovely."

"All flights headed east have been grounded. I was hoping maybe they'd divert us, you know? Like it'd be nice if they could maybe drop us off in, say, Colorado or Iowa or Ohio, but nope. I guess that's not how this works.'

"So what are you going to do?" she asks.

"The airline put us in a hotel for tonight. They gave us some number to call first thing tomorrow for updates."

"Think you'll be flying home tomorrow, then?"

Sighing, I'm not sure how to break this to her gently. "Delilah, they're calling for even more snow tomorrow. And more the day after tomorrow."

"So you probably won't be coming home for a while." She doesn't ask, she only states, and her voice is flat. "Well, that really sucks."

Her words are broken, and from my end of the phone, I physically feel the disappointment in her tone, sinking and powerless. I know thousands of women have babies every single day, but it was important to Delilah that I be there with her. Since we were little girls, we always planned to be there for each other for any and all monumental experiences, and it doesn't get more monumental than giving life to a tiny human being. And I'll be the godmother to her child. This is a moment we'll never get back so long as we live.

"Listen," I say. "I was thinking that maybe tomorrow, I'll head to the nearest car rental place, and maybe I'll just drive the rest of the way? I already did the math, and if I drive for thirteen hours a day for three straight days, I'll be home by Saturday."

"Daph," she says in a way that makes her sound exactly like our mother, Bliss. "You can't drive thirteen hours a day for three straight days. You'll fall asleep at the wheel. It's not safe."

"No, I won't," I say. "I'll stop each night and stay at a hotel. Get some good rest. Be on the road first thing in the morning. The way I figure is by the time I'm almost home, the storm will have passed and the roads will be plowed. It'll be perfect timing. And who knows, maybe by the time I get to Chicago, flights will be back in service and I can hitch one home? I'd be home in, like, two hours."

"You're insane."

"I'm not insane, I just really want to come home," I say. "I hate being stranded. And I promised you I'd be there. Just please, please, please don't go into labor before Saturday."

My sister laughs. "I'll try."

"Okay, well, I'm going to grab a drink at the bar," I say. "My *suite* isn't ready yet."

"Ooh, a suite?" Delilah asks. "Does it have a Jacuzzi?"

"Of course it has a Jacuzzi," I say. "So you know what that

means."

"What?"

"It's New Year's Eve," I say. "I'm going to raid my mini bar and go skinny dipping in my Jacuzzi and party like it's 1999."

"We were third-graders in 1999," she says. "Pretty sure we had a sleepover that New Year's and you and Emma Lancaster got into a hair-pulling fight because you both wanted to play with the same Flower Shop Barbie."

"Those were the days." I sigh. "Anyway, I'm letting you go. Just relax and take it easy so that baby'll stay in a little longer."

"Let me know when you leave tomorrow. I want regular check-ins. Keep me posted. If you're driving and you get tired, just pull off on the side of the road, but at a well-lit rest stop. Or find the nearest hotel. Don't pick up any hitchhikers . . ."

I hold the phone away from my ear as she rambles on. I have to let her do this. It's how she is. Delilah is a grade A, first-class worrywart.

"Got it," I say, pressing the phone against my ear a moment later. "I won't do any of those things. Promise."

"Love you. Drive safe," Delilah says.

"Love you too." Hanging up, I gather my things and scan the perimeter for the hall that leads to the pool that leads to the bar, only my gaze stops halfway and lands on a familiar figure standing behind the check-in desk.

His elbows rest on the ledge, and I watch his shoulders rise and fall as he blows out a frustrated breath.

"Are you absolutely sure you're booked? This is the fourth

hotel I've been to in the last two hours." His tone is curt and the woman with the purple hair stands paralyzed. "I called here twenty minutes ago and was told by *your manager* that you had a room."

"Yes and I'm sorry. That room has since been filled. Things have been a little hectic today. I hope you can understand that."

"He was supposed to reserve the Diamond suite for me," he says. "I gave him my name and phone number and told him I was on my way."

"I'm so sorry." The woman stares up at him through her thick glasses, her expression pale and powerless. "These mix-ups happen from time to time, and I'm really sorry, but there's nothing I can do."

"Are there any other hotels in this area?" He drags his palm down the side of his cheek. "I've already checked the Windermere, the Harriett, and Gateway Plaza. They're all full."

She purses her lips and shakes her head. "I'm afraid not. You'll have to drive two hours to LA to find another. At least another *decent* one. I wouldn't trust the ones in Rockport or Harper's Bluff. Or Crawfordsville for that matter. They're all owned by the same outfit and they're not well managed. Or very clean. Or so I hear."

"I can't go to LA," he says through gritted teeth. "My flight, God-willing, will be leaving from here first thing in the morning."

Someone clearly hasn't been checking the weather.

"Excuse me, miss. Are you in line?" a little old lady asks, placing her wrinkled hand on my arm. It's only then that I realize

I've been standing here, gawking at the shit show happening a mere eight or nine feet ahead like it's some kind of cheap entertainment.

I guess I'm just slightly fascinated by the fact that Prince Charming was all half-smiles and dreamy eyes a few hours ago, and now he's looking like he's about to transform into the Incredible Hulk and smash this entire hotel lobby to bits.

"No, I'm not. Sorry." I step aside. "Go ahead."

The man turns around at the sound of my voice, his face twisted and eyes locking on mine. His expression is distorted now, all hard lines and shadowed edges. He reminds me of this hot-headed Italian boy I met a couple summers ago in Naples. I'd never admit this out loud to anyone, but his temper was oddly erotic for me in a way that I've still yet to understand.

We hold eye contact in a second that feels sort of like forever, his face registering my familiarity in real time, and then he turns back to the lady with the purple hair.

"What am I supposed to do now?" His fist clenches on the ledge of her desk. "Sleep on a park bench?"

Her jaw hangs like she doesn't know what to say and his relentless attention makes her nervous.

"I'm so sorry, sir," she apologizes again.

"Who took the last room?" he asks.

Her gaze passes over his shoulders and lands on me. She doesn't have to say a word, but her answer is loud and clear. My heart thuds in my chest before falling on the floor and shattering at my feet as I'm blanketed in a quick, cold sweat. I can't believe Cool Mom just sold me out like that.

Careening his gaze toward me, our eyes lock, and I swallow the lump in my dry throat. I have no reason to be nervous. I didn't do anything wrong. Cool Mom screwed up. If he has an issue, he should take it up with Cool Mom's manager.

All I want is to settle into my room and figure out how the hell I'm getting out of this place. That's it. Nothing more. Nothing less.

"Daphne, is it?" he asks, his brows meeting. His arms cross and his stance widens. I'm not sure if he's scowling at me or lost in thought or somewhere in between.

"How'd you know . . ." I answer my own question the second I ask it. The license. The airport. God, that feels like forever ago, though now it occurs to me that it's been mere hours. "Never mind."

Pulling in a long breath, his shoulders rise and fall and his jaw tenses. "You took my room."

Scoffing, I clutch my hand across my chest and try not to laugh. Is this guy for real? Is he serious right now? I glance at Cool Mom standing behind him who is officially cowering behind her computer monitor.

Thanks a lot, Cool Mom.

"I'm sorry," I say, my words passing almost too quickly between my trembling lips. I don't know what he expects, but his brooding glare makes me uneasy.

"No, you're not," he snaps back.

My jaw falls. "I'm sorry this happened. I'm not sorry I took your room because that would imply I did it intentionally."

He moves toward me with slow, deliberate steps. "It's been a really fucking shitty day. I need a place to stay. You took my room. Why don't you do the right thing?"

"And what? Give it to *you*?" I scoff, taking a step away from him.

"No," he chuffs. "Share."

"I don't even know you. Sorry. Not happening."

"So you stole my room and now you're going to make me sleep on a park bench tonight? Classy. I hope you sleep well tonight."

Damn it. He has a point. And there's no way in hell I'll be getting any sleep with that on my conscience, though I still maintain the fact that I *didn't* steal his room. At least not intentionally.

"Fine. You can stay with me." For a second, I'm out of my own body. It's like the words traveled from my brain to my lips, bypassing any sort of filter mechanism that may have thrown a red flag on this idea.

The man's face softens but only slightly.

My jaw falls. I can't believe this is happening. This is going to be awkward as hell, I just know it.

"I'm sure there's a pull-out couch or something," I add.

His eyes trace the length of me, and his hand lifts to his hair, running the length of the side of his head and leaving a ruffled, chocolate brown mess in its wake.

I've traveled all over these past few years. I've crashed on dozens of couches with people I hardly knew or friends of friends.

31

I've stayed in hostels. I've shared a dorm room bathroom with six other girls more semesters than I can count. I'm not shy. I'm not stingy. And I'm certainly not about to make this guy sleep on a park bench tonight so I can have the luxury of a soft, warm bed on a night when hotel rooms are impossible to come by.

Okay.

Deep breath.

This is going to be weird.

And awkward.

And at times uncomfortable.

But I can't leave him out on the streets.

"It's up to you," I say casually, brows raised as I adjust my bag over my shoulder.

His stare still hasn't broken, and it's almost bordering on the cusp of uncomfortable.

"All right," he says a few beats later.

"Just don't murder me in my sleep tonight and we'll be fine," I say.

I laugh.

He doesn't.

I think he's still pissed about the hotel losing his reservation, but he's going to have to get over that because it is what it is, and I'm sure as hell not giving up my access to this room.

"Ms. Rosewood?" The lady with the purple hair calls my

name like we're back to being pals again. She cradles her phone receiver on her left shoulder. "Your suite is ready now. Would you like one key or two?"

Wheeling my bag to the front desk, I swallow the uncertain lump in my throat and request two keys.

We're *actually* doing this.

I try not to laugh at the absurdity of this situation.

I don't even know this man's *name*.

"All right," she says, handing off two iridescent silver fobs with a diamond emblem on each side. "The Diamond suite is on our seventh floor. It'll be the last room on the left. 732. If you need anything at all, please press zero. We'll be hosting a New Year's party in the Hixson ballroom beginning at eight. Complimentary champagne and free hors d'oeuvres."

"Thank you." I hand a key to my . . . *guest* . . . and pull my suitcase toward the elevator. His footsteps, heavy and striding, follow behind me.

Stepping onto the elevator, I clear my throat and glance up at him. He towers over me, and his scent fills the small space we share.

"I never caught your name," I break the silence and press the button for floor seven.

He looks down at me, pushing a hard breath through his nose, and the doors close. "Cristiano."

"Do you have a last name, Cristiano?" I don't tell him that I want to know for . . . safety purposes. You never know.

"Amato."

Muzak pipes through the speakers above. I think it's playing some fluted, lyric-less rendition of a Billy Joel song but I can't be certain.

"Hi, Cristiano Amato," I say, extending my hand. "I'm Daphne Rosewood."

He meets my handshake with obvious reluctance, the corner of his mouth drawing upward.

"What are you doing?" he asks. "I know who you are. We met earlier. Several times."

I can practically read his thoughts based on the quizzical expression painted on his handsome face. He thinks I'm crazy. Certifiably. And maybe I am. I mean, I'd almost have to be to let a complete stranger share my hotel room.

"Since we're going to be roommates," I say, "We need a fresh start. Let's forget everything that happened earlier . . . if that's even possible."

He chuckles once, like I amuse him, and then he slides his palm against mine before giving my hand a firm squeeze.

"All right," he says, peering down his straight nose and stifling a smirk. It's good to see him smile again, and it sure as hell beats standing next to his alter ego, *The Incredible Hulk*. "Fine. Nice to meet you, Daphne Rosewood."

We float to the seventh floor, deposited on a cloud of gravity, and the doors ding before retreating into the walls.

"I guess . . . this is us," I say, eyes drawn to the ambient crystal sconces adorning the wallpapered walls. It's an arguably romantic hotel. Higher-end than most. Locally and privately owned, at least according to the brochure I read when I was standing in line earlier. I'm not sure how much this suite runs per night, but I'm thankful it's not coming out of my pocket.

Cristiano stays quiet as we trek to the end of the hall and locate our room. Swiping the fob, the light on the knob turns green and I push the door open. It brushes across the plush carpet as we're greeted with a veil of cold, air-conditioned air. I flick on some lights and immediately move to the balcony, pulling the drapes to let in sunlight.

A king-sized bed centers the oversized suite, and a small group of living room furniture is arranged in one of the corners along with a mini bar and kitchenette. The bathroom door is slightly ajar, and I can already catch a peek of a marble shower and the Jacuzzi tub I have every intention of enjoying at some point tonight.

I'd have really loved to have all of this to myself, but alas, I couldn't be an asshole. My only hope is that this entire thing doesn't backfire in my face because judging by the way Cristiano is slamming his bag on the floor and crouching in one of the chairs tells me he's in a bad way right now.

"You okay?" I ask, almost afraid of his answer.

I never thought I'd be missing the obnoxiously charming version of him I met just hours ago.

He glances up, his face pained and his fingers curled into fists.

"I have to get home," he says, jaw tight.

"You and me both."

"I'm supposed to be in a wedding in New Jersey this weekend," he says. "My best friend is getting married. I'm in the wedding party, and I'm supposed to be there all week."

"Yeah, well, my sister's having a baby any day now," I say. "I'd really love to click my heels and be home too, but that's not happening. We're stuck here. Throwing luggage and going all Hulk-mode isn't going to do you a damn bit of good."

He blows a rushed breath between his full lips and meets my gaze, his expression morphing from hardened to defeated.

"I'm sorry," he says. "It's just . . . I'm supposed to be there. I . . ."

"I get it. Trust me. This really fucking sucks." I plop down on the edge of the king bed, running the palms of my hand over the navy and white duvet. "It's New Year's Eve. You probably wanted to be home with your friends, going out, having a good time. And now you're stuck here in this weird little hotel in some small seaside town with some random girl who chewed you out at the airport earlier for being *too* charming. You have a lot of things to be ticked off about."

I fold my arms across my chest, the way I do when I'm about to lecture my art students when I feel like they're not grasping the weight of my lesson.

"Look," I continue. "I spent the better part of today frantic and anxious and stressed and moody, and it got me nowhere. It did nothing for me. It is what it is and there's nothing we can do but try to get the hell out of here as soon as possible tomorrow."

He sinks back in his chair and glances out the balcony window. "They better have us on a flight first thing in the morning."

Chuffing, I say, "Um, have you looked at the weather out

east lately?"

He pulls his phone from his pocket, his hand engulfing it, and drags his thumb across the screen a few times.

"Well, shit." His head tilts back in defeat as his hand falls against his jeans, landing with a clap.

"I'm checking out first thing after breakfast," I say. "I'm renting a car, and I'm driving home."

"That's stupid." He frowns. "You're going to drive almost three thousand miles instead of waiting for the weather to clear?"

"You sound like my sister." I exhale, rolling my eyes. "I've done the math. Three days of driving thirteen hours a day. I'll be home by Saturday."

He shakes his head. "You have to figure in bathroom breaks, gas, food stops. You might be driving thirteen hours a day, but it's going to be fifteen hours of traveling. Minimum. And you're not accounting for traffic. And what if you get tired and can't do thirteen?"

Lying back on the bed, I fold my hands across my stomach and stare up at the ceiling, groaning. "I know you have some valid points, but I'm also determined to do this, and basically anytime I have my mind made up about something, there's pretty much no talking me out of it."

"Don't let me stop you from being a dumbass," he says, scoffing.

"Yeah, well, I'm going to be home in time to see my sister give birth and you'll still be sitting around Seaview twiddling your thumbs and waiting for the storm to pass so you can *hopefully* find a flight out of here."

"Give it a day or two. There'll be a flight."

"This storm's supposed to last another two, maybe three days. By the time Saturday rolls around, the storm will be gone and the roads will be cleared," I argue. "Besides, I can't sit around and wait. I'll go stir crazy. I'm serious. I can't sit still and do nothing. I just . . . can't."

I glance at him, watching him sigh as he lifts his hands behind his head and stares, dead-eyed, ahead.

"I'm going to make the best of this," I elaborate. "This is going to be a little adventure. I've never road-tripped across the country before." Rolling to my side, I cup my hand under my jaw and say, "I'm probably the most adventurous person you'll ever meet. Just so you know."

His dark gaze flicks my way, and the corner of his mouth pulls up just a hair. "I don't know about that."

"Oh, look, you *can* still smile," I tease. "I was worried you lost that ability down in the lobby."

His expression fades. He's probably not in a mood to be messed with, but I don't care. I'm not spending the next fifteen hours holed up in this hotel room with a six foot three, male model version of Grumpy Bear.

"I think I liked you better at the airport, when you were trying to hit on me," I say, though I'm merely trying to get a rise out of him.

"I wasn't hitting on you."

"Bullshit," I cough.

"If I was hitting on you, trust me, you'd know."

"Mm hm." I rise, grabbing my suitcase and tossing it on the bed.

"You shouldn't do that," he says.

"Do what?"

"You shouldn't put your luggage on the bed," he says. "In case of bed bugs. That's how they come home with you. They climb into your suitcase and your clothes and . . ."

"Fine." I yank it down and sit it on a nearby table. This guy is like a wealth of Pro Life Tips when it comes to traveling, and it's kind of annoying. "Better?"

He doesn't answer. He's still in a mood. Must be his time of the month.

That's a thing – male PMS. It's actually called Irritable Male Syndrome.

My sister, Delilah, has her masters in social work, and she's taken several psychology classes, and she verified that some men suffer a drop in testosterone during certain times of the month. It's cyclical. So basically men have a time of the month and it causes them to be irritable jackasses that nobody wants to deal with.

Unzipping my bag, I pull my toiletry pouch from a side pocket and fish out my toothbrush, toothpaste, and some makeup. Shuffling to the bathroom, I freshen up because judging by the state of my haggard appearance, I've definitely seen better days. When I'm finished, I return to my suitcase and pull out a black dress I'd packed just in case. I waited a full hour and fifteen minutes to get this thing back after I'd checked my bag earlier. For a brief moment, I full on panicked. Lost luggage would've been the cherry on top of this shit sundae, but thank God, it didn't come to that today.

"Where are you going?" he asks like he's my father. All he's missing is the kind of mustache that would make Tom Selleck green with envy.

"It's New Year's Eve," I say with a shrug. "I'm going to treat myself to some wine and a nice steak dinner, and maybe some free champagne if I'm feeling saucy."

"Alone?"

Turning slowly to face him, I nod. "Right. Haven't you ever had dinner alone?"

"Hundreds of times," he says, expression bored. He may as well be polishing his nails on his shirt pocket.

Maybe I'm being rude here. Maybe he has a funny way of fishing for an invite.

"You want to come with me?" I ask.

He stares off to the side. "No."

Flinging my dress over my shoulder, I return to the bathroom and shimmy into it. Combing my fingers through my hair, I pile my hair on top of my head and twist it into a loose bun. A slick of red balm on my lips finishes the look. Fishing a pair of heels from my bag, I toss them on the floor and step in.

"Last chance . . ." I say, grabbing my purse and checking that I have my room key. "Sure you don't want anything?"

"Not hungry."

"Okay." My voice is a barely audible whisper as I head for

the door.

Funny how our personas have completely flipped a la *Freaky Friday*. Maybe when we wake up tomorrow, I'll be the bitchy one again and he'll be trying to charm his way into my cold, dead heart.

This is nothing more than an adventure, I remind myself as my heels scuff along the carpet a moment later. The light above the elevator indicates it's several floors above yet and still traveling down. Pressing the call button, I clasp my hands in front of my hips and wait.

Several seconds later, the elevator dings and the doors part, and a man with inky black hair, crystal blue eyes, and a deliciously wicked smile steps aside to make room.

"Good evening," he says with a quick flash in his baby blues. His jacket is a deep shade of blue, and as I step on board, I spot the four gold stripes on his shoulder and a winged badge on his lapel that identifies him as Captain Conrad. "Going down?"

Chapter Three

Cristiano

I haven't moved in hours, and maybe it's pathetic, but I'm sitting here like a pissed off lump, thumbing through my phone, looking at all the pictures and posts my friends back home are flicking up every ten seconds.

It kills me that I'm not there. My body heats up, flashes of powerless jealousy washing over me. I can almost hear them laughing, clinking glasses, toasting to the bride and groom's future together and making memories that I'll never be a part of because I'm stuck here.

Joey's been my best friend since we were ten, and I'm so supposed to be there. In Jersey. With all our friends.

Instead, I have the good fortune of being stranded in Seaview. I'd spent the last month hanging out with my oldest brother, Alessio, and his new wife, Aidy, in Malibu. One of my friends from college moved to Seaview a couple years ago, so I thought I'd kill two birds with one stone. Come visit him. Fly home from here. The flights were cheaper coming out of here than LAX anyway. Nothing but budget airlines nobody's ever heard of.

Worst. Decision. Ever.

And I've made plenty of bad ones in my day.

My stomach growls, but I'm too pissed off to eat.

I check the time. Daphne's been gone for over two hours now. Deep down, I know she's right. This whole thing is what it is. We can't change it. We have to think of it as an adventure. And I, of all people, should have no problem doing that because I came out of the womb with an appetite for adventure.

It's just hard to shake that powerless, trapped feeling that washed over me the second I heard them say our flight had been canceled.

For the first time in years, I just want to go home.

I *need* to go home.

Forcing myself to stand, I head to the bathroom to splash some cold water on my face and take a good look at myself.

It's New Year's fucking Eve.

I'll be damned if I sit up here all night alone and feeling sorry for myself.

Stripping naked, I hit the shower and begrudgingly decide to haul my ass to that party downstairs.

***

A pianist in a penguin suit plays an instantly recognizable Frank Sinatra tune on some makeshift stage in the Hixson ballroom. Dozens of small crystal chandeliers hang from the extra-tall ceiling and guests dressed in varying interpretations of formal wear dance and chat, champagne flutes in hand and carefree smiles on their faces.

"Champagne, sir?" A young male server balances a plate on his flat palm.

I take a flute and mouth the words, "Thank you."

I scan the party crowd a bit more, gaze landing on a dark corner of the room where a man and woman sit with a flickering candle between them. Staring harder, their outlines grow clearer, and I recognize the one on the left as Daphne.

The man on the right has something on his sleeve. Squinting, I can't quite make it out from all the way over here, so I move closer, navigating through the thick crowd. As soon as it comes into focus, I realize he's an airline pilot. A captain no less. And he showed up to this party in full uniform.

Fucking douche.

He just wants to get laid.

I sip my champagne, observing the dog and pony show going on before me. The asshole laughs at everything Daphne says, reaching his hand across the table and finding every excuse to touch her. He sweeps hair from her face. Places his hand over hers. Scoots his chair closer. His attention is laser-focused on her, like she's the only woman in the room, and she eats it up like this is the first time anyone's ever used that trick on her before.

Psh.

The pilot points to her champagne flute and she nods. He lifts it with ease, so it must be empty. He excuses himself, flashing her a devilish smile, and walks off, and I use this opportunity to steal his spot because I'm an asshole like that.

"That was qui-" Daphne freezes when she realizes it's me and not Mr. Sexy Pilot Pants. "Cristiano, what are you doing here?"

Tossing back a sip of champagne, I cross my legs and lean into the chair, making myself comfortable.

"Never mind what I'm doing here," I say. "Can we talk about what's happening here?"

She scrunches her nose, balking.

"Please tell me you're not seriously considering fucking that douche tonight," I say.

Her arms fold across her chest. "I'm not sure how it would be any of your business."

"It isn't." I shrug. "I'm just saying, he came here to get laid. He set a trap and you walked right into it. I don't know you, Daphne, but I'm pretty sure you're smarter than that."

She refuses to look at me. "I can't believe this is happening."

"He's wearing his *pilot's uniform* to a New Year's Eve party for god sakes," I say.

"Maybe he's stranded like us and it's all he had."

"You mean to tell me pilots don't carry a spare change of regular clothes in those little suitcases they wheel through the terminals?"

Her gaze flicks to her right. "He's coming back. Stop talking."

"Daphne," the pilot says when he returns, placing their filled flutes on the table. We make eye contact and I give him a wide smile that more or less says, "*I dare you to fuck with me because I'm onto your shit.*"

Daphne's stunned expression leads the pilot to immediately move closer to her.

"Everything okay?" he asks. "Do you know this guy? Is he bothering you?"

Her lips part and her gaze travels between the two of us.

"He's staying with me," she says to him.

The pilot steps back, his posture straightening like he's suddenly reassessing the situation. He still holds two champagne flutes in his hands, and my gaze focuses on his left ring finger, where a lily-white tan line practically shines in the dark where his wedding ring should be.

"I don't *know* him, know him," she says. "I just met him today."

The pilot snorts, offering an insecure smile as his gaze passes between us. "Look, you seem like a nice girl and all, but I'm not into that kind of . . ."

"No." She rises, her hand splaying across her chest. "It's not like that. That's not what I meant. And he was just leaving anyway."

She motions for him to come back but he continues moving away, his face wearing the phoniest apologetic smile I've seen in my life. Leaning back in my seat, I'm sure I'm beaming with pride because mission fucking accomplished.

She'll thank me later.

"You happy now?" She hunches forward, giving me the evil eye as soon as the pilot's out of sight.

"Exceedingly."

Rolling her eyes, she lifts a brow and says, "I hope you didn't cock block him because you wanted me all to yourself, because I can *promise you* that's not going to happen tonight. Or ever."

Scoffing, I fight a smile and lean in. "You'd be so lucky."

"Are we done here?" She rises, slipping her bag under her arm and scanning the area. I hope to God she's not looking for that asswipe.

"No," I say. "Sit down."

She flashes me an incredulous glare and keeps her feet firmly planted, completely disregarding my request for her company.

"Daphne," I say. "Sit."

"I'm not a dog."

"Clearly."

"What do you want? You don't even know me and you're acting like a crazy, jealous boyfriend. I'm starting to regret taking you in off the streets today."

Chuffing, I rise. If she won't sit with me, then I'll stand with her. "First of all, I'm not the crazy, jealous type. Second of all, you took me in off the streets because you stole my suite. The suite that I reserved."

Her arms fold along her chest and she pulls her shoulders back, nose lifted. "And is there a third?"

"Yes." I clear my throat. "You should be thanking me right now."

"For what?" Her face is pinched.

"That pilot you were about to fuck was married," I say. "Or did you not notice the indentation on his left ring finger?"

Daphne glances to the side, and I watch her expression change from angry to confused. "I didn't look at his finger."

"Yeah, well, I did." I shrug, boasting like a proud asshole. "Anyway, maybe you're into screwing married men. I don't know."

"I'm not," she says with a sigh. "But I wasn't going to fuck him. For the record, I wasn't."

"Mm hm."

She smacks me across the chest. This girl has balls. "Just stop, okay?"

"Stop what?"

"Gloating," she says, re-crossing her arms. "And stop following me around. And stop trying to intervene with literally everything I'm doing. I can't get away from you. And you're kind of a know-it-all, which annoys the hell out of me, but you're also extremely attractive and those two things put together confuse the hell out of me."

Inhaling, I let her words marinate for a bit. I suppose, from the outside, it seems like I'm following her around. I'm not. I understand her concern, but if she was truly that concerned, I doubt she'd have offered to share her suite with me.

"I get that you're pissed about being stranded," she says, "and you were probably bored up there in that room all alone, but coming here and ruining the perfectly enjoyable evening I was having is beyond shitty."

Our gazes meet, but I can't get a read on her. It's like she's sad and angry and confused and maybe even slightly . . . turned on? Her chest rises and falls and her full, bee-stung lips are slightly parted.

"I didn't know he was married, Cristiano," she continues. "On my life, I didn't. And I wasn't going to screw him. I just thought it'd be nice not to have to spend New Year's alone. He was funny. And he had so many incredible stories because he's traveled all over the world. Do you know how rare it is to meet someone like that? Someone who's traveled to all the places I want to go? Someone that's slept under the Eiffel Tower and climbed Mount Kilimanjaro? We were just talking . . . as *new friends* . . . having a nice time. And then you showed up."

Her gaze falls to the floor and she turns her face away. I don't care what Daphne says or how she spins this, that pilot wanted to fuck her. And who wouldn't? She's beautiful. Long legs, platinum blonde hair, full lips and baby blues. Everything about her is perfection from the tip of her pointy nose to the subtle sway in her hips when she walks.

"Guess I'll just go up to the room," she says. "Happy fucking New Year, Cristiano."

Chapter Four

Daphne

Lying on my back in the middle of my hotel bed, the ceiling tiles above me spin ever so slightly when I hear the barely audible beep of the lock on the door.

He's back.

Stifling a monstrous groan, I roll to my side, away from the door, and curl my body around a pillow.

"Daphne," he says.

Squeezing my eyes, I exhale and wait three beats. "What?"

"I'm sorry."

I'm not sure what exactly he's sorry for or if it even matters at this point. After leaving him in the ballroom like Cinderella at the stroke of midnight, I hurried back to the suite, changed into pajamas, and promptly did a little Googling in hopes that I could prove Cristiano wrong.

The pilot's name was Alistair Conrad and he was from Rhode Island. That was about all I gathered about him from our conversation earlier. That, and he worked for North Patriot Airlines. It didn't take long to find his bio on their website, confirming that he was, in fact, a married man. A cursory Facebook search revealed his and his beautiful wife, Becca's, profiles, which were chock full of family photos of the two of them with their three adorable little children.

My stomach churns.

"You were right," I say, voice flat and slightly muffled by the pillowcase. "He was married."

I wait for Cristiano to say "I told you so," but he never does.

Maybe a tiny part of me hoped that Alistair was special. That our meeting on the elevator was kismet. That we were destined to stay up all night talking and sharing stories in between kisses. That the way he looked at me, like I was the most fascinating creature he'd ever stumbled upon in all of his worldly travels, was actually genuine.

Now I know, he was just another shameless asshole trying to get laid.

Rolling to face Cristiano, I open my eyes. He's standing halfway between the door and the bed, his hands shoved in his jeans pockets and looking at me like he feels sorry for me. Maybe he picked up on something earlier. Maybe he heard the desperation in my frustrated rant. Maybe he *smelled* the loneliness on me.

"I've never climbed Kilimanjaro," he says, expression steady. "But I have slept under the Eiffel Tower, believe it or not."

I sit up.

"I've also been skydiving in Switzerland," he adds. "Although we didn't jump from a plane, it was a helicopter. I thought I was going to die for a second because my first chute didn't open at first. It was crazy. And intense. And I loved every heart-pounding second of it."

Looking at him in a new light, I pull my legs up and wrap my arms around them.

"I've sailed in a boat off the coast of Buenos Aires just to watch a pod of orcas swim at sunset," he continues, "and I've pulled an all-nighter just to see the sun rise in Antigua, how it turns the water all pink and orange. I've shopped the *souks* of Marrakesh, which smell incredible, by the way. I've danced like an idiot in Ibiza after taking a handful of questionable pills I bought from some shirtless girl who called herself Tinkerbell."

"Why are you telling me all of this?"

He steps closer yet still keeps a safe distance. "I don't know. Guess I feel bad about ruining your night. But in all fairness, I think your night would've been ruined after waking up the next morning, hungover, and seeing that dent on his ring finger as you crawl out of his bed. Don't you think?"

I don't answer because I know he's right.

I didn't plan on sleeping with Alistair, but even the best laid plans often go awry.

"I've been around the world, Daphne," he says. "I know I come across as an obnoxious know-it-all, but I've done a lot of things. I've *seen* a lot of things. I'm good at reading people. I know when to call bullshit. And I refuse to sit back quietly when everything in my gut tells me someone's about to be taken for a ride. But anyway, if you want stories, I've got stories. We can stay up all night if you want, and I'll tell you some crazy shit. I won't even try to sleep with you, how's that?"

Pulling my shoulders back, I lift my eyes to his. "Why do you care so much about what I'm doing, anyway? You don't know me."

He exhales, running his hand through his messy hair. "I don't know." His lips pull into a careful smirk that lights his face. "How's that for ironic? The know-it-all has no fucking clue."

I fling myself up from the bed and pad across the carpet, heading toward the bathroom.

"What are you doing?" he calls as I pass him. We nearly brush shoulders.

"I'm going to soak in that tub for the next hour," I say, "and when this year is finally over, I'll emerge, smelling like roses, literally, and I'll sleep like a baby."

"So that's it?" He turns to face me as I linger in the bathroom doorway. "You're just going to call it a night? Ring in the new year alone?"

Shrugging, I nod. "Yep."

"Surely we can salvage this."

Lifting a brow and pursing my lips, I shake my head. "Doubtful. I pretty much just want to forget tonight ever happened."

Stepping inside the bathroom, I grip the edge of the door and prepare to close it, which feels strongly like a metaphor for this moment.

For this past year, really.

"Wait," he calls before I get the chance.

But I don't.

My mood is ruined.

This *night* is ruined.

I just want to drown myself in a million bubbles and a soapy broth of self-pity. Maybe do some reflecting on this last year or so and all the wrong turns I've taken. When I'm through with my introspections, I'll watch them circle the drain and emerge a brand new woman.

Hopefully.

Locking the door behind me, I bid so long to this past year and run myself the hottest bath I can stand.

***

Wrapped in a fluffy robe, my skin red and steamed, I run my palm along the fogged up bathroom mirror and give myself a good, hard look.

I'm not sure what time it is or if the people several floors below have already finished their midnight countdown, but I figure it might not be too late to make a new year's resolution.

I don't want to be lonely anymore. I'm sick of getting my hopes up. I'm tired of having my heart broken.

But I can't think of a single resolution that would prevent any of those things from happening.

Drawing in a long, slow breath, I try and focus on the positives . . . the things I can control . . . the things I want out of life.

And then it hits me.

Completely out of nowhere.

The thought feels wildly surprising yet completely organic.

I know what my resolution is going to be . . .

This year, I want to experience more priceless moments. The kind money can't buy. The kind I can't assign a dollar amount to or order on the Internet with the click of a button.

This year, I want to revel in those immeasurably valuable moments that could never be worthy of a price tag.

I want adventure.

I want to make memories.

I want experiences.

I want to be so busy living that I forget about everything else.

Feeling resolute, I scrape my spirit off the floor and pull in a cleansing breath. I force myself to smile in the mirror, which feels awkward but somehow lifts my mood just enough that I think I can emerge from the bathroom and not bite Cristiano's head off when he opens that smart mouth of his.

Cinching my robe belt, I reach for the doorknob and yank the door open, finding myself face to face with my temporary roommate.

My heart leaps, startled, climbing in my chest and pounding like it wants out. The way he looks at me sucks all the air from my lungs, and before I have a chance to fully comprehend what's happening, his hands are circling my waist and his mouth is moving to mine. Each step he takes moves us, in tandem, until my back is pressed against the bathroom door and there's nowhere else to go.

"Ten . . . nine . . . eight," he says, his voice like a whisper only meant for me.

"Cristiano."

His right hand cups the underside of my jaw, angling my mouth upward.

"Seven . . . six . . ." he continues.

"What are you doing?"

"Five . . . four . . . three," he sighs, his mouth coming closer. His lips brush against mine, and I inhale a hint of mint and Scotch on his breath. "Two . . . one."

His mouth comes down on mine, his fingers lacing through the damp hair at the nape of my neck. He doesn't slip me the tongue. He doesn't make this dirty or raw or animal. He doesn't kiss me in a way that makes me feel threatened or unsafe. For all intents and purposes, considering what this is, he's a perfect gentleman.

My eyes close and my thoughts are muted.

I want to touch him.

I want to reach for him.

But I'm not sure if that would be appropriate. I have no idea why he's kissing me or what his intentions are, and I'm not sure why I'm standing here letting him do this, my body all but offering itself up to him on a quaking, quivering silver platter.

But we're kissing.

He's kissing me.

And it feels so good to be kissed that I could cry.

I could weep like a baby.

Nobody's ever kissed me this way; so gentle, so sweet. Like I'm fragile. Like I'm breakable. Like I'm precious.

All my life, I've known how people see me.

They see this spitfire personality with opinions blasting from her lips every five seconds. They see someone who regularly jet sets across the globe like she's some kind of fearless. They see someone who's had her heart smashed dozens of times and has the audacity to try, again and again, foolishly, to fall in love.

But what they don't see is how truly delicate my heart is. They don't see how heavy it is when I think about how much love it has to give. They don't see how fast it beats when I lock eyes with a man who could potentially hold my entire future in the palm of his hand.

I want to love.

And I want to be loved.

And I want someone who kisses me like this, so soft and slow it makes me forget how to breathe.

He pulls his mouth from mine a moment later, our eyes meeting in a veil of lust-struck confusion, at least on my end.

His lips, subtly pink from kissing me, pull up at the sides just enough. "Happy fucking New Year."

Chapter Five

Cristiano

Holy shit.

Did I just fucking kiss her?

My mouth pulses in time with my pounding heart.

Daphne stares up at me, all wide-eyed and bewildered, her full lips swollen from my kiss.

I'd been sitting on the sofa a minute ago when I realized it was almost midnight. All I meant to do was rap on the bathroom door and tell her it was almost the new year. Despite the fact that she damn near bit my head off earlier, I didn't think it was right to let her miss it.

But then she opened the door, enveloped in a cloud of steam, her light blonde hair stuck to her soft skin and little hints of her tan, bare flesh playing off the white robe that covered her wet body. I saw her, and I just lost all control.

I had to kiss her.

My hands finally leave her trembling body, and I step away. I think about apologizing and then immediately talk myself out of it because I'm not sorry. I kissed her, and I won't apologize for it because it was fucking fantastic. Her lips were pillow soft and tasted like champagne, and when the scent of roses left her damp skin, it was the perfect storm.

Neither of us stood a chance.

She lifts her fingertips to her mouth, gently touching the spot I'd claimed moments before. I expect her to ask why I kissed her. I almost expect her to slap me across the face. But she just stands there, stunned and staring.

I have to own this now.

"You're a beautiful woman, Daphne," I say in all sincerity. "And it's midnight on New Year's Eve. A woman like you should be kissed like that on a night like this."

Despite the fact that I sound like some cheesy male lead in a romance movie right now, I mean it. I mean every word of it. Pulling in a deep breath, I ready myself with a disclaimer. I want to tell her this doesn't mean anything, that I'm not trying to get laid. That I'm not like that.

But when her eyes brim with tears and a single track rolls down her cheek, I silence myself.

Fuck.

She brushes past me, wiping her eyes on the back of her left hand.

"I'm sorry. Shit. I'm so sorry." I go to her because I can't stand back here and witness her falling apart at the seams because of something I did. Out of instinct, I place my hand on the small of her back because it doesn't occur to me that touching her after I just kissed her like that, without permission, might not be the greatest idea. "Daphne, talk to me."

She says nothing as her shoulders heave and fall with silent tears. Her hands cover her face now.

"Daphne," I say, almost tempted to spin her around to face me. "I'll stay somewhere else tonight. I'll sleep on a park bench if you want. I didn't mean to upset you."

Turning, our gazes meet. Her hands fall to her sides and her cheeks are wet with tears. "That was really nice of you."

Trying not to laugh because I'm not quite understanding, I ask, "What?"

She faces me completely, gazing up and drying her cheeks on the sleeves of her robe. "The way you kissed me. It was nice. Nobody's ever kissed me like that before."

Releasing a held breath, I relax a little. "Oh, yeah?"

"I know it didn't mean anything," she says, waving her hand. "I . . . I guess it just stirred something in me. It unraveled me."

I'm not sure what to say, so I play it safe and lend her an ear and one hundred percent of my attention. I try not to let my mind wander, but I can't help but assume she's probably one of those girls who cries after sex.

Never would've pegged her as one of those. She seems so . . . strong-willed? Stubborn? Mouthy?

"God, I feel like an idiot right now. I'm so embarrassed. Really. I am." She laughs through misty eyes. "You have every right to think I'm certifiably insane after today. I think you've seen just about every side of me all in the span of about ten hours."

"Lucky me." I flash a half-smirk that lets her know I don't mind.

She laughs.

"I don't think you're crazy," I say. "Complex maybe. But not crazy."

Daphne bites her lip as she looks up at me. "Can we pretend like this didn't happen?"

"What? Pretend I didn't kiss you or pretend you didn't cry?"

She glances down, pushing a breath through her nostrils. "Both."

Smoothing my hand along my jaw, I chuff. "If that's what you want."

She plops onto the edge of the bed, her hands falling loosely in her lap. Exhaling, she says, "That was, easily, the best kiss I've ever had in my life. And now, every time I look back on this moment, I'm going to cringe."

I take a seat next to her.

"Story of my life," she says, shaking her head. "All the good moments somehow become cringe-worthy."

"That's a sign that you're doing it right," I say.

"I don't know about that."

Leaning back on my elbows, I say, "Yeah, you're right. I don't know if that means you're doing it right. It just sounded good in my head."

Daphne laughs, and I'm relieved. Her smile lights up her whole face, like it's almost too big, and her eyes crinkle in the corners.

"Thank you for your honesty," she says. Her smile fades

gradually, and she turns to me. "Have you really been to all those places and seen all those things?"

I nod. "I have."

She rolls to her side, cupping her hand under her chin, and studies me with furrowed brows. "You're adventurous."

"Are you asking or stating?"

"Observing."

"What about you? You do any traveling?" I ask.

She nods. "I lived in Paris for a year. We'd take weekend trips sometimes. Mostly places like London, Dublin, Brussels. Sometimes Amsterdam. I always wanted to veer off the beaten path. I wanted to seek adventure and try everything there was to try. But the guy I was with at the time, he only wanted to go to art museums and clubs where his name was permanently etched on VIP lists."

"Was he famous, this guy?"

Daphne rolls her eyes. "In the international art scene, yes. I'm sure he's nobody you've ever heard of."

"Try me."

"Pierre DuBois. He's a painter. An abstract expressionist. And a womanizer." She exhales. "But anyway."

"Sounds like a tool."

Daphne laughs. "He was a tool. A total tool. Just wish I'd have known that at the time. I thought he was pretty amazing for a while. He crushed me."

Her smile fades, and her eyes grow despondent. She's looking at me, but she's not.

"He was my first love," she says in a way that almost makes my heart break. Her voice cracks and then she chuckles one time. "I was twenty-three, and I didn't know much about the real world, but I was certain I knew what love felt like and I would've sworn on my life that he truly loved me."

"First loves do that to you," I say. "They rip your heart out and you never really get it back. You might get bits and pieces. But it's never intact and it's never the whole thing."

"Ain't that the truth." Her lips twist in the corners. "A year ago, I thought I was in love with this football player. His friend was dating my sister, that's how we met. And we just . . . clicked. We stayed up all night talking once, and I fell hard and fast and without any kind of warning. It wasn't gradual. It just . . . happened." Daphne glances at the comforter beneath her and then reaches to pick at a thread. "But the more I got to know him, the more we talked about our pasts and poured our hearts out, the more I realized he was still in love with his ex. She was his first love, and he never really got over her. So I let him go."

"Psh." I scoff. "Sometimes people need time. Maybe you were going to be the one to help him get over her?"

"Doubtful."

"Now you'll never know," I say. "You pushed him away before you had the chance to see."

"I pushed him away because I saw the train wreck about to unfold in the distance," she defends herself. "It was inevitable, and it was pointless to stick around waiting for my heart to break."

"So what happened when you told him he was still in love with his ex?"

She's quiet for a moment, inhaling softly. "He denied it at first. And I thought maybe I was wrong. But the next day we met up and he told me he'd stayed up all night thinking about all the things I said. And he told me I was right. He still loved her."

Pushing a hard breath past my lips, I wince when I see the hurt reliving in her baby blues. I can only hope talking about this is somewhat cathartic for her because she's practically radiating pain.

"They got back together," she continues. "At least for a while. I heard they broke up again."

"You should reach out to him."

Her face scrunches and she shakes her head hard. "No, no. He tries to get a hold of me sometimes, but I let his calls go to voicemail. I don't know what he wants, and I don't know what I'd say to him."

"Do you still miss him?"

Her eyes flick into mine. "Like crazy sometimes. Other times, I refuse to let myself think about him because what's the point? What good does it do me to dwell in the past?"

"Did you love him?"

Her eyes narrow. "I thought I did. I also thought I loved Pierre. I don't think I know what love is anymore."

"Fool's love," I say. "There's love and then there's fool's love, kind of like how there's gold and then there's fool's gold. Sometimes it looks like love and it acts like love and it feels like love, but it's just a cheap imitation."

"So how do you tell the difference?"

Rolling on my side, I face her, our eyes locking. "I don't think there's always a way to tell. At least not at first. And maybe that's the beauty of it. You have to wait it out. The real love always lasts. The fool's love kind of . . . falls apart at the seams the second shit gets real."

"I guess that makes sense."

"It's okay not to have all the answers, Daphne," I say. "Sometimes you just have to live your life and not worry about if and when and how you're going to get hurt next."

Her mouth pulls up in one corner. "Easy for you to say. I bet you've never had your heart broken before."

"That's not true," I say, hoping she doesn't ask me to tell her about the girl who obliterated my heart years ago. I'm not in the mood to talk about her.

She rolls her eyes. "Mm hm. Right."

Curling the corner of my mouth, I say, "What's that supposed to mean?"

"You look like a heartbreaker," she says. "That's what that means."

"And what does a heartbreaker look like, exactly?"

"A heartbreaker walks with confidence, knows how to command a room, and has a stare that makes a girl go weak in the knees," she says. "He's handsome. Sometimes too handsome. And he knows it. He's used to getting what he wants, and God save the woman he sets his sights on because she won't stand a chance."

Trying to hide the fact that she just flattered the hell out of me, I shrug. "Yeah, well, I don't know about all of that."

Daphne sits up, taking in a long breath and letting it go. Her body relaxes and she gently punches my shoulder.

"Thanks," she says. "Thanks for putting up with my crazy mood swings today. And thanks for letting me vent. It was nice to take my mind off the fact that I freaking *cried* after you kissed me."

She buries her face in her hand as if she's ashamed, but she's slightly laughing. When she comes up for air, our eyes meet, and without warning, my stomach knots and my mouth goes dry. Focused on her plump, rosy lips, it's all I can do not to crush them with another kiss.

I've been around the world.

I've kissed a lot of girls in a lot of countries.

Maybe I've broken a few hearts along the way.

I've done a lot of things.

I've jumped from helicopters. I've snuck into ancient pyramids after hours. I dove from cliffs overlooking the Mediterranean.

But something tells me Daphne Rosewood is about to become my greatest adventure yet.

"Daphne," I say, my breath low in my throat.

Angling herself to face me, her expression fades. "Yes?"

I sit up, inching closer to her side, and swallow the lump in my throat. "I'm going to kiss you again. And I don't want you to cry this time. I want you to feel it. I want you to enjoy it. Can you do that?"

Her crystal eyes widen and she nods slowly, staring at me through long, curled lashes.

My hand lifts, enveloping the side of her face as our mouths move closer. There's an endless second that lingers between us, causing my heart to stop until our lips brush together. My fingers lace through the hair at the nape of her neck, guiding her mouth against mine.

I kiss her soft at first. Slow. And then I gently take her lower lip between my teeth, releasing it before soothing the sting with another sweet kiss. Daphne reaches for me, the tips of her fingers grazing the flesh along my jaw, and the bed shifts as she scoots closer.

She moans between kisses. It's subtle. Barely audible. And I'm not sure she knows she's doing it. But I fucking love it. I don't want her to stop.

Kissing her harder now, she moans into my mouth a little louder this time, and when she exhales, her breath is warm on my face and she pulls herself away to catch her breath.

"God, I could let you kiss me like this all night," she breathes, lips warm and swollen.

My mouth crashes onto hers, stealing another kiss, and I feel her lips curve as she smiles. There's a hard ball in the pit of my stomach, only it feels empty, and the more I kiss Daphne, the heavier it feels.

It grounds me. It weighs me down. It fills me up.

It tingles, as if it's coming to life. It feels just as real as the heart galloping in my chest.

I don't know this woman, but I love kissing her.

I love the way she needs me to kiss her.

Daphne's lips part, and our tongues meet in a beautiful, inevitable hesitation. Each quiver of her breath, each desperate, needy sigh, makes me want more of her . . . makes me want all of her.

If she were any other girl, I might have my way with her and not feel a thing. I'd feel every inch of her, inside and out, and my mouth would travel her body, reveling in her sweet taste and the way she responds to my touch. But there's something different about this one. She's fragile and broken and vulnerable, and at the same time she's strong and hopeful. She's an enigma, and she's not like the rest.

I'll kiss her tonight.

I'll kiss her *all* night.

But I won't break her because she deserves better.

I hardly know her, and already I know she deserves better than me.

Chapter Six

Daphne

A sliver of sunlight peeks through the break in the hotel room curtains, but the rest of the room is so dark I can hardly see my hand in front of my face. My lips tingle, like they're slightly numb, and I reach for them, sliding my fingertips along my swollen pout.

He *kissed* me. He kissed me *all night*.

The bed shifts, and my attention jerks to my left.

Oh, god.

He's in bed with me.

Squeezing my legs together and running my hand down my front, I softly exhale when I find myself still fully clothed in last night's pajama-and-robe ensemble.

Pressing my head into my pillow, I stare at the ceiling and steady my breathing. Bits and pieces of the night before come back to me.

He saved me from hooking up with a married pilot.

I yelled at him.

I took a bath.

He kissed me.

I cried.

He kissed me some more.

We fell asleep in bed together.

I'm not sure this is the kind of thing I had in mind when I made my priceless moments resolution, but this is definitely not the kind of experience money can buy, so I guess it counts.

Glancing his way, my eyes trace the shadowed outline of his face. He wears a peaceful expression, his breath steady as he exhales.

I watch him sleep, admiring his chiseled features and calming aura, when out of nowhere waves of humiliation wash over me. In the span of less than twenty-four hours, I showed this complete stranger every last one of my true colors, and I'm quite certain that any minute now, he's going to wake up and bask in the very same awkwardness that's consuming me in this moment.

Reaching toward the nightstand, I grip the alarm clock and turn it to face me. It's a quarter after seven. There's a rental car company down the street that opens at seven-thirty. Gently pulling the covers off my legs, I slide out of the bed, one foot at a time, and tiptoe to the bathroom to wash up, stopping to grab some clothes from my suitcase on the way.

I take my phone with me so I can call the company the second they open. With all these stranded travelers, I can imagine business is booming, and I don't want to be stuck without a way home.

Staring at my reflection, I chuckle to myself when I see how swollen my lips are. My jaw hurts too. Cristiano kissed me *so good* and so hard last night. There were times my self-control wavered, and my mind teetered while I was on the verge of ripping off my clothes, climbing on top of him, and commanding him to do with me what he pleased because any man who can kiss like that is probably amazing at all those other things too.

But I had the good sense to stop myself because there's a difference between priceless and reckless.

I never went there.

And he never tried.

Cristiano was the perfect gentleman, and oddly enough, it wound up being the perfect way to ring in the new year, all things considered.

Slipping into a pair of worn-in jeans and a vintage Dior t-shirt I bought from a Paris flea market a couple years ago, I give myself a once-over in the mirror and finger comb my hair into a messy top knot.

The second the clock hits seven-thirty, I'm making my phone call, packing my bags, and setting my sights on the eastern horizon. It's going to be me and several thousand miles of open road, and I'm kind of excited.

I take a seat on the edge of the bathtub, phone in hand, and dial the rental company a few minutes later.

The line is busy.

Hanging up, I immediately try again.

And again.

And yet again.

For fifteen minutes straight, I try them, and for fifteen

minutes straight, the line is busy.

A sick swirl in the depths of my belly threatens to give me a minor panic attack. I can't stay here another day. I can't hang out and do nothing. All I want is to leave this hotel, avoid any awkward exchanges with Cristiano, and forge ahead on my journey.

Pulling in a deep breath, I try again.

This time it rings.

With my heart beating in my ears and my grip tight around my phone case, I hold my breath until someone answers.

"Goodman Rental Services. This is Tanya. How may I help you?" the voice of an angel asks.

"Yes," I say, releasing the breath I'd held far too long. "I'd like to rent a car as soon as possible."

She's quiet, but I'm hopeful. The clicking of keyboard keys in the background and the endless seconds that tick by threaten to steal my optimism.

"Okay," she says, her voice void of any chipper qualities. "We have two cars left."

"Oh, thank god."

"A fifteen passenger van," she says. "And an economy car."

"I'll take the economy car. Do you deliver?"

"We do."

"How soon could you have it here? I'm at the Blue Star

Hotel on Sierra Vista Parkway."

Her end of the phone is muffled briefly, like she's talking to someone else, and when she returns, she says, "Our morning is full. We could have it to you by one p.m. if that would work?"

"You're right up the road from my hotel, right?" I ask. "I could just walk there."

"No, sweetheart," she says, "this is the Chase Boulevard location. The Sierra Vista location closed last year. We're about ten miles from you."

My heart sinks, but my determination is unbreakable. "Is there any way to get it sooner?"

"I'm afraid not."

"I'll pay extra."

"It doesn't work that way. I'm so sorry."

"My sister is about to have a baby," I say, injecting some genuine desperation into my tone, "and I'm trying to get home. Every hour counts."

Part of me thinks I should hang up with Tanya, call another rental agency, and try to secure a different car, but if Goodman only had two cars left in their fleet and there are hundreds if not thousands of stranded travelers in Seaview, I might be shooting myself in the foot by letting this one go.

Tanya sighs, her end of the line keeping silent for far too long.

"I have a soft spot for babies," she says, her voice muted and muffled like she's talking from the corner of her mouth. "Just had a baby girl eight weeks ago."

"Congratulations," I say.

"It's your sister, you say?"

"Yes. My twin sister."

Tanya clicks her keyboard in the background. "All right. I moved some things around. Your car should be arriving by eight fifteen. It's a navy blue Toyota."

"Thank you!" It's all I can do to keep from squealing, and if I could reach through the phone and hug her, I would.

"All right, now I just need your credit card," she says.

I rattle off the numbers and Tanya responds shortly after with a confirmation number. I'll be paying a premium for this rental since it's a one-way trip and I won't be returning it to this agency, but I can deal with that. By the time I hang up, it's almost eight, and my car will be delivered in fifteen minutes.

Creeping out of the bathroom, I try to re-pack my bag as quietly as possible. Cristiano's buried under a mountain of covers now, breathing hard and rolling from his left side to his right.

From the corner of my eye, I spot him reach his hand toward the empty side of the bed, and I watch as his brows meet and his face winces.

Pulling the zipper slowly around my suitcase, I hoist it off the luggage rack and onto the carpet just as he sits up.

"Daphne?" He reaches for the lamp above the nightstand and clicks it on. "Where are you going?"

His hair is sticking up on the side, but it's equal parts sexy and adorable. My gaze lingers on his lips a second too long, and in that second, I can almost remember what it felt like to kiss him.

It's like he's kissing me all over again, and it's just as delicious as it was the night before. There's a swirling, tickling sensation in the center of my belly, but I force it away. It has no business being there.

Zero.

"My car is being delivered. I have to head downstairs. Just check out by eleven, okay?" I force a smile and grip the handle of my luggage.

"Whoa, whoa, whoa." He flings the covers off and rises, hands resting on his hips and lips pursed. "You're serious about this road trip thing?"

I nod. "Of course. I'm going home. I told you, I can't sit around and wait all week for a flight. I'll be home in three days."

"No," he says, stepping toward me. He's standing in front of me now, shirtless and in a pair of pajama pants. He must have changed sometime after I fell asleep last night. "I can't let you do this."

Laughing at his audacity, I say, "Yeah, well, I can't let you stop me."

He reaches for me, his hand landing on my arm and his fist curling around my flesh. I don't particularly enjoy the feeling of being anchored, so I jerk myself away.

"I know you want to get home," he says, "but I'm telling you, this is not the solution."

"And *I'm* telling *you*, I'm going to be home in three days."

He shakes his head, his lips pressing flat. "You can't drive thirteen, fourteen, fifteen hours a day for three straight days."

"Says who? Says *you*?" I pull my bag toward the door and he follows, arms crossed.

"I'm coming with you."

Stopping, I turn to face him. "No, you're not."

"I am. I'm coming with you because you can't do this alone. It's not safe. You could fall asleep and cause an accident. You could get carjacked. You could break down on the side of the road on a deserted highway."

My amusement fades as I watch him pulling clothes from his bag. A shirt falls out and he stuffs it back in.

He's serious about this.

I check the time on my phone. "I'm doing this. And my car's almost here, so . . ."

"Wait," he says. "I'm almost done."

Cristiano tucks a wad of clothes under his arm and heads back to the bathroom, only closing the door halfway. When he emerges a minute later, he's dressed in pale jeans and a navy polo and his hair is wet and neatly combed. He shoves the rest of his things into his suitcase and makes his way toward the door.

"You're insane," I tell him. "You're not even complex, you're certifiably insane."

He takes my bag and we head to the elevator.

I can't believe this is happening. Surely he'll change his mind once he wakes up a bit more and comes to his senses.

As soon as we're deposited on the main floor, I pull him aside. Standing next to a potted palm, I look him square in the eyes and simply state, "You can't come with me."

Balking, he takes a step back. "Why not?"

"I don't want you to."

His brows meet, forming a line between them. "I don't care what you want. You're clearly not thinking straight. It's a matter of safety."

I shake my head, placing my hand on his chest. "I really don't want you to come. This isn't a joke. Or a game. I'm not kidding. I don't want you to come with me."

"I can't let you drive damn near three thousand miles in three days. Do you realize how completely crazy that is?" He seems genuinely concerned for me. "I can't let you get in that car by yourself. You need a driving partner. We could drive three thousand miles together. But you sure as hell can't do it by yourself."

His staunch declaration serves as a challenge, making me want to prove him wrong, but I know in the end, proving him wrong is pointless because I'm never going to see him again. I also know that he has a point. An image of myself stranded in the desert, my engine steaming and some kind of predatory bird circling overhead comes to mind. Plus, I can't deny the fact that it'd be nice to have someone to share the driving with.

"Fine." I place a hand on my hip after giving it some careful consideration, but I may as well be waving a white flag. "You can come with me. But I have some rules."

"Okay." He lifts a brow.

"I'm the pilot. You're the co-pilot. I call the shots. I make the final decisions. You're not allowed to backseat drive, and the driver controls the radio."

"Fine."

Heading to the desk, I check out of the Diamond Suite and turn to see a shiny, tiny Toyota parked in the drop-off lane.

"That's us." I exhale as he grabs our bags and wheels them past the sliding doors.

An attendant from Goodman rental agency stands beside the trunk, greeting me with a pen and a stack of paperwork. When I'm through signing my life away, he climbs into another car with a similarly-dressed man, and they speed away.

Glancing at Cristiano, I find a puzzled look on his face. His forehead is wrinkled and his hands rest on his narrow hips.

"What's wrong?" I ask.

"It's a small car." He states the obvious. And then I glance at his long legs. Forty-plus hours in that chicken-nugget-on-wheels with his long gams isn't going to be fun, but I refuse to pity him because this is exactly what he wanted. What he all but *begged* for.

"It's all they had left. You coming or what?" I wave to get his attention.

Pressing the trunk release button, I stand back as he hoists our bags in. They fit side by side, leaving little room for anything else. Climbing in the passenger seat a moment later, he scoots it all the way back. Still, his seat fully configured, his knees are a couple of short inches from the dash.

I take the driver's seat and stick the key in the ignition and turn to accessory mode. The dash lights up and the air begins to blow, pointed at our faces. With my foot on the brake, I start the engine, buckle my belt, and turn to him.

"You said you have a wedding in Jersey, right?" I ask.

He nods.

"I'm going to New York," I say. "Upstate."

"If you can get me as far as Scranton, I can get a ride from there."

Nodding, I pull up the GPS on my phone and plug in Scranton, Pennsylvania as our destination. The automated voice tells me to drive fifty feet to Sierra Vista and turn right. The interstate is ahead on the left, and I can spot the shiny sign from here.

"I need to call my sister first." Swiping my phone out of a cup holder, I pull up Delilah's number and press the green button.

"What's up?" she answers on the second ring.

"How are you feeling?" I ask, pulling out of the parking lot.

"About ripe for the picking. Where are you?"

"I'm on the road . . . heading east . . ."

"I can't believe you're really going through with this. I thought you were joking yesterday. You're clinically insane," she says. "And I diagnose people for a living, so I'm certified to make that judgment call."

Rolling my eyes, I flick my blinker on and merge onto the eastbound interstate. Traffic is light this morning, then again it's a Wednesday. And a holiday. The rest of the world is hung over, sleeping in, or lounging in pajamas in the comfort of their home.

"If all goes as planned, I'll be home by Friday night," I say.

"Don't you think that's pushing it a little? Maybe shoot for Saturday? I don't want you doing all that driving in such a short amount of time," she says, sounding once again like our mother.

"It's fine," I say. "I found myself a co-pilot."

She's quiet, just like I knew she'd be when I dropped this bombshell in her lap. I can only pray this doesn't make her go into labor. It'd completely defeat the purpose of this entire endeavor.

"Daphne," she says, voice low. "Is someone in the car with you right now?"

"Mm hm," I say, lips pressed into a closed smile.

"Daph-ne," she says, her voice staccato.

"De-li-lah."

From the corner of my eyes, I notice Cristiano's watching, his lips painted in a smirk like he knows where this conversation is headed.

"What's his name?" my sister asks.

"Cristiano," I say, meeting his gaze.

"I want to talk to him. Put me on speaker," she says.

I press the phone against my chest first and turn to him. "She wants to talk to you."

I put her on speaker and hand him my phone.

"Hi, Delilah," he says. "I'm Cristiano, and I'll be escorting your sister across the country."

"Hi, Cristiano," she says. "I hope you don't mind if I ask you a few questions."

"Not at all."

"What's your last name?" she asks.

"Amato."

"How old are you?"

"Twenty-six."

"Any brothers or sisters?" she asks.

"Four brothers."

"Names?"

"Alessio, Matteo, Dante, and Fabrizio," he says.

"And where do you fall in that line up? Oldest, youngest? Middle?" she asks.

Oh, god. She's psychoanalyzing him. I should've known this is exactly what my sister would do.

"Second to the youngest," he says. "I'm number four."

"Would you say you're inclined to have middle-child tendencies?" she asks. "Would your family say you're the 'peacemaker' of the bunch?"

He laughs, and I kind of love that he's humoring her. "Yeah, sure. I just like to have a good time. I don't get caught up in drama. I don't take sides. I'm pretty peaceful."

"Would you say you have realistic expectations in life?" she asks. "Would you say you're used to sharing the spotlight?

And you handle disappointment well?"

"Yes." His tone is serious, but he flashes an amused smirk my way. "Yes to all of that."

"Good, good," she says, her voice growing distant. I can imagine her sitting there, a pen and notebook in her lap as she takes notes. "Would you say you had a fairly typical childhood?"

"Not at all," he says.

Delilah's end is silent. I know my sister, and I know she wants to dig deeper. If there's anything to be uncovered about anyone, Delilah can't help herself. Like our father always said, it's just how she was built. She practically came off the assembly line curious about anyone and everyone and what made them tick.

She clears her throat. "Where did you attend college, Cristiano? And what did you study?"

"I attended a private college in Massachusetts," he says, "on a full scholarship. Pre-law. Actually finished law school last year, but I never sat for the bar exam."

"And why was that?"

"I wanted to explore the world instead. I didn't want to feel stuck in one place, working long hours with no life outside the office," he answers. I'm sure my sister is eating this up right now, the wheels in her head spinning faster than her questions can keep up with.

"Delilah, enough," I say. "I said you could talk to him. I didn't say you could do a full psychological evaluation."

"I just have a few more questions and then I'm done," she says, speaking more like a professional than a sister.

"*No*," I say.

"*Yes*," she says, harder.

"De-li-lah." I reach for the phone and Cristiano hands it over. "I love you, and I'll call you tonight when we find a hotel. Bye."

Hanging up, I stick my phone in a cup holder and grip the steering wheel, eyes on the road.

"I'm not going to apologize for her," I say. "You signed up for this when you hopped in my car. She has every right to worry about me traveling across the country with a complete stranger."

"A stranger that you made out with for hours last night," he adds. "Daphne, it's totally fine. I don't care. She means well."

"All right. Just wanted to get that out there." I clear my throat and pull my shoulders back.

It's quiet for a few beats.

"What kind of music do you like?" I ask, reaching for the radio and scanning stations. The presets are set to mostly country, oldies, and talk radio.

"Classic rock. But you're driving. You pick," he says. "Your rules, remember?"

I decide to be nice and tune in to a classic rock station. The Rolling Stones' *You Can't Always Get What You Want* comes on the radio, and I wonder if I'm going to associate this song with this moment for the rest of my life.

Probably.

There are a lot of songs that have latched on to epic

moments in my life, good and bad. I can't listen to Louie Armstrong's version of *La Vie En Rose* without thinking of the night Pierre kissed me outside a little café in Bordeaux just before midnight. The song was piping through outdoor speakers as his hands found my hair and his lips pressed onto mine with such feverish passion that the world stopped spinning.

Buena Vista Social Club's *El cuarto de Tula* reminds me of the night I met Weston, the football player. There was a live band playing on an outdoor stage at some Cuban bar in downtown Miami, and when I asked him what this song was, he didn't know, so he ducked inside the bar to flag down the owner to find out for me. When he came back out, he took me by the hand and twirled me beneath the streetlights when I told him I wished I knew how to salsa dance. We laughed and then he wrapped me in his arms in a single second that felt like sweet eternity.

The Darkness' *I Believe in a Thing Called Love* was practically the soundtrack of my entire relationship with my high school boyfriend, Corbin Dietrich. Every time I hear it, all I can think about are those never-ending summer nights, picnics at the falls, school formals, Friday night football games, and aimlessly cruising around Rixton Falls in his shiny black Firebird with the windows down. Corbin left for college the summer before my junior year of high school, and I never heard from him again. I heard he's married now, with a kid on the way, and I often wonder if he thinks of me – of us – when that song comes on the radio.

The GPS instructs me to take an exit a quarter of a mile ahead, and I check my mirrors before getting over. I spot him checking the mirrors as well, though he's trying to be sly about it.

"No backseat driving," I remind him.

"Excuse me?"

"I saw you checking the mirrors."

"I didn't say anything."

"Just the fact that you had to double check my mirrors tells me you don't trust me driving," I say, slightly teasing. "If you're having reservations about this, I'm more than happy to drop you off at the nearest gas station so you can call a cab to take you back to Seaview."

"Zero reservations," he says. "And I checked the mirrors because I'm your co-pilot. I'm fifty-percent responsible for a safe arrival at our destination, and these California drivers are crazy."

"I'm from New York. We invented crazy drivers. Ever heard of the New York State Thruway?"

"I'll see your thruway and raise you one New Jersey turnpike."

"This isn't a competition," I remind him with a smirk in my tone. "Just sit back, relax, and enjoy the ride."

Reaching for the radio knob, I turn up the volume and focus on the road. Cristiano stays quiet as the mile markers pass, and the music droning from the speakers does very little to drown out thoughts of last night. If I concentrate hard enough, I can still feel his weight over me, the pressure of his mouth against mine, and the feel of his hand cupping my jaw. Even the tingles radiating down my spine. It's like they're right there where I left them.

Turning off the radio twenty miles down the road, I pull in a deep breath and prepare to address the hot pink polka-dotted elephant in the room.

"Can we talk about last night?" My brows meet as I turn to him for a second.

He sits up, dragging his palm along the stubble on his chiseled cheek. His gaze narrows at me and his lips press flat.

"All right," he says.

"It's just, if we're going to be spending the next few days together," I say, "after last night . . . after yesterday, really . . ."

I don't know where I'm going with this other than the fact that I want to prove to him I'm not crazy.

And I want to make sure he isn't either.

"Let me start over," I say, waving my hand in the air like I'm erasing a chalkboard. "You ever have one of those days when everything goes wrong and you're not feeling like yourself?"

He shrugs. "I guess?"

"Well, yesterday was one of those days. For me. And I didn't mean to bite your head off in the airport. Or at the hotel. Let me just apologize for that because it wasn't me at all."

"Okay."

"And the kiss," I say. "I've never cried from a kiss before. I'm embarrassed, honestly, and it's been bothering me all morning. I really need you to know that I'm not usually this big of a . . ."

"Hot mess?" he finishes my thought.

Exhaling, I turn his way and offer a sheepish hint of a grin. "Yeah. Hot mess."

We're focused ahead, and I change lanes the second we get behind an elderly couple in a Buick driving an irritatingly ten miles under the posted speed limit. We've got to make good time.

"Is this weird for you at all?" I ask. "I mean, after yesterday. After last night . . ."

I glance at Cristiano, whose gaze narrows my way. His brows meet and he shakes his head.

"No, Daphne. It's not weird for me. But it's weird that you're making it weird."

"I'm not trying to make it weird, I'm simply asking a question."

"We made out last night," he says, exhaling. "It's not like we fucked. If you don't make it a thing, then it won't be a thing."

His phone rings, and he has to contort himself in this cramped little car in order to retrieve it from his left pocket.

"Hey, Joey," he answers. "Yeah, still no flights. I found a way back though. I won't miss your big day . . . I'll be there . . . promise . . . how you holding up? You doing all right?"

I try not to eavesdrop but when he's sitting twelve inches from me, it's kind of hard not to.

"Don't stress," he says. "Like I said, I'll be there. Everything'll be fine. Hoping to get back Friday night. We can all go out. Maybe get a beer or something to calm your nerves."

He chuckles, and then he ends the call.

"Cold feet?" I ask.

"Who the hell knows," he scoffs.

"Is it just me, or is everyone our age either having weddings or babies?"

Cristiano nods, his mouth drawn up in one corner. "Feels like it."

"Do you want to get married?" I ask. "I mean, do you ever see yourself getting married someday?"

Without hesitation, he sits up straight and looks my way. "Yeah. I do. Guess I'm old-fashioned that way."

"How crazy is it that in this day and age, marriage is considered old-fashioned?" I muse.

"How about you? You want to get married someday?"

I shrug my shoulders, hands clasped on the wheel. "Maybe? I don't know. Depends on the day. Somedays I think I do. Other days I'm one hundred percent sure that I don't. Don't get me wrong, I want to be with someone. I believe in love and soul mates and all of that good stuff, but marriage?"

I stick my tongue out.

"I made a pact," he says, staring wistfully ahead. "This girl I grew up with. If neither of us were married by thirty, we were going to marry each other. Have kids. Settle down. All of that. Kind of always thought it'd be her. But she's with someone now, so I don't think it's ever going to happen."

"I know we just met, but I honestly can't imagine you settled down living the quiet married life in the suburbs," I say. "It's probably for the best."

His gaze falls to the dash. "Yeah. You've got a point."

"You want kids though?" I ask.

"Yeah," he says. "I think so. Maybe ten years from now. One or two would be nice. You?"

Releasing an audible half-groan, my shoulders slump. "I don't know. Maybe one. Maybe ten years from now. There's just so much living I want to do, you know? And if I have a baby, I want to be able to give it my undivided attention. I want to give it all of me, and I can't do that if I'm staring out the window wondering what it'd be like to be snorkeling in Fiji or skiing in the Swiss Alps. I hope that doesn't make me sound selfish."

"Quite the opposite," he says.

"I grew up in a big family. There were six of us altogether, my parents, two sisters, and a brother. The house was always noisy and chaotic and people were always coming and going. I used to lock myself away in the storage room in the basement, flip on a radio to drown out the noise, and just paint and draw for hours."

"You're an artist?"

"I studied art, yes," I say. "I have my MFA in Drawing, though I love oil painting just as much, if not more. I was actually interviewing for a job at a fine arts college in Seaview this past week. Anyway, I heard you tell my sister you have four brothers?"

"Yep." He sighs. "Bet my house was a hell of a lot noisier than yours. Anyway, speaking of noise and peace and quiet and all that, I'm going to catch a quick nap. Someone had me up late last night, and we should switch off every three to four hours. Figure we'll need to stretch and grab gas or food or whatever. It's more efficient this way. And safer."

Chuffing, I let him have his way. He's clearly taking this whole safe arrival thing seriously. And I have to admit, it's kind of nice having him here, even if he is an obnoxious, overprotective know-it-all.

Chapter Seven

Cristiano

The click of the car door wakes me, and for a split second, I forget that I'm trekking across the country crammed in some Micro Machine-sized car. Reaching for the door handle, I give it a tug and swing the door wide.

I don't know what state we're in or exactly how long we've been driving now, but I see red mountains in the distance and desert sparse with cacti and other greenery. My eyes focus on a sign by the road that says welcome to Fort Reed, Arizona.

"Morning, sunshine." Daphne shoves the gas nozzle into the side of the car and smiles wide. "You took quite the nap. Welcome to fabulous Arizona."

I rub my eyes, and my stomach growls. The bright mid-day sun nearly blinds me when I step out from under the awning above the car.

"Think you can man this thing while I head inside and grab some food?" she asks.

I make my way toward the gas pump, watching the numbers tick by slowly, like they've got all the time in the world. Daphne drags her feet through the dusty gravel parking lot as she heads in, her blonde hair blowing in the tepid breeze. There's a slight chill in the air, but the sun provides enough warmth that it's not so bad.

Making my way around the car, I check the tires, kicking them and pressing them and making sure they're all properly inflated. The gas pump clicks once the tank is full, and I turn my attention that way to complete the sale.

By the time I'm done, I climb into the driver's seat, preparing to take my turn behind the wheel. Attempting to get comfortable here is no easy feat, especially when my knees are jammed under the steering wheel despite the seat being moved all the way back.

Groaning, I remind myself that it is what it is, and then I check my phone. A few friends from back home have sent texts, asking if I'm all right and if I'll be there for the wedding. I assure them all that I wouldn't miss it for the world, and I tell them not to sweat it. I'm coming home. I'll be there soon.

It hits me a few minutes later that Daphne seems to be taking an awful long time, especially considering the fact that we're in a bit of a hurry here, so I glance at the gas station storefront to see if I can spot her inside.

Only she's standing out front, next to a newspaper rack, surrounded by a couple of men in flannel, tight jeans, and cowboy boots.

Their backs are to me, but I can see her face. She's smiling, nodding. Her mouth is moving and her arms are full of snacks and beverages. She takes a step toward the parking lot but they move with her, blocking her almost. From here, I see her smile fade for a second, and then she gazes my way.

Before I have time to think twice, I fly out of the car and make my way toward Daphne and her new friends.

"What's the hold up here?" I rest my hands on my hips and

glare at the cowboys. They turn to me, their tanned faces weathered and their expressions unwelcoming.

"Who the hell are you?" one of them asks, head cocked.

"I'm with her," I say. "Who the hell are you?"

"They were just asking if we needed anything, directions or whatever. I told them we have a GPS and we're fine," she says, words rushed. She releases a nervous titter. "Anyway, we should hit the road."

I shoot the assholes a look and slip my hand on the small of Daphne's back, escorting her back to the car.

"Anybody ever tell you not to talk to strangers?" I chuff when we climb inside.

Her arms are full of chips and candy and bottled waters, and she begins organizing it neatly in every cup holder and cranny she can find.

"This should last us a while," she says. "I guess the Pittz Pit Stop has never heard of bananas or dry roasted almonds. It was nothing but junk in there."

"Daphne," I say, starting the engine. My jaw is tight. "Did you hear what I said?"

She pulls her seatbelt across her lap and fastens it with a satisfying click. "Yep."

"Those guys were looking for trouble," I say.

Daphne swats her hand. "They were harmless. They were potato farmers from north of Prescott. People in these itty-bitty towns aren't used to seeing strangers. They were just curious."

"I watched you try to walk away from them and they followed," I say, pulling back onto the main highway. "They weren't going to let you go that easily. I'm not sure if you're choosing to be naïve about this or if you truly are naïve."

She groans, resting the side of her head against the glass of her window. "Really not in the mood for one of your lectures, Cristiano."

Reaching for the radio, she cranks up the music.

I crank it back down before returning my tight grip to the wheel. "Just, don't talk to strangers, okay?"

"Have you always been this overprotective?" she asks. "God help you if you ever have daughters."

Fishing through the snacks, she offers me a chocolate bar and a bottle of water.

Messing with the radio again, she tunes it until she finds a classic rock channel, and then she rolls down her window, sits back, and tears into a bag of red licorice, singing along to the Led Zeppelin tune in between bites.

Checking the GPS, it looks like five hours from now we'll be somewhere in Colorado, and if we can make it a few hours past that, we'll be able to stop for the night and get some rest.

"FYI, I was perfectly capable of escaping those *Deliverance* guys on my own, but thank you for taking it upon yourself to come to my unnecessary rescue," she says, snapping a piece of licorice from between her teeth. She grins wide, her eyes teasing. "It's cute that you're protective. And annoying too. And I promise not to talk to strangers again. Though you're technically a stranger, so where does that leave us?"

"Sweetheart, we're hardly strangers," I chuff. "I think we passed that point when we woke up in bed together this morning."

"Whatever." She pulls another strand of licorice from the bag and stares ahead with a smirk. "Just drive, Amato."

Chapter Eight

Daphne

"You sure this is our *only* option?" I ask as we pull up in front of a giant Victorian house in a creepy little town called Silver Hollow in eastern Colorado. It's almost nine o'clock and we've been on the road nearly thirteen hours today. I'll never admit this to Cristiano, but driving all these hours really wears a girl out, and these last forty miles, I've been struggling to stay awake.

There's a wooden sign out front with a giant cross and the words Holy Cross Bed and Breakfast painted in intricate gold cursive. A smaller wooden sign hangs off the larger one, indicating rooms are available. The house is painted in shades of plum and goldenrod and hunter green, and ominous weeping willows fill the expansive lot. The turret to the right of the front porch spans three stories and finishes with a pointed metal cross that points to the darkened skies.

"I feel like we're seconds from experiencing our own personal horror story," I say. "If we get murdered tonight, I'm blaming you."

"This keeps us on schedule," he says. "It's getting late and we need a place to crash. Next hotel isn't for another eighty-six miles."

I kill the engine and climb out, legs stiff and throbbing. Stretching my arms over my head, my shirt rises up just a little, and I catch Cristiano stealing a two-second glimpse.

Grabbing our bags from the trunk, we walk to the front door and ring the bell. My heart races, drowning out the sound of some rogue swarm of birds circling the trees above.

It feels like we're legitimately standing in some Alfred Hitchcock scene, seconds from meeting an ill-timed fate.

The porch light flicks on with a hum, and we hear the sound of metal locks and latches clicking on the other side of the door. A second later, an elderly woman with a shiny silver bun on her head and a knit shrug swings the door wide.

Her lips are turned down in the corners and her beady eyes scan our faces.

"Are you Mrs. Snodgrass?" Cristiano asks. "I'm Cristiano Amato. I called about an hour ago. We're passing through and needing a place to stay for one night."

Her brows meet as she scrutinizes us, and her brows lift, covering her forehead in dozens of fine lines.

"Where are your rings?" she asks, her voice brittle and quaint despite the fact that I get the feeling she's anything but.

"I beg your pardon?" he asks, turning to me and then back to her.

"Your rings," she says. "This isn't some Moonlight Motel on Route 66. We don't cater to philanderers, adulterers, or those engaging in pre-marital relations."

"Oh." I place my hand on my chest. "No, no. None of that here. We can assure you."

She peers over a thin set of glasses that rest on the tip of her nose, and then she reaches for the silver cross brooch above her heart, tracing the tiny inset crystals with her fingertips.

"So you're married." She isn't asking.

Cristiano and I exchange looks. He lifts his brows. I lift mine higher. Something tells me if we want a place to stay, we have to tell this woman what she wants to hear.

"We're brother and sister," he says, taking this in a completely different direction than I expected.

It would've probably been easier to tell her we were married and not wearing rings. We could pretend to be married. Easily. We can't pretend to be brother and sister when we look absolutely nothing alike. He's dark and brooding and full-blooded Italian. I'm blonde as they come with pale baby blues.

"Brother and sister?" she crosses her arms, eyes squinted.

"Our aunt is ill," he says. Liar, liar, pants on fire. "We're headed to Omaha to see her. She doesn't have much time left. We just need a place to rest for the night and we'll be out of your hair first thing in the morning. You don't even have to make us breakfast."

Her hands move to her hips. She sucks in a long breath and then purses her lips until they're flat as a pancake.

"I only have one available room," she says. "The others are booked."

"It's fine," he says. "I'll take the floor and my sister can have the bed."

Mrs. Snodgrass searches our faces, like she's some kind of human lie detector, and steps back from the doorway, finally ushering us in.

"All right," she says. "It's ninety dollars for the night. I'll show you to your room. The kitchen's closed but it's late so I assume you've already had dinner."

"We have," Cristiano says.

"I've got homemade chocolate chip cookies in the oven for the turndown service," she continues. "I'll bring them up when they're ready."

We follow her past the living room with its wallpapered walls, marble fireplace, and brass chandelier, and head toward the steps, taking one creaky stair at a time until we reach the top. She waddles past a series of closed doors, each one polished and stained in rich mahogany. When we reach the last door at the end of the hall, she pulls out a set of skeleton keys and shoves one in the lock, twisting with all her might.

"Here you are," she says, turning the crystal knob and letting the door creep open.

"Thank you." Cristiano takes the key she offers him and wheels our luggage in.

Mrs. Snodgrass stands in the hall just outside the doorway and watches us like she's still trying to figure out whether or not we're brother and sister.

"Thank you." I say, closing the door. I listen for her footsteps and hear nothing. Leaning in, I whisper in Cristiano's ear, "I think she's on the other side of the door, eavesdropping."

He smirks.

"If I wasn't so tired, I'd give her something to eavesdrop on," he whispers back.

I swat him away and move toward one of the dressers, flicking on a fringed lamp that illuminates a tiny corner of the bedroom. He flicks on the lamp by the bed, which looks to be a full-sized bed of all things, and I jump back, startled.

"What is it?" he asks, scratching the side of his head.

"Oh, my god." My heart races and I clutch at my chest as I try to steady my breath. "All these . . . *dolls*."

He glances around, taking a step toward the center of the room. Everywhere we look there are little porcelain dolls with shiny eyes and glassy stares and frilly dresses. They're all looking at us. Watching.

"Good god," he says, exhaling. "Talk about creepy."

"Talk about horror movie. We're so getting murdered tonight." I take a seat on the edge of the bed because dead center of the room feels safer than the doll-filled corners. "I feel like now would be a good time to tell you that I have a genuine, creeping fear of horror movies and ghosts and creepy things. I used to get nightmares as a kid because my brother let me stay up one night with him and his friends for a scary movie marathon. I've been traumatized ever since. And there was this one . . . with porcelain dolls that came to life . . ."

I shudder, running my palms along the sides of my arms, hugging myself.

"You're joking, right?" He laughs. "They're just dolls, Daphne. They can't hurt you."

My gaze lands on one doll in particular. She's got pitch-black hair that's folded into two braids that run down the front of her emerald green dress. Her eyes are black almost, and she's smiling. Staring.

"Here." He moves toward a cedar chest, popping the lid up and pulling out some folded blankets. Moving around the room, he covers them all up. "Now we can't see them and they can't see us."

I look at him then back to the mounds of blankets littering the room now. "Just because I can't see them doesn't mean they're not there. I feel like they could pounce on us at any moment."

Dragging his hands through his hair, he turns to me, and then he rests his hands on his hips.

"So what? Do you want to leave? You want to drive another hour and a half and hope we can find another room somewhere?" he asks.

"Don't be annoyed. Please." I'm laughing, but this is no laughing matter. "I'm legitimately scared of these dolls. I'm not trying to be cute or funny. This is terrifying to me."

Hoisting his luggage on a nearby rack, he turns his back to me.

"What are you doing?" I ask.

"I'm going to take a shower. And then I'm going to bed because we're hitting the road first thing in the morning. I suggest you do the same."

"But . . ." I suck in a breath and shiver, though it's not cold in here. Quite the opposite. It's hot and stuffy. Little tremors take over my body. If my siblings were here, they'd get a kick out of this.

Cristiano throws a pair of navy sweats over his shoulder and heads toward the en-suite bathroom.

"Are you really that scared?" he asks, turning to face me.

I nod, shoving my hands under my arms to hide the trembling.

"Fine." He exhales.

"Fine what?"

"Fine . . . I'll sleep next to you tonight. Will that help you feel less . . . *scared*?" He's fighting a smirk, and I'm questioning why my body is all of a sudden changing gears. There's a heat in my core, a tingle in my belly, and a burn on my lips when I think about sharing a bed with him tonight.

A kiss from Cristiano sure would distract me from the creepy dolls under the blankets . . .

"You don't have to do that," I say, mentally scolding myself the second the words leave my lips. *Of course* he has to do this. I'm terrified. I won't sleep tonight if he doesn't, and I need to sleep. We've got a long day tomorrow. "But I don't want to make you sleep on the wood floor. That's not right. We can share the bed."

He tucks his lower lip behind his teeth before his mouth pulls up at the corners. He's totally onto me. Disappearing behind the door, I perch on the edge of the bed and listen to the shower run.

After a few minutes of convincing myself that my fears are completely irrational and that I'm capable of ignoring them, I change into pajamas and grab my soap and toothpaste in wait of my turn in the bathroom.

The shower's still running. It feels like he's taking forever, and there's no TV in here to pass the time, so I check my phone and fire off a quick text to Delilah, letting her know where we are and that our first day on the road went smoothly. I don't tell her about the Deliverance guys in Fort Reed, and I don't tell her about the lovely bed and breakfast we're seeking refuge at tonight. Details aren't important, especially when I have a sister who obsesses over them.

A moment later, the door swings open, and Cristiano emerges in a cloud of soap-scented fog, nothing but a towel wrapped around his waist.

"Oh . . . hello," I say, keeping my eyes on his and pretending like I have no desire to lick the rivulets of water that are currently trailing from his muscled shoulders down to his rippled abs. My mind chooses now as a good time to point out that the only thing separating me from him is a thin white towel and a whole lot of self-restraint.

Good god, he's sex on legs.

His dark hair is loosely finger-combed to the side, his body glistens under the dim light, and his body is pure muscle, lean and strong.

There's a lump in my throat that I try my damnedest to swallow away before he asks me a question, because I know all that'll come out will be squeaks and air.

"Did . . . did you need something?" I rise from the bed, going toward his luggage.

"Yeah," he says, half-smirking. He takes his place at my side, unzipping a leather pouch on top of his clothes and pulling out a few items . . . a toothbrush . . . a comb . . . I'm not sure what else he grabs because I'm completely flustered and all my energy is being funneled into my feeble attempt to remain calm.

A knock on the door forces my heart into my throat, and I jump back, swallowing a gulp of air. Gathering myself, I don't consider the fact that Cristiano's wearing nothing but a bath sheet before I decide to go ahead and open the door.

"Mrs. Snodgrass," I say. "Hi."

The smell of warm chocolate chip cookies floods the small space between us, and I glance down to see the tray of milk and cookies in her hands. Her eyes flick over my shoulders and into the room, landing on a half-naked Cristiano.

Her fingers clutch the sides of the tray and her lips form a hard line. "I'm here for the turndown service."

My jaw hangs. "It's not what it looks like . . . we're just . . . he was grabbing something . . ."

There's nothing I can say or do in this moment to ease the shock Mrs. Snodgrass is feeling right now. I can only hope she's not going to have a heart attack in the next sixty seconds.

Shoving the tray into my arms, she lifts her nose in the air. "I want you two out by dawn. Leave the money under the lamp on the fireplace mantle."

"Yes, ma'am." I say.

Quick footsteps carry her away, and I shut the door softly behind her.

"She hates us," I say, carrying the cookies to a small table and chair set by the bay window on the far wall. "And now she's definitely going to murder us in our sleep tonight."

Cristiano shoves a melted, gooey cookie in his mouth. "I'd like to see her try."

He heads back to the bathroom, shutting the door only halfway behind him, and emerges fully dressed in sweats and a t-shirt and smelling like spearmint. I take my turn after him, and when I come out, the room is pitch black save for the bright screen of his phone illuminating his face.

Heart racing slightly, I tiptoe across the wood floor and climb into bed beside him. There's at least a good eight inches between us, which says a lot since this is a full-sized bed and I'm on the very edge, teetering on the verge of falling off because I don't want to seem presumptive. And I don't want to make him think my intention was to try to get a reprise of last night's events.

His screen darkens and I hear the click of the screen as it lands on the nightstand. The bed shifts and he moves closer, slipping his arm underneath me and pulling me into him like I'm no heavier than a rag doll.

"What are you doing?" I ask, heart beating harder and faster than ever. My mouth is dry and my tongue grazes my lips just in case he decides to plant one on me in the coming seconds.

"Protecting you from the dolls," he says. He yawns before burying his face in my hair, his chin resting on the back of my shoulder.

His body forms to mine.

We're spooning.

But at least the dolls can't get me tonight.

My lips form a wide smile in the dark, one that he can't see. I can't help but laugh about all of this. Never thought I'd find myself holed up in some Victorian bed and breakfast, surrounded by creepy dolls, and wrapped in the arms of one of the most attractive men I've ever laid eyes on.

Just another priceless moment, I suppose . . .

Chapter Nine

Cristiano

"If you could have one super power, what would it be?" Daphne asks, her knees on the dash. She licks the tip of her pointer finger and turns a page in some stupid book she insisted on buying from the gas station when we fueled up this morning. She thought it'd be a fun way to pass the time since we've got another thirteen-hour day ahead of us, but I'm pretty sure I'd rather gouge my eyes out with a rusty fork.

"I don't know." I squint at the sun as we head east, feeling around for the five-dollar sunglasses I picked up yesterday at one of our stops. Sliding the cheap aviators over my eyes, I say, "I guess maybe the ability to heal people? Just touch them and then, boom, they're good to go."

"Aw, that's cute," she says, paging through the book and scanning the pages for another question. "I was expecting you to say x-ray vision or something that could be used for perverted stuff."

"You think I'm a pervert?"

"You're a twenty-something-year-old guy, so . . . yeah." She fights a smile and then punches my arm. "I'm kidding. Okay. Next question. Best childhood memory?"

"My eighth birthday," I say. "Money was tight. We'd just moved to Jersey. Mom was working two jobs, doing it all on her own. My oldest brothers, Alessio and Matteo, pooled their money so they could throw me a birthday party. The five of us went to Chuck E. Cheese. Played for hours. My brothers, most of them were too old for that place, but they knew I wanted to be there, so they made sure we had a good time."

"That's really sweet." She flicks another page, her voice soft. "They sound like good guys."

"They are."

"What's your biggest secret?"

"Whoa, whoa, whoa." I take my eyes off the road for a second so I can shoot her a look. "You can't just go from like, 'what superpower would you want' to 'what's your biggest secret.'"

"Why not?"

"Several reasons, but for starters, I hardly know you."

"You know me well enough to jump in my car and drive across the country with me."

"I'm not telling you any secrets."

"Why not? It's not like we'll ever see each other again after this. As long as you're not confessing to, like, murdering anyone, I'm not going to kick you out of the car."

I drag in a ragged breath and focus on the dotted white lines on the road ahead. Two semis are crowding the lanes, blocking the flow of traffic as we head up a hill. We're not even halfway home and this drive is taking for-ev-er.

"Fine. You go first. Tell me your deepest, darkest secret, and then I'll tell you mine," I say.

"We didn't say deepest, darkest," she says. "Only biggest."

"Is there a difference?"

"Of course."

"All right, what's your biggest secret?" I ask.

I watch her from my periphery, her mouth twisting in one corner as she stares off to the side.

"I'm waiting," I say after what feels like a solid minute.

"I'm thinking, hold on." She waves me away before closing the book in her lap. "Okay, when I was a senior in high school, I hooked up with my art teacher. Nobody knows. Not even my friends at the time. It was a one-time thing. I was at his house, dropping off some supplies that I'd borrowed from him – things we didn't have access to at school – and he invited me in. We were talking, and then he took me to his in-home studio to show me some of his paintings. There was this one of this girl . . . she looked like me . . . and she was nude. It was weird but oddly flattering, and I don't even know what happened after that. Everything got dark and blurry and then we were kissing, and it was over before I knew it."

"Jesus, Daphne." I exhale, searching her face for signs of distress. "Were you upset? Did you tell anyone?"

"No." She glances down to her lap, her fingers knitting. "At the time, I sort of had a little crush on him. I was glad it happened. He moved that summer. Took a non-teaching job in another state. Never did find out where he went. His name was John Smith. It doesn't get any harder to find than that."

"What an asshole."

She chuckles. "I know, right? Looking back, yeah. It was wrong. But you couldn't tell eighteen-year-old me anything."

"I have a feeling not much has changed in that regard."

"Anyway," she exhales, sitting up straight and tugging her shirt into place. "Your turn. What's your biggest secret?"

"I have two," I say. "I'm not sure which one to tell you. They're both pretty big."

"Two?" She leans closer, her lips drawn wide. "I get two? This is amazing. Spill it!"

"First one." I draw in a long breath. "Nobody knows this about me. Not my mother . . . not my brothers . . ."

She's quiet, which I take as a sign that she's all ears.

"I never graduated from law school. Everyone thinks I did. I was screwing some girl who worked in the registrar's office, and I convinced her to put me on the list for the ceremony. They give out that fake diploma anyway, so it didn't matter. It was all for show. I just wanted to make my mom proud."

"Damn."

"I just want to explore the world, as cheesy as that sounds. I realized halfway through law school that I didn't want to practice law. I didn't want to sit in an office all day, putting in fifty, sixty-hour weeks, hoping someday someone would make me partner. So I quit after a year and traveled on my own for a bit. Went back to campus to clear out my apartment, ran into that girl, and it all sort of came together. It was her idea actually, but I gave her the green light. I feel horrible for lying though. One of these days I'll come clean, especially to my mother, but when I look at her and see the pride in her eyes . . . I'm just not ready to let her down yet."

"People drop out of school every day," Daphne says. "There's no shame."

"I realize that now. If I could do it over again, I wouldn't have done that." I run my fingers through my hair, tugging on the ends. "God, I'm a fucking asshole."

"No." Daphne shakes her head. "You made a mistake. We all make mistakes. Learn and move on. Dwelling on them doesn't do a damn bit of good. Now what's your next secret?"

My lips curl up in one corner. There's a slight heat in my cheeks. I'm getting all flushed and second-guessing my decision to reveal this one, but in my defense, my intention was for it to be a bit of comedic relief.

Because it's fucking hilarious.

Drawing in another breath, I change lanes. "All right. Secret number two has to do with my source of income."

Daphne's eyes squeeze tight. "Please, please, please don't tell me you're a drug mule."

"God, no. Guess again. You're cold. Very, very cold."

"Hitman?" She winces.

"No."

"Stripper?"

"Nope."

"Porn star?"

"Not . . . quite."

"I don't know?" Her eyes squint as she looks me up and down, sticking the tip of her thumbnail between her top and bottom teeth.

"I pose for romance book covers," I say the words I've never spoken out loud to anyone in my life.

Her face is washed in relief and she clutches at her chest. "You scared me for a second. I was assuming something really, really bad. But you're a model. That's respectable."

"Not just any model," I say, fighting a ridiculous smirk because I know how lame I'm about to sound. "I'm Jax Diesel."

"Jax Diesel?" She wrinkles her nose, just like I expected her to.

"It's like a stage name," I say. "I didn't want to use my real name, for obvious reasons, so in the romance world, my face is associated with that name. I even have a Facebook page with about fifty thousand likes."

"Damn. I'm going to look it up now."

"Please . . . don't. I don't want to . . . turn you on."

She laughs, tossing her book aside and grabbing her phone. I suppose if she wasn't going to do it now, she'd be doing it later.

"Holy . . ." she says, her thumb gliding across her phone

screen in rapid succession. "These pictures . . . um . . . wow."

"Okay, enough," I say.

"How much does one of these fetch? If you don't mind my asking?"

"About fifteen hundred."

"Dollars?!"

"Yes."

"For one photo."

"Yes."

Her hands fall in her lap, the phone nearly sliding onto the floor. "That is insane."

"That's how I pay the bills. And travel the world."

"And nobody knows?"

"Nope. Not a soul."

"Why haven't you told anyone? I'd think your mother would be proud. You're a success, *Jax Diesel*."

"My mother will never see these photos." I cringe at the thought of her seeing smoldering, sexy photos of her half-naked fourth son.

She's grinning from ear to ear as she reaches for her phone. Within seconds, she's thumbing through another photo album.

"Oh my god, this is awesome. Never knew I'd someday be in the company of an Internet celebrity."

"I'm not an Internet celebrity."

"Eh, I beg to differ on that, *Jax*. If people want your autograph, you're basically famous." She holds up a photo of me at a book convention signing autographs behind an eight-foot banner with my half-nude likeness on it. Ladies are lined up by the dozen. Smiling. Grinning. Patiently waiting for a chance to take a picture with me or have me sign their unmentionables.

Rolling my eyes, I swat her phone from her hand, grabbing it and placing it in the door on my side of the car.

"Enough," I say. "Now kindly un-see what you've just seen."

"Never." She reaches for her stupid book and flips to a page in the middle. "This is really fun. I'm so glad I bought this. Okay, next question. Where do you see yourself in five years?"

"Next," I say.

"What?"

"This isn't a fucking job interview. That question is lame. Give me something better."

"Most embarrassing moment?"

"I don't get embarrassed."

"Bullshit," she coughs. "You've got to have something."

Pressing my lips together, I debate whether or not I want to tell her the one and only most mortifying moment of my life.

"You so have something," she says, nudging me with her elbow. "Come on."

"Fine." I clear my throat. "When I was twelve, one of my friends dared me to try to fit into one of those baby swings at a nearby park. I was a pretty skinny kid. A confident kid, too. So I took the dare."

Her hand clasps over her mouth, her eyes wide. "You got stuck, didn't you?"

I nod. "Mm hm. Got stuck and while my friend ran off for help, a family came up with their baby. Put their baby in the swing beside me. Stared a bit but didn't say much until they finally asked if I needed help. By then a firetruck was pulling up and my friend was running my way. They had to cut me out of it."

Daphne snorts, her hands covering her face. "That's freaking hilarious, Cristiano."

"No, it was fucking mortifying. The whole neighborhood came to watch. Everyone saw the firetruck and decided it was a good time to stand on the corner and gawk. Including the girl I had a major crush on that summer."

She's still laughing, only this time she has tears in her eyes. "I'm sorry. It's just . . . it's just, I can picture it so clearly . . . and . . . I'm sorry it happened to you . . ."

"All right, all right. Get it out of your system." I motion for her to wrap it up. "Next question. That is, if you still want to play this stupid game."

She fights her smile, stifling her laughter, and pages through her book to find another question.

"Okay," she says, "Have you ever had your heart broken?"

Exhaling hard, I don't respond. "You sure know how to pick 'em. There's no finesse to your line of questioning. We need to work our way to these big questions."

"Most of the questions in here are superficial," she says in all seriousness. "I'm not much into superficial conversation. I could give two shits what your favorite color or season is. I don't care what your favorite basketball team is or your favorite movie. Those kinds of things never make for good conversation. We've got a lot of miles to cover, Amato. Let's make 'em count."

"Next question."

"No," she says. "Answer it. Has anyone ever broken your heart before?"

"Of course. Next."

"Elaborate, pretty please."

"No thanks."

"Fine. I'll go first." She situates herself in the passenger seat and shuts the book in her lap. "I've had my heart broken a few different times. The first was my high school boyfriend. The second was that artist in Paris, the one you've never heard of. The last was Weston – a professional football player I met one summer. It was one of those whirlwind things. You know, the ones where you're obsessed with each other. Everything clicks. You can't get enough of each other. Your family loves them. There's never been anyone more perfect for you. You see forever when you look at them . . . and then it's over just as fast as it started. Ever have one of those?"

"Nope."

"Lucky you."

"I'd hardly call me lucky."

"Then who was it, Cristiano? Who broke your heart?"

"Just a girl."

Daphne scoffs. "I highly doubt she was just a girl."

"Yeah, well, that's all she was. Just a girl who lived next door to me. Didn't feel the same way I felt. She wanted to be with someone else. I let her go. The end."

"The end?" Daphne twists her body toward me. "That's all you're going to give me?"

"Yep."

"She's the only one who's ever broken your heart?"

"Yep."

Daphne slinks back in her seat, hopefully sensing my reluctance to speak more on this subject, but I have no interest in revisiting anything remotely as painful as that experience was.

"Cristiano?" she asks a moment later. We're coming into some thicker traffic, so I'm hoping her question-and-answer session is coming to a halt.

"Yeah?"

"I just want to say that," her voice is light, "you're not so bad when you're not being a pompous, overly protective know-it-all."

"You're not so bad when you're not pretending to be something you're not," I zing back.

"I beg your pardon?" Daphne sits straight, her hand over her heart and her jaw slack. She's approaching the verge of offended, but I'm only messing with her.

Kind of.

"Yeah," I say, "you try to act like you're this free-spirited, adventurous type, but you're actually a Type A control freak."

"I. Am. Not."

"I saw the way you rearranged the soap in the bathroom this morning."

"I was bored."

"And you re-routed us three times because you didn't like how crooked our original route looked. You wanted more of a straight line."

"The crooked route had too many detours through small towns."

"You ironed your jeans," I add. "That lady wanted us out of her bed and breakfast, but you took the time to iron your jeans."

"They were wrinkled from my suitcase."

"When you mixed your coffee this morning at the gas station, you added creamer. Stirred. Added sugar. Stirred again. Then added creamer. Then you replaced the lid and swirled it like it was a goddamned martini. Like you had it down to a science. Like it wasn't your first time."

Daphne shrugs. "Okay, particular about things doesn't mean I'm Type A."

"The hell it doesn't."

"Fine. I can be both Type A and adventurous, can't I?"

"You can," I say, "but don't pretend you're only one or the other when you're both."

She exhales loudly, pressing her cheek against the passenger glass.

"I only brought it up because I thought it was cute," I add, hoping to soften this situation. "I'm teasing you. I guess I forgot that you don't know me that well. You probably don't get my sense of humor. Guess it just feels like we're friends, and shit, maybe we are now. You know my secrets. I know yours."

Daphne glances my way from the corner of her eye. "Lucky me."

Her phone rings from my side of the car, and I remember that I'd confiscated it a few miles back.

"Here," I hand it off, catching the name DELILAH on the screen.

"Hey," she answers the call. "Everything okay? You didn't have the baby, right?"

It's quiet, and I catch Daphne biting her thumbnail again. Must be a nervous habit of hers.

"Okay," she says, "I'm so relieved. We're making good time. Everything's going smoothly. I should be home by Friday night. We're headed to Chicago now. We'll stay the night, and then from there, we'll head to Scranton, Pennsylvania so I can drop him off, and I'll be home three hours after that . . . I promise . . . love you too."

She hangs up with her sister and buries her phone in her purse, reaching for the backseat and grabbing a photography magazine she bought at one of our pit stops.

"Everything okay with your sister?" I ask.

"Yeah," she says, flipping a glossy page.

"You're quiet."

"Just anxious to get home."

"I'll get you there." I think about calling my friends back home to reassure everyone that I'm getting close, but Joey'd probably give me shit for calling with an update. If I say I'm going to be somewhere, I'm always there. I'm a man of my word.

Checking the GPS on my phone, I note that we'll hit Chicago around eight o'clock, which is nice because then we can avoid rush hour. Daphne made us reservations at an actual chain hotel, one with clean, modern furnishings, a bar and grill, and a pool. I'm looking forward to a good night's rest tonight, that's for damn sure.

She even made sure there are two beds in our room, and the odd thing is, when she told me we wouldn't have to share a bed tonight, the smallest part of me felt a twinge of tightness in my chest.

It's been kind of nice lying next to her at night. Plus she's soft as hell and she smells good, too. Like lavender and oranges and clean laundry.

Last night I passed out by the time my head hit the pillow. Driving all day took its toll on me. But had I kept an ounce of remaining energy, I'm not sure I'd have been able to keep my hands off her.

It's easy to be around her. As annoying as she is. As stubborn as she is. Something about being with her just . . . works. It fits. It feels right. I'm comfortable around her. I don't feel the need to turn myself into some Prince Charming to get what I want. I'm myself. And she's herself. And neither of us apologize for it.

She's genuine. She isn't trying to be cute. She isn't trying to get me to fall in love with her. She isn't playing some pseudo-girlfriend role just because we've found ourselves in this coupled situation.

She's just . . . herself.

And shit, if things were different, I might even entertain the idea of . . .

Nah.

It would never work.

We're almost too similar.

I'm not the settling down type, plus the last thing I need when I'm traipsing around the globe is some girlfriend back home worrying about me.

Glancing at her through the corner of my eye, I watch her tug her bottom lip between her teeth as she stares blankly ahead at the cars in front of us. I'm seconds from asking what she's thinking about, because I'm genuinely curious, but for some reason I stop myself.

"I'm going to take a nap, all right?" she asks, yawning and reaching for the backseat to retrieve a neck pillow we picked up at a gas station yesterday. "Wake me up when you need me to drive."

Chapter Ten

Daphne

"When the sign said World's Largest Turtle, I expected it to be real. Not some painted, fiberglass turtle sculpture thing." I stand in front of a fifty-foot plastic-looking turtle painted in the most garish shade of puke green. The painted smile on its face is comically crooked, and the eyes are two dark empty windows. There's a sign that says you can pay five bucks to go up into the turtle's head, but I think I'll pass. "You going to take the picture or what?"

Cristiano lifts my phone and snaps a couple of pics. We're in some tourist trap on the border of Iowa and Illinois called Turtle World, which happens to be conveniently located in Turtle County.

"All right, your turn." I walk toward him, reaching for my phone.

"I'll pass."

Sticking my tongue out at him, I say, "Don't be so boring."

"If not standing in front of a giant plastic turtle makes me boring, then I'm as boring as they come. Come on, let's get back on the road. We're making good time. Let's keep it going."

We trek through the dusty, pea gravel-filled parking lot and head toward our car. In the passenger side is a white plastic sack of snacks and random turtle items I bought from the turtle shop when he was fueling up the car.

He climbs into the passenger side, moving the bag and then peering into it. "I'm fucking starving. What'd you get?"

Biting a smile, I slide into the driver's seat and start the engine.

"What . . . the hell." He pulls out two saran-wrapped gas station-quality sandwiches that happen to be cut in the shape of a turtle. Next, he retrieves a shiny red bag with a chocolate turtle on the front. "What are these?"

"Turtle chips," I say.

His nose wrinkles. "I'm not eating fucking turtle."

"No, they're potato chips covered in chocolate and drizzled with caramel. No turtles were harmed in the making of those chips."

"Did you get any regular food?"

"Ha. Did you honestly expect a place called Turtle World to offer regular food? There's a burger place up the street."

I guide us out of the gas station, passing the giant turtle on our way to the highway, and follow the iconic golden arches so that my fellow traveler can have some non-turtle sustenance.

A minute later, we're fourth in line at the burger place, and he's squinting to read the menu from clear back here.

"Hang on," he says, pulling his phone from his pocket. He presses the green button on the screen and lifts it to his ear, though I had no idea it was even going off. "Hey, what's up?"

He's mostly quiet, like he's listening, and I hear him say,

"Mm hm." He nods, his eyes narrowed on the glove compartment. The line moves, but he's still on the phone. He doesn't seem preoccupied with his growling stomach anymore.

"Everything'll be fine. We can talk about this more when I get there," he says. "Just don't freak out. You'll make it worse. Yeah, I wish I was there too, but I'm not. I'm here if you need me. Just stay cool. I'll be home in two days."

He hangs up, and I pull the car forward again. It's our turn to order next.

"Who was that?" I ask.

"Joey." He pushes a hard breath through his nose, concentrating on the lit menu on our left.

"Everything okay?"

His lips form a flat line. "Cold feet, that's all."

He orders a combo, shouting over the driver's seat, and we pull forward.

"Cold feet is normal," I say. "Or so I hear. I wouldn't know. But I feel like if someone's at the point where they've already committed to marrying someone, they're probably making the right choice. I mean, if you go so far as to give someone a ring and propose to them, you had to have wanted to be with them at some point. Maybe I'm not making any sense. I just think that the week of the wedding is kind of the worst possible time to second-guess your decision. You're stressed and feeling irrational and not thinking clearly. You have to trust your gut and trust that the non-stressed, rational version of yourself made the right choice."

I quietly pat myself on the back because I feel like Delilah would be proud of me right now. I'm well aware that I suck at psychoanalysis most of the time. Art is my strong suit. Give me something abstract, and it makes perfect sense. But this . . . I feel like I made some sense here.

"Nah," Cristiano says, his chin jutting forward. "Those two have no business being married. I've tried to get my point across for the last two years. Not sure what they're thinking, but if it were up to me, I'd stop the wedding in a heartbeat."

"Oh."

"Biggest mistake of their lives, if you ask me. They're all wrong for each other. And Joey deserves better."

We pull forward to the next window, and he hands me a ten-dollar bill to pay.

"If more people would listen to you, the world would be a better place, right?" I tease, trying to lighten his mood.

"I don't know about that, but a lot less people would be getting fucked over. That's for damn sure."

Chapter Eleven

Cristiano

"The hostess won't stop staring at you." Daphne fights a smile as she peers over a laminated drink menu in a booth at the bar and grill attached to the Family Comfort Inn Hotel and Suites.

"She wants me," I tease, polishing my nails on my shirt and stretching my arms over my head. Lacing my fingers behind my neck, I toss her a wink and a smile that makes her blush and spin on her heel. She nearly bumps into a busboy. "It's nothing new."

"Women stare at you a lot. I've been noticing that the last couple of days. Everywhere we go, you literally turn heads. The gas stations . . . the rest stops . . . the restaurants . . . driving seventy-five miles per hour down the freeway . . ."

"And your point?"

"It's weird, don't you think?"

I shake my head. "It is what it is."

"I hate that saying."

"Me too."

"I'm ordering two drinks tonight. Just an FYI." She flips a page in her menu, studying her options.

"Two? You lush." I scan the bar area for our server. We've been seated for five minutes now, and I'm starving and I haven't seen a single server in sight. A group of people are huddled in the corner, and every so often laughter erupts.

"What's going on over there?" Daphne peers over her menu, squinting toward the group of people.

"I saw a sign by the door when we came in. Palm reader or something."

"Palm reader?"

"It's just some stupid gimmick bars use to lure people in. Come for a palm reading, stay for a drink. Or two."

"I want my palm read."

"No, you don't."

"Is it free?"

"I think so, but it's also fake, so it's a huge fucking waste of time."

"Have you ever had your palm read?"

"Never."

"Then how do you know it's fake?"

"Because I know everything. I'm a know-it-all, remember?"

She rolls her eyes and drops the menu. "I'm going over there."

If I've learned anything about Daphne Rosewood in our short time together, it's that once she gets an idea in her head, there's no stopping her. Within seconds she's clear across the bar, standing in line for a palm reading.

Pulling in a deep breath, I slide out of the booth and join her. I want to hear what this scammer says because God forbid she tells Daphne to go out and buy a grand worth of lottery tickets on the second Wednesday of next month . . . and she actually does it. These people tell you what you want to hear. I learned that a couple of summer ago in Rome, when a gypsy read my "fortune" and declared that I was going to be wealthy beyond my wildest dreams by the time I was twenty-five.

Twenty-five came and went, and I was just just some random guy posing for book covers making a comfortable living.

"Oh, hello," she says when she sees me. Her lips pull wide and the white of her smile brightens the dark. "Decide to get a reading, did we?"

"Nope." I fold my arms across my chest and pull my shoulders back. "Just making sure you don't get ripped off."

"How could I get ripped off? It's free."

I shrug. "They have ways. It's what they do. She might try to sell you some kind of potion or some shit."

Daphne bursts out laughing, covering her mouth. The man standing behind her cranks his head to shoot her a dirty look. Apparently people in this town take their psychic palm readers very seriously.

"I would so buy a potion from her," Daphne says.

"Wait, what?"

"Where else, in this country, can you get an actual potion? A potion!" She punches my arm, her face lit. "Do you know how freaking awesome that sounds?"

"I don't even know if she makes potions, I was just saying. She's got bills to pay and there's no such thing as a free lunch, so just . . ."

"Cristiano. Stop." She places her palm flat on my chest. "I'm a big girl. I can handle this."

"Who's next?" the woman calls her, her accent vaguely Romanian, though it could very well be fake.

Daphne steps forward and takes a seat at a round table covered in a lace cloth. A flickering candle rests between them as well as a deck of Tarot cards and a crystal ball. If Daphne believes in any of this shit, I'm going to be really fucking disappointed.

"Palm or tarot?" the psychic asks, peering down her wire-frame glasses. Wild gray waves cascade down her shoulders, and she's wearing some sort of purple velvet dress. Her fingers are covered in giant rings with various crystals, ruby, and emerald centers, and bangle bracelets clink around her wrists when she moves her hands.

"Palm, please." Daphne is beaming. She's excited about this. Her hand flies to the center of the table, palm-side up, and she shoots me a wink.

"Ah, yes. Okay." The woman holds Daphne's hand in her own, examining it, rolling it from side to side and lifting it closer to her vision. "Very interesting."

"What is it?" Daphne asks, eyes flicking from her palm to the lady and back.

The woman traces the pad of her finger along Daphne's ring finger. "This. This tells me you're very creative. You're very left-brained. You think outside the box. Abstract."

Daphne's smile fades, maybe from shock. The lady is one-for-one.

"This line here, between your index and pointer finger," the psychic says. "Tells me you're the baby of the family. I'm guessing . . . fourth child?"

Daphne's jaw hangs, though she says nothing.

"This line here," she says, "these are your children. Well, looks like you're only going to have one. A little girl. No time soon. You'll have her later in life."

"What else do you see?" Daphne scoots forward, even more invested than she was a moment ago.

"This is your marriage line." The woman drags her nail down the center of her palm. "You'll only get married once, but it will be forever." Closing her eyes, the woman says, "You will marry a man you've already met. He is your soulmate, but you don't know it yet."

Daphne bites her lower lip, concentrating on the psychic's face, clinging to her every word. "You can tell that by looking at my palm?"

The woman nods. "Well, that, and I just . . . know things. It's very complicated. But I've always sort of . . . known things. Ever since I was a little girl. Call it an exaggerated gut instinct. Mine just happens to be a bit stronger."

"Anything else?" Daphne lifts her brows, hopeful.

With her eyes on Daphne's palm, she smiles slowly. "Yes, you're going to have a long life. I see here you'll live until your upper eighties."

Daphne pulls her hand back, pressing it against her chest. "Thank you."

"Young man, would you like to go next?" The psychic turns to me with a smirk on her face. I'm sure she's been doing this long enough that she can spot a skeptic from a mile away.

"Do it!" Daphne nudges me closer to the table.

"No, thank you." I back away.

"Come on. What do you have to lose? She was spot on with me," Daphne says. "She's legit."

I don't want to offend this woman, and I don't want to cause a scene. A group of women standing behind are mumbling to each other, probably complaining that I'm holding up the line.

"I'll pass," I say.

"Please? Where's your sense of adventure?" Daphne presses her hands into prayer formation and stands on her toes.

Fuck. She has a point.

But I still don't believe in this shit.

"Fine." I yank the chair out and take a seat, placing my palm on the center of the table.

"No, no." The woman lifts her nose, her lips pursed. "I won't be reading your palm."

The second I go to stand, she places her hand over mine.

"Sit. Stay," she says, like I'm a goddamned dog. "I won't read your palm. But you're getting a reading."

The woman presses her fingers against her temples,

scrunching her face and closing her eyes tight.

"He is sorry," she says.

"Who?" I fold my arms, chuffing. "There are a lot of people with a lot of reasons to be sorry."

"He is sorry he could not be the father you deserved. But he is happy for you. He is proud. You make him proud. You *all* do."

There's a tightness in my throat. A burn in my chest. My eyes water. Hell, I didn't even know they could do that. Can't remember the last time I shed a tear over anyone or anything. Sure as hell have never cried over that drunk bastard, at least not in my adult life. As a kid, I was too young to be broken. As a teenager, I was too rebellious to care. As an adult, I'm too intelligent to waste my time mourning that sorry son of a bitch who couldn't keep a roof over our heads or his hands off my mother.

"Also, are you going to a wedding soon? I'm being told there's a wedding and that you're a very important part of it." She cocks her head to the side, peering down her nose. "I feel like you have reservations about this marriage, but it's important that you show your support to the bride and groom. Their day isn't about you."

Chills run up and down my spine and my arms are covered in gooseflesh.

"I don't want to do this anymore." I rise, pushing the chair out, and make my way back to the booth.

Chapter Twelve

Daphne

My cheap ballpoint pen drags along a pad of hotel paper, my mind ignoring the bright blue logo across the top. Making crosshatch after crosshatch, I sketch Cristiano's likeness, and when I'm done, I've captured his mood.

The sullen look on his face.

The furrowed brow.

The flare of his nostrils as he exhales.

He's seated beside me, staring at the flickering hotel TV, though I'm pretty positive he's doing anything but paying attention.

"What are you thinking about?" I break the silence between us.

He's been in a mood ever since his psychic reading. Maybe he's thinking about his late father? Maybe he's thinking about the wedding he's trying to get to? I have no idea because he's been quiet since dinner, offering little more than a few, "Mm hms," and grunted yesses when I try to engage in conversation.

Cristiano's chest rises and falls as he pulls in a deep breath, like I've woken him from a trance, and then he turns to me, his gaze narrowing on my face first and then falling to the pad of paper in my lap.

"What's that?" he asks.

Handing it off, I say, "It's you."

He pulls it closer, examining my masterpiece. "You did this?"

"Who else would've done it?" I half-chuckle.

"I mean, you did this with a cheap hotel pen and pad of paper?" He scratches his temple, staring at his sketched image. "I'm impressed. It looks so . . . real. But do I really look this pissed off?"

I swipe the drawing from him and nod.

"Yeah. You do. You mad about something?" Before he answers, I sign my name in the corner and hand it back. "Here. Keep it. Maybe someday when I'm a famous artist, it'll be worth something to someone."

The corner of his mouth pulls up. It's good to see him smile. He hasn't smiled in hours.

"Not going to answer my question?" I circle back to that.

"Not mad, just thinking."

"About?"

He shakes his head, biting his bottom lip and turning his attention to the TV screen once more. "Anyone ever tell you that you ask a lot of questions, Daphne?"

My lips curl. "Pretty much everyone since the dawn of time. Yes. I ask questions. It's what I do. There's nothing wrong with being inquisitive, but since you're not in the mood to tell me what you were thinking about, forget I asked."

Gripping my pen, I scan the room for something else to sketch. I'm bored. And despite the fact that we've been driving all day, I'm not nearly as tired as I expected to be. Drawing relaxes me, and tonight it's my Ambien.

"I'm not mad," he says a few beats later, exhaling with a soft groan. "Just thinking about things . . . people, mostly. People you don't know. Things you don't know about. My thoughts would bore the hell out of you."

"I doubt that."

"Anyway, we're getting up in six hours." He shuts off the TV before reaching for the lamp by the bedside. The room has two queen-sized beds, and the plan was not to sleep in the same bed tonight, but he hopped on mine earlier because I had a better view of the thirty-two-inch flat screen.

Scooting down, he shoves two pillows under his neck and clasps his hands over his chest, staring at the popcorn ceiling.

"Oh, um." I place my pen and pad on my nightstand and click off my lamp. "I could take the other bed if you want."

"I thought the other bed *was* your bed."

"It doesn't matter. I just thought since I put my stuff over on this side of the room . . ." I exhale, placing one foot on the floor. His silence is making this awkward. Or maybe *I'm* making this awkward. I seem to be good at that these days.

"Fuck it. We can both sleep in this bed." He pulls the covers down and scoots over.

Fighting a smirk, I say, "Don't act like you're annoyed. It's not like you're doing me a favor. There's another bed, and I'm perfectly capable of sleeping by myself for the first time in days."

The AC kicks on behind me, sending a quick chill into the air. I have to admit; it's been nice sleeping next to someone for the first time in a long time. And tonight is our last night together. Forever.

"Okay, while you're over there weighing your options, I'm going to be over here sleeping," he says, rolling over. He punches the pillow, tucking it under his neck and situating his body under the blankets, silently conveying a "now or never" message.

Sucking in a lungful of stale, air-conditioned air, I climb under the covers beside him. There's a dent in the blanket marking the space between us void of human contact. You could fit another person in that space, easily.

The sliver of light between the drawn hotel curtains illuminates our section of the room and highlights the contour of his rounded, muscled shoulders, and his body slightly shifts as he breathes steady, quiet breaths.

The AC unit kicks off, bringing silence to our room, and I immediately miss the droning hum because I'm wide awake, and white noise would be welcome. Rolling to my side and facing away from him, I close my eyes and try to relax. I'd love to text Delilah right now, but it's late back home and I'm sure she passed out hours ago.

Moving to my back, I can't seem to get comfortable. I stare at the ceiling, whipping my attention toward the curtains, when I see flashing red and blue bleeding through. Someone must've been pulled over in the parking lot.

Exhaling, I twist my body back toward Cristiano, burying my cheek against the cool, white pillow, only this time he's facing me, eyes wide open.

"Daphne," he says, voice low and calm. "Go to sleep."

"I'm trying."

"No, you're not. You're tossing and turning. Shut your mind off and close your eyes. You should be exhausted by now."

He's such a know-it-all.

"I think it's that rum and Coke from earlier. It had caffeine in it."

"You mean the two rum and Cokes?" he corrects.

"Yeah. I'm wired now."

"Just try." He closes his eyes, pulling in a breath and pushing it through his nostrils like he's frustrated with me. I know he's tired. I should be more compassionate. I should hop over to the other bed and let him get some rest. He did most of the driving today, but it was purely by accident. The first day we had a system. A schedule. Today we played most of our stops by ear, and we got better gas mileage than we expected in Nebraska and Iowa because it was so flat, so we only had to fill up twice.

A gradual relaxation claims his expression, and I get the sense that he's well on his way to dreamland right now, so I take the opportunity to stare at him. Really stare at him. I study his features, mentally sketching them out. The curve of his jaw. The hint of a dimple in his chin that I hadn't noticed until now. His chiseled cheekbones. The tufts of thick dark hair that hang over his forehead. His perfect brows. Those long, chocolate-hued lashes. Those lips. Those full lips with the cupid's bow arch.

No wonder women go nuts over him.

He's literally a work of art.

Slowly scooting toward my edge of the bed, I quietly slide my phone off my nightstand and Google the name *Jax Diesel*. I have a wild hair to check out the romance covers he's graced. It doesn't take but a few clicks and I've hit the jackpot. There's one indie romance author, Hadley Caldwell, who seems to have used him for multiple covers. Clearly she's a huge fan. I even find a photo of the two of them from a signing in Colorado Springs last year. She's young. And pretty. And smiling bigger than I've ever seen anyone smile before.

I continue clicking through Google images and come across a photo of him at a book convention, signing autographs and taking pictures with fans. There's another picture of him with a whole group of ridiculously attractive men. I'm assuming they're all cover models. Studying their faces, I keep going back to Cristiano's.

He blows the other guys out of the water.

No contest.

"What the hell are you doing?" Cristiano's voice sends my heart sailing into my throat.

Clutching my lit phone against my galloping chest, I turn to him, breathless. "I thought you were asleep."

"Why are you looking at pictures of me?" he sits up, resting on his forearm.

"I wanted to see some of your book covers."

"Didn't look like you were looking at book covers. Looks like you were Googling me."

"So?" I defend myself with a single word that means absolutely nothing in this argument. I did it. I Googled him while he was lying next to me because I couldn't sleep. I'm sure I look like a freaking weirdo. Guilty as charged.

"Why would you want to look at pictures of me when I'm right in front of you?"

I don't know how to answer that question. It's a damn good question, too.

"No reason, really. I told you earlier. I'm just a curious girl." I shrug, placing my phone on the nightstand and slinking back under the covers. "Goodnight, Cristiano."

"No, no, no," he says, scooting closer and closing the gap between us.

"What?"

"You tired all of a sudden?"

"No?" I'm not sure what he's getting at. "You should probably go back to sleep."

"I'm wide awake now." He lies back, running his hand through his messy hair and blowing a breath through his lips. "So thanks for that."

"Sorry."

Rolling on his side, he props himself up again. I meet his gaze and even in the darkness of our hotel room, I know his stare lingers on my mouth.

"It's going to be different," he says, voice low. "After tonight, I mean."

"What are you talking about?"

"This is our last night together." I pick up on a hint of something bittersweet in his tone.

"You getting all sentimental on me?" I fight a smirk. "Doesn't seem like your style, Amato."

"How would you know my style?"

"I don't. But you don't seem sentimental. You seem like someone who's stuck in the moment. And maybe that's a good thing. But I don't think you think much about the past. And people who don't think about the past can't be sentimental."

"That's where you're wrong." He licks his lips, eyes locked on mine. "I think about the past every single day, Daphne. Sometimes I wish I could forget it."

My heart hammers in my ears, and in some ways, I feel like I'm looking at him for the first time all over again. He's not just a beautiful man. He's a complicated man. Broken. I couldn't see that before, but I see it now.

"Did you do something bad?" I ask, my voice a sheer whisper. The second the question leaves my lips, I'm doubting whether or not I want his answer. "Don't answer that. Sorry."

"Daphne?" he asks, brows narrowed. Somehow he feels closer now, like he'd moved my way without me noticing. The space between us is tight, and his warmth brushes lightly against my skin without us touching.

"Yes?"

Cristiano brings his hand to my face, cupping my cheek in his palm before his gaze lowers to my lips. My heart hammers in my ears. A ripple of tingles passes through my core, radiating through to my fingertips. So much for sleeping tonight. My body's alive and electric, completely entranced from the way he's looking like he's about to devour me.

"I'm going to kiss you," he says, his voice steady and unmovable like a freight train.

Swallowing, I try to speak, but forming a response feels insurmountable at this point.

His mouth crashes on mine, his soapy scent invading my lungs as I breathe him in. Fingers cupping the side of my neck and tangled in my hair, he presses his lips against mine with a feverish need.

Our bodies meet in the middle of the bed. In a matter of seconds, I'm pinned beneath him, anchored. His hips press against mine, and my body drinks in the comfort of how good it feels to be wanted, even if it's only temporary.

With his hands gathering my hair, he tugs until my mouth is again lifted to his, bringing his lips down on mine all over again.

I run my hands along his sides, feeling the subtle ripple of his muscles beneath his t-shirt as his body moves atop mine. An unquestionable hardness pressed against my sex takes this entire thing to a whole new level. He's hard. For me.

I'm completely immersed in this moment. I think he is too. I wonder if this is what he does: stays locked in these moments as a way of running or hiding from his past. From the intrusive thoughts that steal his joy out of nowhere.

There was a certain sadness in his dark gaze earlier. Whatever it was, whatever he refused to talk about, I have a feeling it's always there . . . residing just beneath his polished veneer.

Cristiano grinds his hips against mine, and I release a moan into his mouth. My core tingles with a palpable ache. It craves his touch. His fingers inside me, stroking. I imagine the way he might tease me with feather-light strokes first, building with hurried penetrations. First one finger, then two, and then . . . whatever else he'd like to do to me. Just looking at this man, I'm one-hundred percent certain he knows how to rain all kinds of pleasure down upon me.

"You're so fucking beautiful, Daphne," he whispers, his lips grazing mine. His minty breath fills my lungs, and all I can think about is whether or not he can feel how fast my heart is beating in my chest. "I've never met anyone like you before."

His hips press harder into mine, grinding with a slow rhythm that tells me we're straddling a very fine line here. This could easily go one of two ways. Grinding my hips against him, I nudge us in the only direction that feels right in this moment.

It's official. I want to sleep with Cristiano.

No.

I *need* to sleep with Cristiano.

A hot ache in my throat accompanies the fever pitch of anticipation. I'm doubting whether or not he's picking up what I'm putting down, but the moment he slides his hand beneath the covers and his cool fingertips graze the warm flesh of my belly, I struggle to breathe.

In an instant, his hand slides beneath the waistband of my panties, sliding down my wet seam. My stomach caves and my body tenses at his touch. I'm hyperaware of every breath. Every move. His finger presses harder, inviting itself inside of me one teasing inch at a time, and the sudden awareness of his touch is a sensation I welcome, my thighs falling limp and powerless. His strokes are soft and gentle at first, and his eyes meet mine. When he plunges a finger deep inside me, I release a held breath that may as well symbolize his name on my tongue.

This man is all over me. Inside. Outside. I'm fully immersed in the Cristiano Amato experience and loving every second of it.

My mind travels, thoughts racing through my mind at warp speed. Does he enjoy this? Is he watching me? Does he like the way my body reacts to each plunge of his finger? My eyes squeeze tight. I don't want to see. I don't want to know what he's thinking anymore. I only want to feel. I only want to enjoy.

His body lifts slightly above mine, and the covers have fallen. My body trembles, and I'm not sure if it's because it's freezing in here or because he's making my body feel things it hasn't in well over a year.

Rising on his knees, he tugs my pajama bottoms down all the way before pulling my panties off. Sitting up, I yank my tank top over my head before working on my bra. The sooner I'm completely naked with this Greek Adonis, the better.

He smirks, the hint of his white teeth lighting the dark. "God, I could never get tired of looking at you."

His fingers return between my thighs, slipping down my slit as his thumb circles my clit with gentle pressure. His caresses are restrained, but the glint in his eye tells me he doesn't intend to rest until he's enjoyed all of me. Closing my eyes, I sink back into the pillow, feeling the shift of his weight on the bed and, suddenly, the warmth of his tongue dragging the length of my seam.

"Oh, god," I say, exhaling. Wasn't expecting that.

His warmth and wetness mixing with mine is sheer heaven, and I reach for a fistful of sheets to gather as my jaw unhinges.

Cristiano, quite simply stated, is amazing at this.

His tongue circles my clit, his free hand pressed flat against my tensed stomach, holding me down. He devours me, and yet, at the same time, there's a gentle sensuality in the way he touches me.

Within minutes, I find myself getting close, pulsing, throbbing, craving the real thing. I suck in quick breaths each time I feel that tingle between my thighs. Staving it off isn't easy, and I'm not sure how much longer I can fight it.

Rising to his knees, he leaves the apex between my thighs. Moving closer and holding his body over mine, he brings his lips down on me once again. I taste my arousal. I taste the sweet musk of what he's done to me as he deposits an owning kiss on my waiting, wanting mouth.

Reaching for the hem of his shirt, I pull it over his head, yearning for the feel of his skin against mine. Cristiano presses his body down against mine, his hips flush against mine until I feel every inch of his hardness. We're separated by the fabric of his sweats and the endless, tortuous seconds that precede the inevitable.

I help myself, guiding my hand down his sides, grazing his muscled torso until I find the band of his sweats and pushing them down the sides of his muscled, flexing ass. Slipping a hand beneath the silky fabric of his boxers, I wrap my palm around his rock-hard cock, my heart leaping in the process. The skin is hot, throbbing in my palms as I pump his length. Meeting his gaze, I bask in the seductive half-smile he gifts me.

"Do you want this, Daphne?" his voice is a soft growl as he lowers himself, pressing kisses into the flesh above my collarbone.

Pressing my lips together, I nod. "Mm hm."

Moving to the side, he grabs his wallet from the nightstand and retrieves a gold foil packet. Ripping it between his teeth, he shoves his boxers down and wastes no time sheathing his hardness and returning to his space between my spread thighs.

A pulsing knot in my stomach makes its presence known in the seconds that lead up to his body pressing against mine all over again. His mouth finds mine in the dark as his hand grips the base of his cock, teasing my entrance with the tip before pushing his length inside me with one delicious thrust.

He fills me, stretching me with a pain that hurts so good, but after several thrusts it washes over me, evaporating into sheer ecstasy. I want more. I want all of him inside all of me. Every inch of us connected. Every inch of us made for this moment. It hasn't been but a minute, and already I'm burning with the kind of desire I've never known before. I don't want this to end. Ever.

Cristiano's mouth descends on me again, his hand cupping my jaw and his fingers wrapping around the nape of my neck. His kisses linger, like he's savoring every moment. Like he knows this isn't just the first time . . . it's also the last.

After tomorrow, I'll leave him in Scranton. He'll go his way. I'll go mine. And that'll be it. There won't be anything else.

Just tonight.

In this dreamily savage moment, I am his and he is mine. My soul melts with his kisses, my body melts with his touch.

He brings his mouth on mine again, our tongues meeting as

he thrusts himself faster inside me. His lips are warm and sweet, and I bring my hands to his face, cupping his chiseled jaw and feeling his dark hair beneath my fingertips.

My body shivers.

I can't fight it anymore.

I hold onto the wave, riding it out and letting it crash into me. Cristiano pumps harder, needier, bringing himself to a climax that elicits primal moans and stiffens his body from head to toe. His neck strains and his back arches as his cock pulses inside me.

When he's done, he kisses my mouth, resting on top of me, and then rolls off the bed and heads to the bathroom.

I'm exhausted, basking in this post-coital stupor and barely capable of forming a fragment of a thought. All I know is my body feels like a million bucks, and at the same time, there's a tinge of sadness washing over me because something like this will never happen again.

And I kind of wish it could.

***

Friday morning, I wake to the sound of the shower running. Sitting up, I blink a few times, adjusting to the glow of the small desktop lamp across the room. It's still dark out, but the alarm beside me says it's time to get up. We've got to hit the road by seven. It's six hours to Pittsburgh and another two to Scranton. After that, I've got another two hours until Rixton Falls.

Grabbing my phone from the nightstand, I spot a missed call from Delilah's husband, Zane.

"Shit." I dial him back as fast as my fingers will allow and pray to God he answers on the first ring.

He answers on the fourth.

"Hey," he says, almost whispering.

"Please tell me she hasn't gone into labor yet." I rise off the bed, spotting a covered dish on the table in the corner. Cristiano must've ordered breakfast for us. Not sure how I slept through room service, but after last night, I slept harder than I have in months.

"Not yet," he says as I uncover my plate and take a seat. I'm famished, which is probably also a result of last night's activities. "We went to the hospital around three o'clock this morning. We thought it was the real deal. Delilah was in a lot of pain, but she was still only dilated to a two. They sent us home. Said to monitor the contractions. I guess they weren't close enough together or something. I don't know how any of this works. Anyway, she's sleeping now, but I wanted to let you know because she'd asked me to call you. The doctor thinks we're getting close. Says the next time this happens it might be it."

My heart races.

I'm so close.

"I'll be home tonight," I say. "Tell her not to worry. We're leaving Chicago in the next hour and hitting the road. How's the weather, by the way?"

"Storms have all passed. They're just cleaning up now. I heard western Pennsylvania is okay but the farther east you get, the messier it is. Drive safe, Daphne."

"I will. Please tell my sister I'll be there, and I can't wait to see you guys."

"Will do."

My stomach rumbles when Zane ends the call, but now I'm too anxious to eat. The bacon and eggs and toast before me hold about as much appeal as a bowl of sawdust.

"Hey." The bathroom door flings open and Cristiano stands, fully dressed, hair damp, and smelling like a million bucks. "I was about to wake you up. We've got to hit the road."

"Yeah, I know. Delilah's getting closer."

"You'll be home tonight," he says it like it's a sure thing.

But a lot can happen in six hundred miles.

Chapter Thirteen

Cristiano

"Shouldn't you be resting? Why are you drawing?" I glance at the passenger seat where Daphne sits, knees on the dash, sketching something on that chintzy little pad of hotel paper.

"Not tired."

"Guess that's not surprising considering you drank a venti double shot Frappuccino two hours ago. You're going to be dragging by the time it's your turn."

"I'll deal."

Ever since she talked to her brother-in-law this morning, she's been quieter than normal. For the last three days, this woman has chatted my ear off. She always has something to say. A question to ask. A statement to make.

God, I hope this isn't because of last night.

Last night was fucking amazing.

It's a night I'll never forget as long as I live. Her scent, her soft skin, the way her lashes fluttered as she bit her lip every time I thrust my cock inside her sweet, tight pussy. She offered herself to me, and I took it, and I loved every fucking minute of it. In fact, I couldn't get enough. The second it was over, I wanted her again but I knew we had an early morning, and she was finally getting tired.

There's a tightness in my chest – a feeling I don't recognize because it's attached to a thought I've never felt before. At least a thought I've never felt about a woman I hardly know. Most of the time, I have my fun, call it an adventure of sorts, and go on my merry way, never seeing or hearing from them again. But the thought of walking away from Daphne several hours from now, never knowing what becomes of her or if anything would've become of . . . us . . . is almost sad.

I don't want this to be the end, and I'm not sure how to grapple with that notion. It's an unfamiliar feeling, like a foreign language that is as difficult to speak as it is to comprehend. Twisting the volume on the radio, I turn up the music and decide to let these thoughts mellow for a bit. Maybe I'm still worked up over last night, still reveling in how fucking amazing it was.

Definitely.

That's got to be what it is. It's the only logical explanation. A few more hours, and I'll be back to my old self.

"What are you drawing?" I ask above the musical stylings of Steely Dan.

"This bistro in Paris," she says, head tilted as if she's recalling a fond memory. "I used to grab breakfast there every day. They had the best chocolate croissants and espresso. I'd give anything to go back."

"Why don't you?"

She lifts a single shoulder, mouth bunched in one corner. "I don't know. I'm sure I will. It's just that if I get that job in California, teaching at that fine arts college . . ."

"What teaching job?"

"I was interviewing for a position at Seaview School of Fine Arts," she says. "That's why I was in California this week."

"Okay, so what about this job?"

"If I get this job, I'll be in California. They want to fill the position as soon as possible. I'd be starting spring semester. Apparently the drawing instructor they had decided to have a fling with a student – a high school student – and has been placed on unpaid leave pending the investigation."

"It wasn't that same guy, was it? The one you . . ."

"Oh, god, no. I don't think so? Guess I didn't ask his name. That'd be pretty meta though, wouldn't it?"

"Okay, so if you get the job in California, you can maybe go to Paris this summer, right? And if you don't get the job, you can go whenever you want."

Daphne snorts through her nose. "Not everyone's made of money, *Jax Diesel*. I can't just pick up and fly to Paris because the mood strikes me."

"What if I took you?" I make an offer I've never made anyone ever before . . .

. . . and I'm met with silence that sucks the air from both our lungs.

"I couldn't let you do that," she says.

"Why not? We obviously travel well enough together. We could go. As friends. It'd be a great time. I have friends in Paris, believe it or not. We could crash at their place. Or get a hotel. Whatever you want. I've been meaning to go back."

My phone vibrates in my pocket, and I slide it out.

Fabrizio's name flashes on the caller ID.

"Hey," I answer.

"Just checking on you," he says. "Everyone's asking about you. Wedding's tomorrow, so we're all just getting kind of nervous. Joey especially."

"Tell Joey I won't miss it for the world. I'll be there soon. Another four hours and I'll be in Pennsylvania. I'll call you when I get close to Scranton. You're going to have to pick me up. Bring some fresh clothes for me, will you?"

"Yeah, yeah, yeah," Fab says. "Just get your pretty boy ass home. And watch the roads. Eastern PA is still a frickin' mess."

Snowflakes fall on the windshield, giant flakes that dance in the wind and melt the second they hit the glass. I glance at Daphne, intending to point them out, but she's curled in a ball, her legs on the seat and her head resting on pillow wedged between her neck and the passenger door.

She's out cold.

Chapter Fourteen

Daphne

My body wakes with a snort, and I spring up in my seat. The remnants of dried drool stick to the corner of my mouth, and the reality that I woke myself up by snoring hits me square in the ego. Leaning forward, I squint toward the mid-day sun, searching for an interstate sign to orient me.

Snow.

Nothing but undriven, alabaster snow in the meadows we pass.

But the roads are clear, thank God.

"We're in eastern Ohio," he says.

"Oh, shoot. We were supposed to switch in Toledo," I say. "I'm sorry."

"It's fine. You needed the sleep."

"Pull off at the next rest stop, and I'll get behind the wheel." I grab my phone, checking to make sure I haven't had any missed calls. The screen is empty, but I decide to call Delilah anyway. I'm sure she'd appreciate an update. Lifting my phone to my ear, I nibble on my thumbnail and silently count the rings.

One . . . two . . . three . . .

"Hey, what's going on?" Delilah's voice is groggy, and she

breathes hard into the phone, like she's sitting up in bed. "Everything okay?"

"Yeah, everything's fine. You just get up?"

"No, I've been up for hours," she says. "I'm trying to make my way from the living room to the bathroom before my bladder explodes. Sure would be nice if someone could roll me there."

"Where's Zane? Make him help you."

"He's outside with Weston. They're shoveling the driveway."

My heart lurches into my throat, depositing a hard lump I can't seem to swallow away. "Weston's there?"

"Yep," Delilah says. "He flew in last night. Zane wants him here for the birth, you know, since he's the closest thing Zane has to family, really. They're like brothers. I told him he has to wait in the waiting room though, and he was fine with it." She chuckles. "Anyway, he was asking about you this morning."

"What? What did he say?" I chide myself for wanting to know, but alas, I'm the curious type. It's my fatal flaw.

"What you were up to . . . where you were living . . . if you were seeing anyone . . ."

My heart rate kicks up a notch.

"He still cares about you," Delilah says. "I get the impression he wants to be with you again. Or he wants to try."

"What about Elle?"

"They broke it off last year. You didn't want me to tell you anything about Weston after you ended things, remember?"

"Can we not have this conversation?" I glance at Cristiano through the corner of my eye. He's steering us toward an exit ramp toward a rest stop, and it'll be my turn to drive soon. I don't want a heavy heart or a heavy mind when I'm supposed to be focusing on the road. Talk about impaired driving.

"Of course," Delilah says. "I just think maybe you shouldn't be so quick to write him off. And I wanted you to know he's here. Didn't want you to be blindsided when you walk in tonight and he's standing there looking like he's two seconds from falling in love with you all over again."

"Anyway, I'll see you soon. We just passed Canton, so I should be home in about seven hours. Maybe eight." I'm anxious to wrap up the conversation as the car crawls to a stop in a narrow parking spot in front of a brick rest stop. "Call you when I get closer."

"Okay. Love you." Delilah hangs up, and I slip my phone back into my bag, pushing a long, slow breath past my lips.

"Everything okay?" Cristiano asks.

I turn to him, studying the concern washing over his face.

"Yeah," I say, forcing a smile. "Everything's fine."

Yanking on the door handle, I step out and stretch my legs. Swirling snowflakes dance around me, and my shoes crunch in a light dusting of snow on the pavement that can't decide if it wants to stick or melt.

Cristiano comes around the front of the car, stopping in front of me. "You sure you're okay to drive? You seem . . . out of it."

I wave my hand in front of my face. "I'm fine."

Stepping around him, I make my way to the driver's seat, slide in, shut the door, and adjust my backrest. Cristiano's messing around in the trunk, pulling something small from his bag and tucking it under his arm before he takes his seat.

Within a minute, we're back on the interstate, heading east and music piping lightly through the speakers.

"My ex," I say, chest so tight I can hardly breathe. The rest of the words get caught.

"What?"

"My ex is back home," I blurt. It feels good to get it out. I don't think I could possibly contain this for the next however-many-hundreds-of-miles. "I haven't seen him in over a year, and he's going to be there, and I'm kind of freaking out."

Cristiano settles back in his seat, lifting his hand to his jaw and staring straight ahead. When he exhales, I can't tell whether he's deep in thought or annoyed that we're about to have this conversation about some guy he knows nothing about.

"I'm sorry," I say. "We don't have to talk about him. I just . . . I just feel like I was blindsided by this. I mean, I knew Weston was going to be around in some capacity. He's Zane's best friend. I just didn't know he was coming to Rixton Falls. I figured he'd visit them in Chicago or something. I . . ."

"You thought you could avoid him," Cristiano finishes my thought. "Yeah, well, sounds like you can't, so you better figure out a way to be okay seeing him."

"Honestly, seeing him is the least of my worries."

"Then what's the issue?"

"Delilah thinks he still has feelings for me." I swallow the hard ball lodged in my throat. My mouth is dry. "And I've spent the better part of the last year trying to get over him."

"Did you love him?"

"I think so. Everything happened so fast, but yeah. I think I did because it wouldn't have hurt so bad if I didn't, right?"

"Do you still love him?"

I let his question marinate, my hands gripped at ten and two as I forge ahead. Snowflakes dust the hood of the car, and the ones that land on the windshield thaw on impact. I flick on the wipers, but the liquefied flakes smear across the glass, temporarily blurring my vision.

"Are you thinking about your answers or are you avoiding the question?" he asks.

"Do you still love that girl? The one that broke your heart?"

"Isn't that how it works when someone you love breaks your heart? You always kind of love them? Maybe not as much as you once did." He shifts in his seat and clears his throat. "I don't think those feelings ever completely subside. At least not until you find someone else. Someone to love harder. Someone to love you better than they ever could."

Inhaling, I switch lanes. "I don't know if I still love him. I just know I feel . . . something . . . and I have no idea what that something is. And that makes it really hard to want to see him right now."

"Maybe when you see him, you'll know," he says, retrieving a small leather-bound book. Cracking it to the middle, he scribbles something down with a pen that had been functioning as a bookmark.

"What's that?"

"Travel journal. Had to write something down before I forgot."

"I didn't know you had a journal."

Chuffing, he says, "You and the rest of the world."

"How long have you been doing that? Documenting your travels?"

He shrugs. "A while. Few years maybe? I don't know."

"Have you written about our road trip?"

Turning to me, he smirks. "Yeah."

"Read what you've written."

"Not a chance."

"Why, is there something *bad*?" I nudge him with my elbow.

"No. It's just not something I want to read. It's private."

"Did you write about me?"

"This isn't some teenage girl's diary," he says with a smirk. "There are no juicy secrets in here."

"Then read it."

"These writings aren't meant to be shared. Don't take it personally." He shuts the book and tosses it to the backseat before reaching for the radio knob, a subtle hint that he's done with this conversation. I guess I respect that. I'd be annoyed if he were prying into my personal musings. A moment later he whips his phone out and thumbs across the screen. "We should be in Scranton in about five hours."

From the corner of my eye, I watch him tap out a text message and slide his phone back into his pocket a moment later.

It's weird . . . five hours from now, we'll say goodbye. These last few days have flown by and now they're coming to a screeching halt. Forever. In the span of four days, I went from loathing this complete stranger to feeling an unexpected pang in my stomach when I realize this is the end of the road – literally – for us.

Squinting over the dash, I find myself struggling to see the taillights of the car ahead.

"Is it just me or is it snowing harder now?" I ask.

Cristiano leans forward, staring ahead, "Huh. Yeah."

Taking his phone out, he drags his thumb down the screen and mutters something under his breath.

"What?" I ask, hands tight on the wheel.

"There's another snowstorm hitting eastern Pennsylvania."

"I thought the snowpocolypse was over?"

"Nah," he says, gaze narrowed on his screen. "It was supposed to start again on Sunday, but I guess it's moving faster than they thought. It's here two days early."

My heart rate quickens. "We're still going to make it, right?"

We pass a car in the ditch, its tail lights cherry red and lit. It hasn't been there very long.

"I'm not one-hundred percent certain, but I could've sworn that car passed me a few miles back," he says slowly.

"I think you're-"

Thump. Pop. Whoosh.

My foot is pressing the gas pedal, but it feels as though we're slowing down. Gripping the steering wheel within an inch of its life, I glance at Cristiano with pleading eyes though every cell in my body is trying not to freak out.

"We blew a tire," he says, remaining calm as he reaches for the hazard lights button. "Hold the wheel steady, foot off the gas." Checking the mirrors and our perimeter, he adds, "Get over here on the shoulder, come to a gradual stop. Let it coast until you're off the road."

Shaking, I follow his orders, appreciative of the calm he brings to this literal storm. It's snowing faster now, the flakes dense and heavy, hard enough to quickly cover the glass if the wipers aren't moving fast enough.

Without saying another word, he flies out of the passenger side and heads around back, knocking on the trunk. I hit the trunk release button and feel the car rock as he digs around in the back. A minute later, he climbs back in, face red and wind-kissed.

"Fuck," he says, slicking his hands together and blowing his warm breath between them. His dark hair is sprinkled in snowflakes and there's a clean crispness in the air that might feel refreshing if we were anything other than stranded.

"What? What is it?"

"Spare's flat."

Gripping the wheel, I bang my forehead against it and groan. "Okay. What do we do now?"

"I'm calling a tow." When I look up, his phone is already pressed against his ear.

I refuse to believe this is happening.

We're. So. Close.

Hours from home.

Literally. Hours.

"Yes, I'm needing a tow as soon as possible," he says. "We're on I-80, just past the Coalfield exit."

His face says it all, from the clench of his jaw to the flattening of his lips.

"Are you sure? . . . There isn't anything . . . all right," he hangs up, exhaling loudly.

"When are they coming?"

"They're not." He performs a search on his phone, pushing a hard breath through his nose. "Apparently the storm's worse about ten, twenty miles from here. All the trucks have been called out already, and they're thinking the DOT's going to enforce a tow ban in the next couple of hours. I'm checking somewhere else."

Sinking back in my seat, I close my eyes and listen to him make phone call after phone call after phone call.

They all say the same thing.

They're busy. The trucks are all in service. It's going to be several hours before they can get to us and even then they might not be able to.

Chapter Fifteen

Cristiano

I throw our luggage on the bed of yet another hotel room and watch Daphne collapse in the middle of one of the beds. She buries her face in a pillow, though I don't think she's crying. She's too disappointed to cry.

I am too.

We were supposed to be in Scranton by now. Instead we waited for three hours for a tow truck and a lift to the nearest town. The tire shops in this area were closing by the time the tow truck showed up.

The driver dropped the Toyota off at a nearby shop and gave us a lift to this chlorine-scented Superior Inn Express.

"We'll be on the road by eight o'clock tomorrow," I say, sinking back into the second queen bed. Eyes closed, I slip my hands behind my head. "We'll be in Scranton by noon. You'll be home by two."

"Just stop." Daphne huffs.

"What?"

"Stop being so positive about everything. We're stranded. It fucking sucks. And knowing my luck, my sister's going to have the baby before I get home. And how do you know the roads won't still be closed tomorrow? We might get halfway to Scranton and have to call it a day. Again. And why aren't you worried about missing your friend's wedding? How can you just sit there and act like we're going to get home when you don't know if we're going to get home?"

"We're going to get home." I place as much conviction in my tone as I can.

"When, huh? *When*?"

Standing next to the dresser and unfastening my watch, I glance over at her bed. She's sitting up now, her blue eyes stormy and slightly bloodshot as they bore into me.

"I'll get us home," I say. "I promise."

"Don't," she says, face twisted as she slides one foot off her bed. In a blurred rush of seconds, eyes bleary and squinting, she storms to my side, finger pointed in my face. "Don't make a promise you can't keep."

"I'm going to *try*," I add. "I promise I'll try to get us home. Better?"

"Now you're just telling me what I want to hear."

Chuffing, I drop my watch on the dresser top and tug my t-shirt over my head. I can't win with her. Not tonight. Not when she's in this . . . mood. Stepping around her, I unfasten my jeans.

"What are you doing?" she asks. "Shouldn't we make more phone calls? Try to line up a new rental or something?"

"I'm hitting the shower." I lift my brows, my hands paused at my zipper. "That okay with you?"

"You don't have to ask permission."

"Really?" I spit sarcastically.

"What's that supposed to mean?"

"You're fucking priceless, you know that?" I smirk, scraping my hand along the underside of my jaw as I stare past her and focus on a mass-produced portrait of a lighthouse hanging on the wall behind her.

Her jaw hangs. "Are you trying to insult me? Last I checked, being priceless was a good thing."

"Depends on the context," I say, making my way toward the bathroom and trying to ignore the fact that she's following me. "You know, we've only known each other a few days, and already you're acting like you're my goddamned girlfriend, starting fights and shit."

I shake my head, turning to face her, trying not to laugh when I see how pinched her face is or how tight her arms are across her chest.

"If you were my girlfriend," I add, taking one final dig, "at least I'd be getting laid more."

Smack.

The warmth of her palm precedes a blossoming sting radiating across the side of my face.

She just fucking hit me.

My jaw snaps and then locks. I pop it back into place, my eyes locking on hers.

"All right. Maybe I deserved that," I say, voice low and ego lightly bruised. I pull in a lengthy breath and push it out through flared nostrils. "But I don't deserve you fucking picking fights with me because you're pissed off that the universe isn't bending to your every need. Guess what, Daphne? Life doesn't work that way. Never has, never will. Don't take shit out on me. I'm just the guy that saved your ass when you thought driving three thousand miles across the country by yourself was a good idea."

"You didn't save me. I didn't need saving." Her hand flies to her hip.

"Really Daphne?"

"I don't understand why you have some sort of super hero complex," she says, brows meeting in the middle.

If she only fucking knew . . .

"I'm going to hit the shower," I say, keeping my voice even and steady, though I can't look at her right now. I need to calm down, or I'm going to say something I'll probably regret. "Why don't you go down to the bar, have a drink. Get some space. We've been together twenty-four seven for the last several days, and I think it's starting to get to us."

She rolls her eyes, turning on her heel and waving me off. "Whatever, Cristiano."

"What the fuck do you want from me?" I throw my hands in the air. "I didn't cause any of this. Don't take it out on me."

Daphne's on the other side of the room now, throwing her phone into her purse and muttering under her breath.

I need to have compassion for her. She wasn't in a good place the day I met her, so I don't know why I'd expected that to miraculously change after several days together in a cramped car and winding up stranded at some hole-in-the-wall roach motel.

"I imagine you feel powerless right now. Maybe you're overwhelmed by the fact that we made it this far and now we've come to an impasse? It fucking sucks. I get that. But what can we do?" I move toward her. "Yelling at each other? What's that going to solve, huh?"

She says nothing, and when I glance down, I see her phone resting in her hand, her thumb hovering over her sister's name.

"If I could get you home right now, I would," I say. "But we're stuck here. At least for one more night."

Daphne sits her phone down on a nightstand, her shoulders falling as she exhales. "I hate feeling stuck. And I hate that I'm not with her. And I hate that you're so calm when all I want to do is yell and scream."

"Then yell and scream," I say. "You do you. I'll do me."

She turns to me, her glassy eyes blinking and a hint of a reserved smile appearing across her full lips. "God, you must *really* think I'm a nutcase now."

"Yeah," I say with a chuckle. "You are a nutcase. But I kind of like that about you. Shows you're real. And you're not afraid to be yourself. That alone puts you leagues ahead of everyone else I've ever met."

"You're too nice," she says, burying her hand in her head. "I'm sorry I got upset with you. I just really, really want to get home, and I have all this pent up anger and no where to put it."

"You can hit me again if it'll make you feel better." I'm only half kidding.

Her gaze flicks to mine, and she rolls her eyes when she sees the smirk on my face.

167

"Look," I say, exhaling. "Let's try to make the best of this, all right? After tomorrow, you'll be back home with your sister and I'll be in Jersey, and we'll never see each other again. This'll be a distant memory. All we have is right now. Tonight. Let's make the best of it. It's all we can do."

Daphne's chin tucks against her chest and her stare is pointed at the carpet between our feet. I reach for her face, cupping the side of her cheek and lifting her face. A moment later, her eyes rest on mine once more, and I catch her nibbling her lower lip.

"What?" she asks with a nervous titter. "Why are you looking at me like that?"

"I'm beginning to think I'm the nutcase here," I say.

Her nose wrinkles and her eyes search mine. "What? Why?"

"Because despite the fact that you just freaked out on me . . . despite the fact that you fucking *slapped* me . . . I still find you ridiculously sexy right now. And I still really, *really* want to kiss you. But not only that. I want to slam you against these god-awful wallpapered walls, crush your mouth with a kiss, and fuck you like it's the last time I'm ever going to see you."

I watch her chest rise as she sucks in a startled breath. She wasn't expecting me to say that, but then again, neither was I. The realization that I'm never going to see her again after tomorrow weighs heavy in my bones in a way I didn't expect it to.

She says nothing, locked somewhere between shocked apprehension and piqued curiosity if I had to guess by the confused expression blanketing her face right now. Cupping my hand beneath her chin, I inch her mouth closer to mine, willing this to happen and nudging it in the right direction. All she needs to do is say the word, and I'll make her mine. I'll make her mine so fucking hard.

This woman . . . this infuriatingly complex woman . . . has some kind of hold on me I've never experienced with anyone else before. And maybe it's because we're more alike than we're different. We're both a little broken. A little damaged. A little fucked up. A little crazy. We're both stubborn, feet firmly planted in the captain's seat of our respective choose-your-own-adventure lives. Maybe we're both a little empty too. Searching for something to fill that gaping void we try to ignore by filling our lives full of all the things we're convinced matter most.

Regardless, and whatever it is, my feet are firmly planted in the here and now. With her. It's all I have, and right now, it's all I want.

My body hums with anticipation, my cock hardening at the mere thought of all the things I want to do to this woman. Resting my hands around her waist, I pull her against me, her hands landing flat on my bare chest. Pressing my mouth hard against hers, I feel her exhale against me, her body surrendering as I sweep her closer into my arms.

"I want you, Daphne," I say, my lips grazing hers in the seconds before our tongues meet. My right hand travels up the back of her neck, my fingers tangling in the silky waves at the nape of her neck, making her smile. I gather a fistful, gently tugging and guiding her lips back to mine all over again.

I kiss her. I kiss her harder than I've ever kissed anybody before. In this moment, it feels necessary. My mouth claims hers over and over, reveling in the taste of her sweet lips and how her body fits against mine, her curves filling my angles like we're made to fit.

My palms slick down her sides, tracing the curves of her hips before gripping a handful of her perfect ass. Daphne lifts on her toes, and my hands travel to the waistband of her leggings and panties, tugging them down her long thighs with a quick yank. My hands ride up her bare legs, and the way they quiver at my touch forces my cock to strain against my jeans. Daphne works my pants off, tugging at my boxers until she sets me free, taking my length in her hand and urgently pumping it in her soft palm.

Lowering herself to her knees, she presses her mouth against the tip of my cock, swallowing my girth one inch at a time. Her tongue is velvet and smooth, flicking the underside of my hardness, swirling, pumping. Gathering her hair in my hand, I guide her rhythm, my hips gently fucking the hell out of her perfect, bee stung mouth.

"Goddamn," I groan, tipping my head back. I knew she had a mouth on her, but this . . . this is fucking magical. I let her suck me off a while longer because it feels too damn good to make her stop, but the greedy bastard in me wants more. I want the heat and the friction, the scent of her arousal, her sweet taste on my tongue.

Pulling my cock from between her lips, I reach down and swipe my wallet from my jeans pocket, retrieving a perfectly intact rubber and ripping the packet between my teeth.

"Take your shirt off, Daphne," I command, pumping my cock in one hand.

Following orders, she slowly pulls her blouse over her head, followed by the swift unhooking of the black lace bra covering her perky tits. The dim lamp from the hotel nightstand illuminates her curved body perfectly, and I love that she isn't rushing to shut it off. Moving my mouth toward her breasts, I take a pointed tip between my lips, tugging gently until I hear her release a soft moan.

With my free hand between her thighs, I slide my fingers between her wet slit and massage her clit softly with my thumb. Backing up against the wall behind her bed, she melts into submission, her eyes squeezed and her tongue grazing her lower lip. Falling to my knees, I breathe in her addictive scent, lapping her arousal, swirling my tongue between her soft folds, devouring her pussy because it's fucking perfection.

Her hands find my hair and she takes a fistful before giving it a good pull, and while it's clear she's in heaven, we both know she wants more.

Rising, I sheathe my cock before cupping her peach-shaped ass and pressing her harder against the wall. Depositing a punishing kiss onto her lips, I grind my hips against hers until she moans into my mouth and hikes her thigh up my side in a single wordless gesture.

Dragging my cock against her wet pussy, I give her a tease, eliciting a smile out of her as her mouth waits, open and wanting, for another claiming, crushing kiss. I push myself into her, slowly, deliberately, inch by tortuous inch, and then I grip her long thighs, pulling them both up my sides before pressing her back against the wall.

Her warmth and wetness envelope me in a way that moves beyond carnal. There's a strange comfort being with Daphne . . . it's in the way she looks at me, in the way her body grinds against mine and her fingernails dig into my flesh, the way we've only just begun and get stopping feels like an impossibility. It's as if we both know something about this just works in a way we never could've predicted, and yet we've accepted the fact that we'll only ever have tonight.

Pushing myself inside her, deeper, harder, faster, I press my lips into the feverish skin below her collarbone. Peppering biting kisses along her shoulders, my fingers dig deep into the soft flesh of her curves, holding on with everything I have and giving her every greedy inch.

Carrying her to the bed behind me, I deposit her in the middle, climbing over her. Her legs part, and my fingers trail her slick seam in the seconds before I thrust my cock inside her all over again. She exhales, her head pushing back against the mattress, and I push myself deeper.

I could do this all night. And I never want this endless, snowbound, stranded night to end.

Taking a peaked, rosy nipple between my lips, I swirl the swollen bud, my cock throbbing hard inside her with each thrust. Every inch of this woman is soft and sweet and addictive.

Her hands travel down my sides, guiding the natural rhythm we're creating, and when our eyes meet, my chest tightens and I swear I see a future – our future – flash before me. It's a lifetime in a split second, and it's not something that's ever happened to me before.

I haven't thought about my future in . . . years.

Shaking it off, I plunge and pivot myself deeper inside her, faster, thrusting so hard, she screams out in sensual agony, her hips bucking, meeting my every move. Daphne fucks me back, her body tightening and rocking against mine like she's getting close. The tightness in my balls is the only thing I feel . . . and then I black out . . .

When I come to, I'm lying on top of Daphne, both of us heaving, our bodies stuck together. Climbing off, she crawls out of bed and heads to the bathroom. I'm reeling. Feeling it all. Feeling the things I haven't felt in years; the kinds of things I wasn't sure I was capable of feeling anymore.

She returns a moment later, naked as the day she was born, a satisfied crooked smile on her beautiful face. Crawling under the covers beside me, she flicks out the light on the nightstand without saying another word.

I head to the bathroom, hit the shower, and emerge ten minutes later. Words linger on the tip of my tongue – words I didn't expect I'd ever need to say to this woman.

I want to see her again after this. I don't want to tell her goodbye tomorrow and go our separate ways. There's something between us, I know there is. I feel it. She has to feel it too.

Climbing in bed beside her, I press my body against her, letting mine take the shape of hers and slipping my arm over her.

"Daphne," I say, my voice a careful whisper.

No answer.

On second glance, I see she's already asleep. I won't get to tell her tonight. But tomorrow . . . I'll tell her tomorrow.

Chapter Sixteen

Daphne

"Car's ready." Cristiano ends a call on his phone and turns back to his suitcase, packing yesterday's clothes. His hair is still damp from the shower, and the scent of soap and aftershave fills the cool hotel air. This man loves his showers, that's for damn sure. "They're dropping it off in fifteen."

"Roads are fine," I say, looking up from my phone. Suddenly I'm flashing back to last night, my body enveloped in a warm rush of excitement followed by a quick burst of sadness when I realize we won't have time for a reprise. Cristiano's easily the best sex I've had in my life. And last night was tragically our grand finale. "No closures on the route."

"We should hit Scranton in about three hours," he says. There's less confidence and a bit more exhaustion in his claim, but I don't hold it against him. It's been a long, ridiculously unpredictable week.

I deposit my phone on my nightstand and move to grab my clothes so I can take a quick shower before we hit the road, but the second I walk away, it starts to vibrate, skidding across the wood. Spinning around, I spot the caller ID and answer it in the middle of the second ring.

"Delilah, hey. We're leaving soon. I'll be home in about five hours," I answer.

"Daphne, it's Zane," says a voice I was not expecting to hear. My heart sinks to the floor.

"Zane, what's wrong?"

"Nothing's wrong," he says, his voice calm. "Everything's fine. I was just calling to let you know the doctor's admitting Delilah right now. She's in labor."

"Oh, god." I sink into the edge of the mattress, staring blankly ahead at a watercolor reproduction of a wheat field at sunset.

"She could be in labor for twenty-four hours," he says, a slight chuckle in his tone like he's trying to ease my worries. "Don't freak out just yet. The next five hours could be fairly uneventful. You never know. Just focus on getting here safely, and I'll let her know you're on your way."

My eyes water as powerlessness takes a hold of me. "Okay. Tell her I love her, and I'm going to do everything I can to get there as soon as possible."

"Just don't speed," Zane says.

I chuff.

"I'm just trying to say what Delilah would say," he adds. His voice is slightly breathy, and I hear footsteps in the background. "She's in her new room now. You want to say hi?"

"Yeah." I grip my phone tight. "Can she FaceTime?"

My phone beeps as Zane initiates a video call, and I move my screen in front of my face. The pale peach walls of my sister's birthing suite blur into the white sheets of her bed. I hear my mother's voice in the background, low and soothing, and then I hear a woman talking about measuring contractions and giving her something to "take the edge off."

"Daphne?" Delilah's face comes into focus. She's wearing a thin white gown covered in tiny pink flowers. There's a cuff on her arm and a myriad of wires in the background connected to something off camera. A steady beeping noise drowns out my mother's voice, but I manage to hear her ask, *"Is that your sister?"* in the background. "Hey, sis."

"How are you feeling?" My brows lift, and I force a smile because it's all I can do to keep my composure in front of her. It kills me not to be there, by her side, holding her hand.

"Scared." She laughs through her nose before wiping a tear from the corner of her eye. "Scared out of my freaking mind."

"You can do this," I say.

"I wish you were here." Her head tilts to the side, and then she glances up and over the phone. Zane appears at her side, leaning down and kissing the top of her head. He then takes the seat beside her, slipping his hand in hers. He loves her so much, and I'm glad she has him, but she needs me too. Growing up, we've always felt less than complete when the other one wasn't around. Maybe it's a twin thing, I'm not sure.

"I'll be there soon," I say. "Give me five hours and I'll be right there with you."

"Is that Daphne?" My sister Demi crouches down on the other side of Delilah, waving and grinning wide. "Hi, Daph! We miss you. Wish you were here."

She pouts, and then I spot my mother's bushy blonde hair in the background. My chest squeezes.

"Is everything okay?" my mom asks, brows furrowed as she squeezes in.

"Yes, Mom," I say with a bittersweet smile. "I'm on my way. Don't let her have that baby until I get there."

My sisters laugh, and Mom swats her hand toward the screen. "You want me to put the phone up to her belly so you can tell your nephew that yourself?"

The hotel phone rings on Cristiano's nightstand. He cradles the receiver on his shoulder, mumbles something, and then turns to me.

"Car's downstairs," he says.

"I have to go, guys. I love you, and I'll see you soon." I end the call, directing my attention to Cristiano who's zipping his suitcase now. He hoists it with one arm and sits it by the door.

"Everything all right?" he asks.

"They admitted Delilah. She's in labor for real this time." My eyes water, and I look away.

He moves to my side, running his palms along my sides. Bringing a finger beneath my chin, he guides my gaze onto his.

"I'll get you home," he says, straightening his shoulders. There's a certain sadness in his voice, as if he knows he could be sacrificing something he isn't sure he's willing to sacrifice. "Even if we have to take a detour . . ."

"No," I cut him off before he can make any more promises. Shaking my head, I tell him, "You're not missing that wedding."

His hand slides down my arm, stopping at my wrist as he looks me in the eye. "You'll be home in a few hours. I promise you, Daphne."

Chapter Seventeen

Cristiano

The car is noiseless save for a hint of road noise and the chintzy clicking of the turn signal as I pull off on an exit that'll lead us to Scranton. We've driven most of the last three hours in dead silence, Daphne biting her nails and me wondering when might be a good time to mention that I want to see her again.

A million thoughts run through my mind, most of which reach the conclusion that after the week she's had with me, she may never want to see me again in her life. Granted, it's not my fault any of this happened, but she might associate me with one of the worst weeks of her life so long as she lives. Yeah, the sex was hot. But that's about the only positive takeaway from this week.

Amazing sex, but . . .

Long hours in the car.

Mediocre gas station dinners.

Lumpy hotel mattresses.

The possibility that she could very well still miss the birth of her sister's baby . . .

I pull off the main road and veer toward a Shell gas station, the one I told my brother to pick me up at at twelve-thirty sharp. Scanning the parking lot, I spot his rusty Bronco and pull up beside it, killing the engine. For once in his life, he's actually on time.

"You okay to drive the rest of the way home?" I break my silence.

Turning toward me, her gaze is averted and fixed on my seatbelt strap. She holds her phone up and turns it to me, the screen illuminated with a text that was sent a mere minute ago. I scan the message, reading the words, "DELILAH'S GETTING READY TO PUSH. JUST WAITING ON THE DOCTOR. SO SORRY, DAPHNE."

Fuck.

She buries her face in her hands, exhaling as her shoulders fall.

"I'm so sorry." I rub my hand along her back, but her body is rigid so I pull her into my arms instead. Hugging over the tiny console of this microscopic rental car, I wrap her in my arms and kiss the top of her blonde head, repeating myself because I'm at a loss for words, "I'm so sorry."

"It's not your fault." Her voice is muffled against my shoulder, a melancholy whisper. "I just can't believe the timing . . . we tried so hard . . . I didn't think this would happen."

Cupping the back of her head in my palm, I hug her tighter. I'm not a touchy-feely guy, at least not beyond the confines of a closed-door bedroom, but this feels right. She needs a friend right now.

Daphne pulls away after a moment, glancing at the clock in the dash. "You should get going. You've got a wedding to get to. It's not too late for you, is it?"

Pressing my lips flat, I shake my head. "No. It's not too late."

She forces a smile, dabbing at her misty eyes. "Good. I'm glad this wasn't a total loss for both of us."

My hand still rests on her arm, my fingertips grazing the soft skin just before her wrist. I glance into her baby blues, knowing damn well it's going to be the last time unless I grow a pair and fucking say something. It's now or never. And I don't want to spend the rest of my life wondering what might have happened had I . . .

Knock, knock, knock.

My heart lurches in my chest until I glance over my shoulder and spot my younger brother knocking on my window. Rolling it down, I shoot him a quick glare because clearly he should be able to see I'm busy here.

"Give me a sec," I say.

Fabrizio crouches down, peering through the car toward the passenger side. "You must be Daphne. Let me just apologize, on behalf of the entire Amato family, for the terrible inconvenience of spending the last four days stuck in this chicken nugget with this obnoxious asshole."

Daphne laughs, placing her hand on my shoulder. "Nah, he's been great."

"Get back in the car," I tell him. "I'll be there in a minute."

Climbing out, Daphne follows suit and we reconvene at the trunk as I get my luggage.

"So I guess this is goodbye?" She shoves her hands in the pockets of a hoodie we picked up back in Iowa a couple days ago. It's John Deere green with a bright yellow zipper and a cartoonish ear of corn on the back with the words, *"Do I make you corny, baby?"* screen printed across the back. It's a size too big for her, which she insisted on in case I needed to wear it too.

I guess that's the kind of girl she is, always thinking of everybody else. I think back to the moment I first saw her standing in line at the airport. A plastic ID rested on the tile floor a few spots back from her, and when I swiped it off the ground, I scanned the area for a match, never expecting it to be the girl I'd been admiring from afar.

When I bumped into her at the coffee stand a short while later and made her spill her coffee, she could've lashed out at me. She wanted to. I saw it in her eyes, a quick flash of frustration. But she smiled and told me it was fine.

And at the hotel – she let me stay in her room. Granted, it was supposed to be my room. But if it weren't for that kind gesture, I'd have been sleeping on a park bench, celebrating New Year's Eve all by myself and probably asking myself the kinds of questions a man never likes to think about unless he has to. Instead, I spent it with her. And it was so much better than I ever could've imagined.

I wait for the click of Fab's driver's side door before taking a step closer.

"I had fun with you," I say, locking eyes. "This little . . . adventure . . . I'll never forget it as long as I live."

She laughs through her nose, glancing down at her shoes as she digs a toe into the gravelly parking lot.

"Thanks for coming with me." Daphne lifts her gaze onto mine, peering up through curled lashes. "I know I fought you on it at first. I didn't want you to come. But I'm glad you did."

"I want to see you again." I decide to cut the small talk.

Her eyes widen, as if it was the last thing she expected me to say to her right now.

"These last several days . . ." I pull in a deep breath. "I don't know, Daphne. They've been frustrating and aggravating . . . and wonderful . . . and incredible. I'm not sure if you feel the same way, but all things considered, I wouldn't trade them for a million bucks. Being with you, getting to know you . . . and you're so easy to be around. So genuine. It's effortless being around you, in a way I've never had with anyone else. I-"

"I want to see you again too." Her mouth pulls into a half-crooked smile, and her blue eyes light up. It's as if she'd been waiting for me to make the first move this whole time. "Give me your phone."

I hand it over, and she programs her number before giving it back.

"I have to go," she says, glancing at the driver's side of the rental car. "You're going to call me, right? This isn't part of your whole heartbreaker schtick?"

Smirking, I shake my head. "No, Daphne. I would never break your heart."

Her gaze flicks onto mine. She parts her lips slightly, like she's about to say something, but I silence her commentary with a kiss. A temporary goodbye. A sweet until-we-meet-again.

"I'll call you," I say, coming up for air, missing the sweet taste of her tongue and the cherry smoothness of her lips. "I promise."

"Go," she says, fighting a grin. "Get to that wedding."

Chapter Eighteen

Daphne

"He's so precious, Del." I pout my lips, fawning over my freshly born nephew, Noah. "I'm so in love with him already. Look, he has your ears! And your mouth."

"Yeah, that's definitely a Rosewood mouth," she says, beaming proudly.

Baby Noah's not quite an hour old. I missed his grand entrance by fifty-four minutes and thirty-five seconds.

"I still can't believe I missed this," I say, reaching for my godson's tiny hand. He curls his fingers around my pinky.

"It's fine. Really. Stop beating yourself up about it and just enjoy the preciousness that is Noah Zane de la Cruz."

"Speaking of Zane . . ." I sit up. "And everyone else for that matter . . . where is everyone?"

"Mom ran home to get Dad. Demi left to call Royal. Zane is out in the waiting room making calls." She smiles an exhausted smile, her gaze fixed on her new son. "There was all this commotion and excitement and then they all scattered like leaves in the wind. Wouldn't be surprised if one of them were standing on the roof of the hospital, shouting the good news."

Rolling my eyes, I chuckle. "Well, enjoy the peace and quiet while you can. I'm sure they'll be back any minute now, fighting over who gets to hold him first."

"You want to hold him?"

Sitting up, I meet her gaze. She lifts him off her chest, hands cradling his tiny body as she waits for me to take him.

I love my siblings and I'll always love the children my siblings bring into this world. I can appreciate a drooly smile or a little baby fedora or one of those pacifiers with the mustaches on them because they're freaking hilarious, but as far as actually holding them? That's so not my department.

But he's my godson.

And this moment is absolutely priceless.

I suck in a deep breath and slide my arms beneath his swaddled blanket. Cradling him against my chest, my heart races.

"God, I love him." I lean closer, nuzzling my nose against the tufts of fluffy dark hair that covers his tiny head. "He couldn't be any more perfect, Delilah. I mean that."

I want to stay in this moment for as long as possible, basking in the warm fullness that radiates from my chest. He begins to fuss a little, though his eyes remain closed tight. His cry is squeaky, and he reminds me of a fuzzy little mouse. His mouth opens as he yawns, and his tongue peeks out just a tad.

"That was adorable. Where's Zane? He totally missed a Kodak moment here." I hand my nephew back to my sister, and he immediately melts into her arms, no longer crying. It's like he knows she's his mother, and something about that sends an unexpected twinge to my ovaries and a strange tightness to my chest.

For a flicker of a second, I imagine what I might be like as a mother. I can only hope I'm half as natural as my sister.

"Knock, knock." A man's voice pulls my attention toward the doorway.

The first thing I see is a giant bouquet of flowers.

The second thing I see is a shiny Mylar balloon attached that reads, "IT'S A BOY!"

The third thing I see is Weston.

Chapter Nineteen

Cristiano

"You bring my suit?" I ask Fabrizio as we cross into Jersey.

"Yeah, it's in the back," he says, pointing. "We have to be at the church by three. We're going to be cutting it close since you had to bid farewell to your new girlfriend and all. I suggest you change in the car."

Unfastening my seatbelt, I grab the garment bag draped over the backseat and start suiting up.

"You've been quiet," Fab says, giving me side eye. "Something happen with that girl?"

I don't answer.

"Or is this about Joey's wedding?"

I still don't answer.

"Look, everyone's going to be there," my brother says. "You're going to have to put on a happy face whether you want to or not. You knew Joey'd be the first of us to get married. It's not the end of the world. The end of an era maybe, but not the end of the world."

It's the end of an era all right. And maybe even the beginning of something else entirely, though I can't be sure. Everything feels oddly . . . up in the air at this point.

"You not going to talk?" Fabrizio chuffs, hands gripped on the wheel as he changes lanes. "Fine. Whatever. Suit up though. I'm responsible for getting you to that church, but whatever happens after that is all you."

Chapter Twenty

Daphne

"Can I ask you a question?" Weston takes a sip from his Styrofoam coffee cup as we sit at a corner table in the hospital cafeteria. After an awkward-as-hell hello in Delilah's recovery suite and Delilah's nurse needing to tend to a few private matters with my sister, Weston insisted we give her some space and some time to rest and bond with the baby before she's flooded with visitors again.

"Of course." I sit up tall, eyes fixed on his light blue gaze, finding myself wishing I was sitting across from Cristiano right now.

Months ago, I'd be foaming at the mouth in Weston's presence. Drooling over the way he's grown out his sandy blond locks or the way his shoulders fill out his navy blue polo, his muscles strained beneath the dry fit fabric. I'd be fantasizing about his jaw and the mouth he never quite could keep to himself whenever I was around. There would be hearts in my eyes, clouding up my vision and good judgment.

I haven't seen him in well over a year, and even six months ago, I was still having doubts as to whether or not I'd ever be as happy with someone new as I was with him.

But something has changed. There's been a shift. I'm not sure when it happened, but I don't feel the way I thought I'd feel right now.

Looking at Weston, I'm hit with a flood of memories. They come crashing down on me all at once. The night we met in Miami at that awful club. Walking the streets listening to Cuban music. Staying up all night talking. Exchanging numbers. Flying across the country to visit each other. Lying in his arms in bed, breathing him in and wondering how it was possible life existed before him.

And then the rest of the memories follow . . .

Catching him flipping through a scrapbook his ex had made while he was cleaning out one of his spare rooms. Finding a text from her on his phone. He didn't respond to it, but she was definitely trying to make a connection with him again, and the shift in his mood during the weeks that followed was undeniable.

That's when I knew.

He wanted to love me. He *tried* to love me.

But he was still in love with her.

"Why haven't you taken my calls?" he asks, his voice his signature shade of Weston-calm.

My jaw hangs. I'm not sure how to answer that. Normally when a person avoids another person's calls, they're able to avoid them in real life too. All those times I sent his calls to voicemail, I was never imagining what my explanation would be should he ask for one.

"I thought," he says, pausing and exhaling hard through his nose, "when we ended things, that we were going to be friends. I know that's a thing that people say to people when they don't want to be with them anymore and they're trying to be nice, but I thought we were different. I thought you meant what you said. I know I did."

"Oh. Um." I take a sip of coffee, my toes tapping under the table as I fidget in my seat. "I meant it. At first. And then I came home and I thought it might be easier, for both of us, if we weren't friends. You were with Elle, and I didn't think it'd be respectful if I was still in the picture."

"She wouldn't have minded. I mean, we're over now. It's done. For good this time. But she wasn't like that."

"And maybe a part of me wanted to avoid talking to you because it was a reminder of what we had, and what we lost, and I didn't want to know if you were happy with her because it would hurt too bad. It would only serve as a reminder that you weren't nearly as happy with me." My gaze flicks to a cardboard soup menu resting between us, nestled next to a salt-and-pepper shaker. "Maybe that makes me sound selfish, I don't know. But my radio silence was never about you. I want you to know that."

He gives me a bittersweet, closed-mouth smile, his gentle crystalline eyes trained on me. "I think about you all the time, Daphne. I never really stopped. Probably annoyed the hell out of Delilah, always asking questions about you. She probably told you."

I shake my head, amazed that my sister actually listened to me for once when I told her not to so much as breathe his name around me that first year. "She never said anything. She was kind of under strict orders not to."

He rakes his teeth along his bottom lip before smiling wide. But it isn't a happy smile. There's sadness in his eyes. Regret. Longing.

"I really hurt you, didn't I?" He squints across the table.

Looking away, I inhale sharply. "Yeah. You did. But I

know you didn't mean to."

His hand rests on the edge of the table, his fingers twitching. I think he wants to reach out to me, cover my hand with his, but something keeps him from making the move. It's probably a good thing because despite the forty-year-flood of emotions happening in this depressing, gray-scale hospital cafeteria, I find myself wondering what Cristiano's doing right now . . .

. . . and why it's so easy to sit here with Weston and not want to jump into his arms and start all over again, because something tells me that's where this conversation is headed. He wants to start over again. To make it work. And for the first time in over a year, the idea of being with him holds zero appeal. It's like my longing for Weston dissipated, fading into thin air practically overnight.

"God, it's good to see you, Daphne," he says. It feels good to hear him say that, but it doesn't change how I feel. "You have no idea."

Checking the time on my phone, I rise, cutting this conversation short before it grows wings and flies to heights much too dangerous.

"It's been a long day," I say, wincing apologetically. "I'm going to head home and rest for a bit. Tell my sister I'll be back in a couple of hours."

I don't give him a chance to respond; I simply turn and leave.

Chapter Twenty-One

Cristiano

"She's in there." Joey's mom straightens my tie outside a Sunday school classroom at the church, her lips pulled up in one corner and eyes misty. She smells exactly the way I remember: Charlie perfume, aerosol hairspray, and menthol cigarettes. "You look very handsome, Cris."

"Is she nervous?" I ask.

Her mom swats her hand in front of her face. "Not my Joey. You know how she is. She was at first, but she's been all smiles today. Only thing she was worried about was whether or not you'd make it here in time to give her away."

Connie runs her hand down my lapel and gives me a misty-eyed smile before walking off, her shimmering blue dress swaying with each step.

Rapping on the door, I take a deep breath and wait.

"Come in," she calls.

Pushing the door open, I'm smacked in the face with a little bit of everything all at once.

Confusion.

Guilt.

Regret.

Subjection to the inevitable and that which I have zero control over.

But she's my best friend and she has been for almost two decades, and I'll be damned if I'm not happy for her on her big day. It's not about me. I'll swallow my pride. I'll stuff these emotions deep down, where they belong, and I'll put on a good face.

I almost missed this day; I'll be damned if I ruin it.

"Don't look at me like that, you're making me nervous." She offers an uneasy laugh, reaching for a dark tendril and twisting it around her fingers. "Do I look ridiculous with all this makeup? Please tell me I don't. You know how I am. I don't think I own a tube of Chapstick, and now I'm all glammed up. Feels weird."

Joey's a tomboy through and through. Always has been. It's how she got mixed in with our group growing up. Granted, she lived in our neighborhood, but she was also into riding bikes and playing baseball and video games while all the other girls on the block would've preferred to braid each other's hair and aimlessly page through Seventeen magazine.

"Nah," I say. "You look beautiful."

And I mean it. She looks gorgeous. I don't know what she did different. I know she's wearing makeup and her hair is curly or wavy or some shit. It's long, dripping down her shoulders, and there is some kind of crystal and pearl crown sitting on the top of her head. She looks like a princess.

"You sure? You know you can tell me the truth," she says. "I'd rather hear it from you than anyone else. If you think I look ridiculous, I'll wash it all off right now."

"Nah." I take a seat on the edge of a table beside her. Her bouquet of red roses rests next to me. "Leave it. You look like a million bucks, Jo. Honest."

She smiles, exhaling as if she's releasing tension. "I'm so glad you made it. I was worried for a while. I shouldn't have let you go out of town the week before my wedding."

"Like you could've stopped me." I toss her a wink, arms folded across my chest.

Joey rolls her dark eyes. "Right. You always were my rolling stone. God forbid you gather a little bit of moss every once in a while."

There's a palpable silence that lingers between us for a moment, and her smile fades.

"I wish you'd come home more," she says. "We miss you. It's not the same going from seeing you every single day to seeing you a couple of times a year."

Pulling in a deep breath, I glance up at the ceiling tiles, unsure of what to say. The truth lingers on my tongue, though I have zero intention of speaking it.

"Sometimes I think you left because of me." Her voice is lower now, and when I look her way, I see fingers fidgeting in her lap as her gaze is focused on them. "Sometimes I think a lot of what you do is because of me."

"Joey."

"Cris," she cuts me off. "You weren't the only one whose life changed forever that night."

Her bottom lip trembles. I can't have her crying on her

wedding day because of *this*.

Because of *me*.

"You have to stop blaming yourself . . ." she says, pulling in a long breath and looking to the side. "And you have to stop running when things get hard. You act like you're this world traveler guy, but I know you, Cris, and I know you're just running. I know you don't come home because it's hard for you to see me."

"Come on. Not today. We're not having this conversation on your *wedding* day, Jo."

"No." Her voice booms and her eyes flick into mine. "We have to have this conversation because we have to move on from that night. We *both* do."

Blowing a tight breath past my lips, I fold my arms snug across my chest and give her my full attention.

"All right," I say. "Go ahead. Let me have it."

"I know you don't like Trent," she says, clasping her hand across her heart. "But he loves me, Cris. He loves me *so* much. He's the love of my life, and he loves me exactly the way I am. He knows what he's signing up for with me. And I know that's hard for you to hear because you've always felt like you were supposed to be the one to take care of me, but Trent loves me in a way that you can't. Not because you don't want to, but you know, I'm like a sister to you. You're like my annoying big brother. It'd be really frickin' weird. You remember that time we kissed, right? In tenth grade? It was disgusting."

I crack a hint of a smile, though it disappears in a flash. It's true. I don't like Trent. He lived in his mom's basement until he was thirty. He manages a video game store. And from the outside looking in, I get the impression he has zero motivation in life to ever leave Jersey or make something of himself.

But fuck if he doesn't make Joey happy.

And he's loyal as hell.

He loves her, and he loves her exactly the way she is.

"At some point, you have to stop blaming yourself," she says, reaching for my hand and slipping hers into it. "I'm sure we'd both like to go back three years and make different decisions, but we can't. We went on that spur of the moment road trip, you fell asleep at the wheel and hit that guardrail. You walked away with hardly a scratch and I . . ."

She glances down at her lap.

"It was my turn to drive," she continues. "You were tired, and I was tired, and I asked you to drive just a little bit longer, and you agreed because that's the kind of person you are, Cris. You're selfless. You did it for me."

I pinch the bridge of my nose between my thumb and forefinger.

"I don't blame you," she says. "You're still my best friend, and I still love you, and it hurts so damn bad to see the way you look at me now and to know you avoid coming home because it means you'll have to see me and it means you'll be reliving that night all over again."

Letting my hand fall to my side, I look her in the eye. "You're right. I hate seeing what I did to you. And sometimes I fly halfway across the world just to try and forget it. And when I heard you were getting married, a part of me felt like an even bigger piece of shit, because I'd always vowed to be the one to take care of you."

My chest burns the way it did the summer we both turned thirteen and the weightlessness of childhood faded without warning. Her dad had been diagnosed with terminal brain cancer the day after school let out. And the night before he took his last breath, he'd asked to see me. Mom sent me over with a casserole for Connie, and I was startled when I walked in and saw Joey's dad sitting at the kitchen table. He was bald and frail and pale, and he was wrapped in a thick blue robe, but he was smiling as if nothing was wrong. There was something lighter about him that night, as if he knew it was his time. He called me to the table and asked me to take a seat.

That night he asked me to promise to always take care of his Joey.

"I don't blame you, Cristiano. So can you please stop blaming yourself? And can you please be happy for me? Because I'm so happy and in love. I'm happier than I've ever been, I promise. And for the love of God, will you please push me down the aisle now?" Her face lights the way it does when she thinks about Trent.

"Yeah," I say, standing tall and moving to the back of her wheelchair, letting the burn in my chest fade to a soft fullness. "I'll push you down the aisle now."

Chapter Twenty-Two

Daphne

Crawling under the covers of my childhood bed, I clutch my phone and peer through tired eyes at the bright screen in the dark. I left the hospital an hour ago, stopped for a late dinner with my parents at a local diner, and patiently bided my time until I could be alone with my thoughts again, and exactly as I predicted, they seem to be fixed on one thing.

Pulling up Facebook, I type in the name Cristiano Amato.

I want to see his pictures. I want to know more about him. I want to pull back the curtain and peek into his life one snapshot and status update at a time.

There are only two Cristiano Amatos, according to the search I perform, and I click on the first option. His cover photo is of a city at night. Looks like Paris. And his profile picture, though tiny, is undeniably Cristiano standing outside the pyramid of Giza.

My heart patters as I click through his photo albums. Most of them are pictures from his travels. He doesn't caption most of them; just a few random ones. Some people ask questions and he responds.

Some girl, Joanna Marcuso, comments on almost all of them. Beneath a photo of Cristiano parasailing, she's written, "I thought you were afraid of heights. You sit on a throne of LIES!" It shows he responded, so I click to expand the conversation.

"I've never said I was afraid of heights. You must have me confused with Ben Fletcher," he replies, tagging Ben. "Correct me if I'm wrong, but Ben was the one who climbed the flag pole in sixth grade and pissed himself when he got to the top."

Ben Fletcher replies twenty-five minutes after, saying, "Don't listen to him, Joey. That never happened."

Joey . . .

I click on Joanna's profile, my heart pulsing and my ears heating. Her profile is an open book. Nothing is private, though she doesn't have much to go sifting through. It doesn't take long for me to find a picture of Cristiano with Joey. It's from several years ago. He looks much younger in it, thinner, less brawny. They're smiling ear to ear, their arms wrapped around each other. She's wearing a baseball cap and a Red Sox t-shirt. Flipping through the rest of her photos, I find at least three dozen pictures of the two of them.

My heart sinks.

They look incredibly happy together. Natural. Comfortable. In love.

This is Joey.

This is the "friend" whose wedding he was headed to . . .

The wedding he wanted to stop.

Sitting my phone aside, I decide not to torture myself another minute longer. This feels like Weston all over again. I can't do this. I can't let my heart want another man whose heart is still stuck on someone else.

Closing my eyes, I pull in a deep breath and try to let go of what once was and what will never be.

Rolling to my side, I yank the covers up to my chin and let the day's fatigue soak into my bones. Within minutes, I'm drifting, seconds from succumbing to a bittersweet slumber, when my phone vibrates softly against my nightstand.

Eyes squinting in the dark, I reach for the phone, flipping it over and bringing the screen closer. The caller ID flashes a 973 area code. It's him. At least I'm ninety-nine percent sure. My body freezes, and my mind replays a carousel of images of Cristiano with Joey, smiling, intertwined, inseparable.

The vibrating stops, and the phone quiets, but it's all the same because I can't talk to him. I know where this will lead.

I could answer the phone. I could drown myself in the sound of his voice and imagine his fingers in my hair. I could make plans to see him again and count down the hours until his mouth crushes mine again. I could let him sweep me off somewhere far away, traveling the world by his side and making priceless memories.

But she would always be there in the background, just as it was with Weston. With him, I'd see it in the way he'd look at me, like he was there with me . . . but he wasn't completely there. Sometimes I'd swear he was picturing her in my place, wondering what things would be like if he were sharing that moment with the one who still held his heart in her teeth. And it was never intentional, but it happened.

I was a placeholder. I gave him hope. But in the end, I wasn't enough.

I couldn't do it with Weston, and I can't do it with Cristiano.

I can't play second fiddle.

I can't settle for half of his heart.

I can't sit around hoping I'll be the one to help him move on, and I can't spend the rest of my life trying to convince myself he doesn't always think of *her* when he looks at me.

I just . . . can't.

Chapter Twenty-three

Cristiano

Hunched over the bar at Joey's reception, I lift my empty glass the second I catch the bartender's eye. He gives me a nod, an unspoken promise of sorts, like he knows a troubled man when he sees one, though I'm not sure I'd call myself troubled.

Confused, maybe?

I'd called Daphne earlier, and I've yet to receive a call back. All I wanted to do was make sure she got home all right.

And hear her voice.

I even left her a message.

I could've taken the easy way out and shot her a quick text, but I thought I'd be a gentleman and take the old-fashioned route to show her I cared enough to actually pick up the phone and call her.

The bartender slides me a fresh finger of bourbon, and I slide him a generous tip. Thank God for open bar tonight, the good man upstairs knows I needed a little something to numb the sting of watching my best friend marry Trent Tisdale and hearing her say for the first time that she doesn't need me to take care of her after all.

Maybe it was silly, to put that burden on myself, but for years, that burden was there. I figured I'd travel the world. See everything there was to see. And then come back home to Jersey, face Joey and what I'd done to her, and spend the rest of my life making it up to her. Making sure she'd never want for anything. Making sure she was comfortable. Happy . . . enough.

But she's happy with Trent. That's all that matters.

And she forgives me.

And I'm happy for her. At least I am now.

"Sure you need another one of those?" Two raven-haired women with strands of purple in their hair take the empty seat next to me.

Wait. Shit. No.

It's just one woman.

I'm seeing double.

"I've been watching you all night," she says, waving down the bartender. "You're just sucking those down one after another. Although I do have to say, I admire a man who can hold his liquor. If you were causing problems, then *we'd* have problems. I'll be damned if I let some drunk jackass ruin my cousin's wedding."

"You Trent's cousin?"

She shakes her head. "Nope. Joey's. I'm Ashley."

"No shit?" I remember Joey talking about her cousin, Ashley, growing up. She lived in Minnesota and rarely came to Jersey. Joey and her mom would travel to Duluth every summer to stay with her aunt, and Joey would come back with a funny accent that always seemed to wear off by the time school started again. "You're Cousin Ashley?"

She rises slightly, leaning over the bar to order a draft beer before turning back to me. "In the flesh."

I toss back my drink, her face coming in and out of focus.

"You want a water?" she asks, slowly reaching for my drink, like she's going to try to distract me and take it away.

Joke's on her because I'm not a fucking dog with a chew toy. I slide it away, though in my uncoordinated state, I slide it too quickly and sticky liquor splashes over the rim and onto my hand.

"Fuck," I say, rising from the bar stool and nearly stumbling backward. Ashley hops up, looping her arm through mine to steady me.

"Okay," she says, like she's about to make an executive order. "No more drinks for you. Come with me."

"I'm not going anywhere with you," I say, though I'm ninety-nine percent sure I'm slurring each and every last one of my words.

"Yeah. You are." This one has major attitude. She's feisty.

She pulls me to a corner table with a view of the dance floor. Strobe lights flash on half-empty slices of cake resting on tiny white plates. A disco ball spins in the distance, spilling sparkles of light all over the wooden dance floor. Up ahead, Trent is dancing around Joey, holding her hand as she sways in her chair to Al Green's *Let's Stay Together*.

God, they look happy.

Deliriously happy.

I want that. I want that more than I've ever wanted it before. Maybe it's because I've never had that before? Regardless,

I want it. And I want it with Daphne.

Maybe it's the alcohol talking or maybe I'm still strung up on all those high-running emotions from earlier today, but there's an empty part of me that's making its presence known for the first time in I don't know how long. For years, I ignored this void. Convinced myself it was nothing more than my imagination.

But watching Trent and Joey exchange vows tonight, hand in hand, and watching them tear up the dance floor with dopey smiles on their faces, I'm convinced that love is real. And if that's the case, then loneliness is too.

"Stay here," Cousin Ashley says, speaking to me like I'm a puppy. Or a two-year-old. Same difference.

I kick my feet up on the chair next to me and slip my hands behind my head, watching as more guests head out to the dance floor. Hell, I should be out there too, and I would be if I weren't a safety hazard. Last thing I want to do is bump into a flower girl or step on Grandma Gigi's toes.

Cousin Ashley returns, though I'm not sure how long it's been. I have zero concept of time right now. She could've been gone an hour for all I know.

"Here," she says, dropping a plate of white wedding cake in front of me and then handing me a fork. "You need to eat something. Soak up all that alcohol."

The sight of cake covered in mountains of frosting makes me want to hurl. I'm one of those rare breeds of dog who like cake but hate frosting. I begin to scrape it off, but I'm still not sure if I want to actually eat it. I haven't had much of an appetite since Fab picked me up earlier.

Cousin Ashley digs into her slice, watching me all the while.

"What?" I try to glare at her, but I'm not sure what shape my face has morphed into. Whatever my expression is, she clearly finds it funny because she's laughing. "I don't need a babysitter."

"Eh, you kind of do." She nods her head, like she's agreeing with herself. "It's not like I've got anything better to do. Didn't bring a date. Not in the mood to shadow my mom around like a shy kindergartener. Certainly don't want to sit in a corner and stare at the wall."

"Because those were the only alternatives?" I slur, forking a slice of cake. Lifting it to my nose, I take a whiff. It smells like sweet almonds and vanilla. Taking a bite, I decide it's not so bad.

"So what's your deal anyway?" she asks, leaning closer and speaking above the music. "I've been watching you all night. You're just sulking. You don't want to be here, I can tell."

I shrug. "It's complicated."

Cousin Ashley slaps the table and jolts forward. "You're in love with Joey, aren't you?"

Flicking my gaze at her, I shake my head. "Nope."

She slinks down, brows furrowed like she's thinking. "Did you go through a recent breakup? Going to a wedding after you've just had your heart broken is sheer torture. Trust me, I've been there before."

I shake my head, pushing another bite of cake into my mouth. When I glance down, I see that my plate is now empty, and I have no recollection of eating this entire piece.

Sighing, I shove the empty plate away, lean back in my seat, and fold my arms. I watch as Cousin Ashley finishes her cake and sips her beer and texts someone on her phone simultaneously . . . which reminds me to check my phone for the millionth time tonight.

No missed calls. No messages. Nothing.

Sliding out from the table, I glance at the bar and try to determine if I can make it there without hurting myself – or anyone else. I just want one more drink. Then I'll bid the happy couple goodnight and find Fabrizio and get the hell out of here.

"Hey, where the hell do you think you're going?" Cousin Ashley chases after me, her wild curls bouncing as she runs in heels.

I ignore her. It's nothing personal, it's just that I don't need a minder, and I'm not in the mood to be some bored wedding guest's personal entertainment tonight.

Perching on a bar stool a moment later, I lift my hand and flag down the barkeep again. His lips form a hard line, like he disapproves but knows he's not paid to judge, so he lifts a finger to indicate he'll be with me soon.

"Seriously, stop." Cousin Ashley hooks her arm into mine. "Enough. You're good. One more of those and you're going to be on the floor, and you're about what, two-ten? Two-twenty? Well over six feet tall. There's no way in hell I'll be able to drag you to safety."

"Ashley!" Connie appears from out of nowhere, arms open wide as she embraces her niece. "It's so good to see you, sweetheart. Your mom tells me you moved here for grad school last month? How are you liking Jersey so far? You know if you ever need a home cooked meal, just pop over. We'd love to have you . . ."

Rising from the seat, I forgo another drink for the time being and head outside to get some fresh air. The January wind glides across my warm skin, cutting through this cheap rental suit jacket, but it hardly bothers me. Walking around the building, I find a dark alley away from the smokers congregating out front and slip my phone from my pocket. The screen blurs in and out, my vision not doing me any favors, but I manage to pull up Daphne's number.

I know I shouldn't call her again, but it's ten o'clock on a Saturday night. There's no way she's at the hospital. There's no way she hasn't seen my missed call. The message I left earlier simply asked her to let me know that she made it back safely. How hard is it to return a call? Shoot a text?

Dragging my hands through my hair, it dawns on me.

"My ex is back home . . . I haven't seen him in over a year, and he's going to be there, and I'm kind of freaking out."

Motherfucker.

That's it.

That's why she's ignoring me.

She's with her ex . . . the one who broke her heart . . . the one she clearly still has a thing for.

Fuck. Me.

"Hey, there you are." Cousin Ashley appears from around the corner, her arms folded and her breath like clouds. "I was looking for you."

PRICELESS

Chapter Twenty-Four

Daphne

"You look well-rested, Daphne." Mom pours two cups of coffee Sunday morning and hands me one. "You're glowing!"

I don't tell her it's this new concealer I bought when I was in Seaview. It covers ev-er-y-thing . . . freckles . . . dark spots . . . zits . . . evidence of sleepless nights.

"Thanks, Mom." I take a seat in the breakfast nook overlooking the backyard. The treehouse my father built nearly twenty years ago has seen better days. Some of the boards are weathered and sagging, but I like to think it's the memories that keep it standing tall. "I can't believe the treehouse is still going strong."

"I don't know about *strong*." Mom chuckles, lifting her cup to her lips but not yet taking a sip. "The better you care for things, the longer they last. You know how your father is. The more grandkids we get, the more he keeps lacquering that thing up every chance he gets. Weatherproofing and water sealing it. The whole shebang."

"Where is Dad, anyway?" I ask. "He's usually up before everyone else."

"He went to grab coffee with Zane and Weston this morning then they were going to move some furniture at Delilah's before heading to the hospital." She speaks slowly and takes a sip, her careful gaze moving toward me. "You know, that Weston, he's such a sweet man. Your father really likes him a lot, and that says something because your father doesn't always like everyone."

I lift my brows, exhaling. My stomach twists. I know where this conversation is headed, and I'm not sure I want to take it in that direction.

"Baby Noah looks so much like Zane," I say, changing the subject. "He's, like, twenty-five percent Delilah, seventy-five percent Zane."

"He's a beautiful little boy," Mom agrees, smiling fondly as she stares outside. It's as if she's imagining her grandkids playing in the very same treehouse her children once knew. "Delilah said you and Weston spent some time together last night. How did that go?"

My gaze flicks her way. I'm sure she's asking from the perspective of a concerned mother. She saw the tears. She knows how crushed I was when it didn't work out.

"I really don't want to talk about Weston," I say, shoulders tight and eyes averted. "I'm sorry."

Mom's hand lands across her chest. "I didn't mean to pry about Weston, Daphne. I know that's a sore subject for you. I was just asking . . ."

"No, I know." I lift my coffee mug, blowing a cool breath across the surface and watching the ripples.

"Did something happen?" she asks. "With that young man you drove across the country with?"

My gaze lands on hers, settling on the same baby blue irises that match mine fleck-for-fleck.

"Nothing happened with him. I'm going to hit the shower." I rise, pushing my chair in and taking my cup to the sink. "Then I'm heading over to the hospital in about an hour."

Mom watches me, her expression equally concerned and confused. It's too early in the morning for a weighty conversation, and besides, there's nothing to talk about. Cristiano was a guy that made me think *maybe* he was different. *Maybe* he wasn't like the rest. But it turns out he was exactly like the rest.

He never mentioned Joey was a girl. He never mentioned he was attending the wedding of the girl who broke his heart. In fact, getting any kind of information out of him was like pulling teeth. He was a closed book unless I pried, which tells me he had no interest in getting to know me.

I should've known.

All he wanted was to fuck me.

Lucky him. He got what he wanted. Twice.

And now I just want to move on.

Climbing the stairs to the second level, I stop in my room to grab some clothes before making my way to the shower. Passing my phone, I notice I have a missed call and that they've left a message. It's the same New Jersey area code as Cristian's number, but it's a completely different prefix.

My stomach knots, and I'm torn between listening to the voicemail and letting it go. But in a fog of early morning fatigue and hindered self-restraint, I allow my curiosity to get the better of me.

Pulling in a deep breath, I slide the phone off my dresser and press my thumb over the play button.

Chapter Twenty-Five

Cristiano

"Ah, shit." My head throbs, and I don't have to open my eyes to know I'm not in my own home. Or in my own bed. The sheets feel different. Satin, I think. And they smell like someone else's fabric softener, not the cheap shit I normally use.

Shifting beneath the covers, I feel the cool drag of smooth fabric over my bare legs.

Bare. Legs.

Reaching down, I breathe a sigh of relief when I feel my boxers. Still, that doesn't necessarily mean anything.

I sit up and force my eyes open. There's a white dresser covered in clothes and perfume bottles in the corner, and the comforter is purple and covered in tiny flowers. It smells like a chick in here.

What the fuck did I do last night?

Or, rather, *who* the fuck did I do?

The sound of running water pulls my attention toward a door to my left. It's closed, but light escapes underneath the bottom. This girl, whoever I went home with last night, is in the shower right now.

Fuck.

Climbing out of bed, I scan the messy, clothes-covered floor for pieces of my tux. I spot a black cummerbund and a white button down, but I have no fucking clue where my pants are.

"Looking for these?" Cousin Ashley appears from her bathroom door with my pants in her hand, fully-clothed and hair wrapped in a towel. A toothbrush sticks out from the corner of her mouth.

"Yeah."

She tosses them to me, and I waste no time slipping them back on.

This is embarrassing, but I have to ask because I have no recollection of most of last night. "Did we . . . ?"

I don't *think* I did.

I don't think I *would,* not with my mind set on Daphne . . . and even if I was that kind of guy, I'm pretty sure I had a major case of whiskey dick last night.

She yanks the toothbrush from her mouth, tosses her head back, and laughs. "No. No. No. We did *not* have sex − if that's what you're asking."

She prances to her kitchen, rinsing the brush off under the faucet and tapping it on the stainless steel sink.

"Although you did spend the better part of last night absolutely convinced that I was hitting on you," she says, hand on hip. "Let the record show that I was *not* hitting on you."

I zip my fly and take a seat on her sofa, wondering where the fuck my phone is. This girl has books and clothes everywhere.

"Your phone is on the charger over here," she says. "You

look like you're looking for something, so I can only imagine it's your phone. I had to pry it out of your hands last night after you passed out because the battery died and I figured you'd need it in the morning. I charged it for you. You're welcome."

"Thanks." I rise, moving toward the kitchen to grab it off her charger. No missed calls. No texts. "Want to tell me why I'm here?"

Ashley moves to the fridge, grabbing two waters, and hands one to me. "You were drunk off your ass. Your brother left with some girl. You had no way to get home, and I couldn't, in good conscience, leave you like that, so I took you home."

She moves toward the bedroom.

"Which reminds me, I need to strip the bed. My boyfriend would freak if he came home and the sheets smelled like you," she says casually. "You're lucky he's traveling for work. Anyway, I let you have the bed last night because you kept rolling off the couch. I was afraid you were going to hit your head on the coffee table, and well, I'm not exactly in a position to get sued for medical damages, so I took the couch . . ."

She comes out a few minutes later with an armful of bedding and drops it in front of a closet containing a stackable washer and dryer.

"So who's this Daphne girl?" Ashley rests a hand on one hip and wears a smirk when she returns to the kitchen. "God, you wouldn't shut up about her last night. All night long, it was *Daphne this* and *Daphne that* and *Daphne's so perfect for me* and *I'll never find anyone else like Daphne . . .*"

She mocks my voice, making me sound whinier than I know I am.

I chuff. "I was drunk. I'm sure I said a lot of shit I didn't mean."

"So you didn't mean anything you said about her last night?"

"I don't even know what I said about her last night."

"You said she's beautiful and funny and genuine. That you could see yourself traveling the world with her by your side. That you haven't been able to get her out of your head since you met her. That you want nothing more than to see her again. And then you cried into your pizza at two AM like a drunk sorority girl. It seemed like the proper ending to a hot mess kind of night." Ashley plops down in a leather recliner next to me, resting her chin on her hand. "You have some issues, Cristiano. And I don't say that to be mean or judgmental or whatever, but I think you need to work through some stuff."

"I was just overreacting to something," I huff. "I'm over it now."

"Mm hm."

"Didn't even think about Daphne until you brought her up this morning," I lie.

"Right." Ashley sighs, leaning back. "Anyway, I took the liberty of finding her number in your phone. I figured you'd need a ride home. I left her a message earlier telling her where to find you and to pick you up by ten because I'm leaving for work and you need to be gone by then. Granted, I know Joey can vouch for you, but honestly, we're still strangers and I don't want some random, hungover guy hanging out at my place while I'm gone."

"Tell me you're joking."

Her face is void of expression. "Do I look like I'm joking?"

Dragging my hands down my face, I take a deep breath. "What did you say, Ashley?"

She smirks, glancing up at the ceiling. "Well, let me think. I basically told her that some guy named Cristiano is in love with her and that he needs a ride home and if she loves him too, she can find him at 45 Cherry Street, Apartment 7, in Montclair."

"You did not."

"I did."

"I'm not in love with her. I barely fucking know her."

Ashley's brows lift and she fights a smile. "Yeah, whatever you say, *el capitan*."

"I really wish you hadn't called her." Leaning back in the sofa, I think about what I must look like. What I must *smell* like. I want to see her, but I don't want to see her when I've got remnants of last night all over me.

"Why are you just sitting there?" Ashley asks. "Get off your ass and get in the shower. Just don't use any of Drew's things. I don't want him coming home later wondering why the bathroom smells like his shower gel."

"What, he doesn't trust you?"

Ashley shrugs. "He's got a possessive streak a mile wide. The mere thought of sharing me with another man sends him over the edge."

"That's too bad." I clear my throat. "It's too bad he's possessive, I mean."

Her lips inch up at the sides and her dark eyes light. "Eh. I think it's hot. I'm fucked up like that, I guess. Don't judge me."

Shaking my head, I lift myself off the couch and make my way to the bathroom.

Chapter Twenty-Six

Daphne

I've listened to the voicemail at least four times now.

"Hi Daphne. My name is Ashley. You don't know me, but I have your friend, Cristiano here," she says. *"Anyway, I met him at my cousin's wedding last night. He was hanging out by the bar the whole time, drowning his sorrows. Saddest guy you ever saw. Long story short, he got smashed out of his mind and I took him home and let him crash here. Talked my ear off about you for hours. Maybe it was the alcohol talking, but I'm pretty sure he's in love with you. Or obsessed with you. One of the two. Anyhoo, he's at my place now, and I have to leave for work in a couple hours. If you want to pick him up, he's at 45 Cherry Street, Apartment 7, in Montclair, New Jersey. I'm not sure where you live. Hell, maybe you live in Alaska or something. But if you want to see him, that's where he is. And if you don't want to see him, can't say that I blame you because he's kind of a hot mess . . . okay . . . guess if you're not here by ten, I'll tell him to call an uBer."*

Sinking into the edge of my bed, I let my phone drop to the covers. A Technicolor rainbow of emotions washes over me. The fact that he was talking to someone about me gives me a sliver of hope. But why was he drinking? Was he upset about Joey's wedding? And did he only ruminate about me because it was too late for him and Joey?

My phone vibrates softly against my comforter, sending a

hitch to my breath. Reaching down, I flip the screen over and see a strange number calling. I don't recognize the area code, and I'm not sure who'd be calling me at nine o'clock on a Sunday morning, but I decide to answer.

"Hello?" I ask.

"May I speak to Daphne Rosewood?" a man's voice responds on the other end.

"Yes, this is she."

"Daphne, this is Kurt Greenleaf, professor at Seaview College of Fine Arts," he says, the familiarity of his voice returning. "Sorry to call you on a Sunday, but I'm getting ready to fly out of the country, and I wanted to reach out to you before I left. Do you have a moment?"

Pulling my legs onto the bed, I wrap my arms around them and drag in a deep breath. "Yes, I have a moment."

"The hiring committee has met," he says, his voice just as stoic as I remember. I can picture him so clearly, seated in the center of the table at my interview. He didn't smile once. And he asked all the hard questions. I was pretty sure when we were done that this man hated me for reasons unknown. "And we'd like to offer you an assistant professor position teaching our introductory drawing classes."

My hand flies to my mouth, and I feel it arch beneath my palm as I grin wide.

"Thank you," I manage to sputter. "Thank you so much. I accept. And I'm honored."

"Good, good," he says. "The college is closed for winter break right now, but my assistant, Tina, will be in contact with you first thing Monday. Spring semester starts in three weeks, but we'd like for you to spend two weeks in Paris mentoring under Professor Halbrook. He's teaching at our sister school, *Paris Collège des Beaux-arts*. Halbrook developed our drawing major, and you'll be taking over his classes, so we'd like for you to spend some one-on-one time with him before you start. Are you able to travel overseas, Daphne? You have a passport?"

"Yes," I nod. "And I'm very familiar with Paris."

"All right then. Like I said, Tina will get a hold of you tomorrow. She'll likely have a mountain of paperwork for you to complete, and we'll have you on the next plane to Paris," he says. "I'd like to apologize for the timing of all of this. We weren't anticipating this vacancy. It's not common practice to do everything on such short notice, but we appreciate your flexibility, and we sincerely look forward to having you on board, Ms. Rosewood."

"Thank you," I say. "I can't tell you how excited I am."

My entire body buzzes to life the second I end the call. With trembling hands and a smile that takes up my entire face, I run downstairs to tell my mom the news. She squeals and wraps me in her arms, and we do a little happy dance. And in that sliver of a moment, I temporarily forget about Cristiano.

I forget about the voicemail.

I forget he needs a ride.

I forget that he poured his heart out to some stranger last night in a way that gave her the impression he had some sort of feelings for me.

"Okay," I say, stepping away from my mom. "We can

celebrate later. I'm going to get ready so I can head over to the hospital and love on that baby some more."

"Yes, go," Mom says, smiling proud. "We'll celebrate tonight."

Tromping back upstairs, there's a twist in my belly. An ache. A curious sadness. My thoughts return to Cristiano again, drowning in the what-if and what-might-have-been. Part of me wants to believe I was wrong about him. Part of me wants to give him a chance to explain. But the rest of me, the overwhelming majority of me, is on high alert because truth is, he lied by omitting the facts.

I won't get hurt again. And I knew from the moment I laid eyes on Cristiano Amato that he was a heartbreaker.

Stripping out of my clothes, I run the shower and step in, letting the hot water saturate my hair and drip down my body in slow, grazing streams. Within minutes, I've washed away the day, and I'm sure of only two things:

It's a new year.

And I need a fresh start.

Chapter Twenty-Seven

Cristiano

"I don't think she's coming." Ashley peeks out of her living room curtain, peering into the parking lot below. "Sorry."

I fire off a text to Fabrizio. First I'm going to ask him to pick me up, then I'm going to rip him a new one for ditching me. He was my fucking ride last night.

"I knew she wouldn't," I say. My phone buzzes in my hand. Fabrizio writes back saying he'll be here in an hour.

"So what happened with you and this girl?" Ashley pries, arms folded and head cocked. "I mean, you rambled on and on about how wonderful she was, but not once did you tell me why she wasn't speaking to you."

Raking my hand along my tightened jaw, I stare at the wall in front of me. "Don't know."

"Sure you do," Ashley says. "I'm sure you said something or did something. Think."

Shaking my head, I say, "I met her last Tuesday. Honestly, I don't even know this girl. I was just drunk last night. And seeing Joey get married and how happy she looked . . . it made me think about Daphne."

"Really? You don't know her that well? You sure seemed like you did."

"We were in a car for three straight days. We did a lot of talking. Or she did. She talks a lot. And asks a lot of questions. Guess we got to know each other pretty well. But whatever." I rise, wishing I was wearing anything other than a tuxedo right now. I hate these fucking penguin suits. "It's over. She wants nothing to do with me. Life goes on."

Ashley's mouth bunches at the corner. "You'll meet someone else someday. I'm sure the perfect girl is out there waiting for you to find her."

I laugh through my nose. For a time this past week, I was convinced Daphne was *the* perfect girl for me.

"Yeah, something like that," I say.

She moves to the kitchen, grabbing her purse and jingling her keys. "I have to go to work now . . . I was going to kick you out. Make you wait outside. But since your ride isn't here yet, I guess you can hang out. Just lock the door on your way out. And don't steal anything or my boyfriend will literally kick your ass."

Smirking, I promise her, "I won't touch a damn thing, Ashley."

She looks at me through the corner of her eye, her mouth drawing into a slow smile. "All right. You take care, okay? Chin up and all that."

In an instant, she's gone. And I'm alone with nothing but the thoughts that fill my pounding head.

***

"Ow! What'd you do that for?" Fabrizio rubs the spot on his arm where I've just punched him, and I slam his car door shut.

"That's for ditching me last night. Some fucking brother you are."

He pulls out of Ashley's parking lot like a bat out of hell, nearly side-swiping someone's Ford, and I blame Matteo because Matteo's the one who taught him how to drive.

"Dude," Fab says, "if you would've seen the girl I went home with . . . you'd totally understand."

"Grow the fuck up," I snap, resisting the urge to smack the back of his head. He's lucky he's driving right now.

"But you went home with someone, right? You hook up with that girl with the purple hair?" Fab grins wide, like he's on the verge of high-fiving me.

"No," I scoff. "That was Joey's cousin. She has a boyfriend. And I did not hook up with her."

"Mm hm," he says, as if he doesn't believe me. "Right, right."

"Just fucking drive."

"What the hell is your problem?" Fabrizio asks, coming to a hard stop at a red light. "Is this because Joey got married?"

"No," I spit, face pinched. "Has nothing to do with her."

"Is this about that road trip girl?"

I don't answer. Glancing out the passenger window, I spot a billboard advertising a new international airline with direct flights out of Newark Liberty International Airport, and my next move becomes clear.

I've got to get out of here.

***

"So just like that? You're home for a hot minute and now you're jetting off again?" My mom takes a seat on the edge of my bed. I'm leaning against the headboard, laptop across my legs and credit card in hand as I book my flight to Rome.

Figured I'd crash on a few couches and make my way from Italy to Greece to France to Germany and everywhere in between. Two weeks of eating, sleeping, and drinking my way through Europe should get me back on track. Back in the right mindset.

"Why are you always leaving?" Mom's mouth pulls down in the corner, her voice tinged with a slight Italian accent that always feels like home to me. "Just once, I'd like for you to stay a while. I worry about you, you know. Traveling all over the world all the time, sometimes going days or *weeks* without checking in. It's dangerous."

"Mom," I chuff. "It's fine. This is what I do."

"Sometimes I think you're doing more running than traveling," she says with a sigh, her dark brows arched in concern. "What are you running away from this time, Cristiano? All these years, I figured it was Joey. You took the accident harder than anyone. Even harder than Joey. She forgave you, you know? But I don't think you ever forgave yourself. So you stayed away. Even when it hurt her, you stayed away."

I close the lid of my laptop and cross my arms. "I never meant to hurt her. It was just hard coming home."

Everything was different.

Everything had changed.

And it was all my fault.

"When we forgive ourselves, we set ourselves free," she says. "Forgive yourself, Cristiano. Forgive yourself, and your entire world will change."

My mother's dark eyes soften, and her expression is pained. She hurts too. She hurts for me.

"Stay a while this time, will you?" she asks.

Pulling in a deep breath and letting it go, I regrettably inform her my tickets are booked.

I watch her face fall. "All right then."

"I'll come home after that," I promise. "I'll make it a regular thing."

Her mouth inches up at the sides. "I would love that, *mio amore*."

Mom rises, shuffling across the faded blue carpet of my childhood bedroom and making her way to the door.

"Mom?" I call out.

She turns to me, smiling, which doesn't make what I'm about to say any easier.

"I have to tell you something," I say.

"Of course. What is it?"

"I never finished law school."

Her smile fades. "What are you talking about, Cristiano? I went to your graduation. I watched you walk. Of course you graduated."

Shaking my head, I say. "I paid someone I knew to put me

on the list. I'd dropped out a year before that. I didn't want to disappoint you."

She leans against the frame of the door, her gaze falling to her feet before lifting to meet mine. "You could never disappoint me. If you only knew how proud I am of you. Of all my boys . . ."

"I'm so sorry."

"But it hurts," she adds. "It hurts that you didn't think you could come to me with the truth back then."

"I wish I could have done it differently. Believe me. I've regretted it every single day."

She pulls in a concentrated breath, tilting her head to the side. "I know you were just trying to protect me. For that, I forgive you. But do not *ever* lie to your mother again."

"I promise." There's a lightness in my chest, followed by a partial release.

"So tell me, what are you doing these days for work? Who's footing the bill for all these travels of yours?" She folds her arms, and I find myself speechless. I didn't prepare for that question.

My jaw slacks as I rack my brain.

"Do not lie to me, Cristiano." She points a finger at me, her dark brows meeting in the middle.

"I can't tell you," I say. "And that's the truth."

"Is it illegal, this thing you're doing?" She squints.

"Not at all."

"Okay then." Mom lets her hands fall to her sides. "Tell me when you're ready."

"I will." I neglect to tell her that I'll probably *never* be ready to tell her . . .

"Hold on, just a moment." Mom lifts her pointed finger and disappears, her feet carrying her lightly down the hall. I glance at my computer screen, waiting for the confirmation email with my itinerary to show up, and when I look up, I find my mother standing in the doorway with a paperback book pressed against her chest. The front of the cover is hidden by her wide-spread palm and she takes a step toward me, biting her lip like she's fighting a smile.

Taking careful steps my way, she stops beside me and hands over the book. The title, THE LUMBERJACK AND THE PRINCESS, is scrawled across the front in bold, red font, right across an image of myself in a red checkered, unbuttoned shirt. My jeans are slung low, so low I'm almost giving it all away, and my bronzed and oiled chest is on full display.

"I told you I was in that romance book club, didn't I?" she asks, speaking slowly.

"Not that I recall." Not once in my life have I witnessed my mother reading a romance novel.

Clearing her throat, she says, "Yeah, well, I am. Joined it last year. Anyway, this is the book we're going to be reading next week. I thought the man on the cover looked familiar, but when I opened it up, I saw the model's name was Jax Diesel. Had myself a good laugh because, you know, they say everyone has a twin."

My cheeks burn, white-hot, but I do my best to keep a straight face.

"But then I kept staring at this book cover, and I kept thinking . . . that's got to be my son," she says, bringing the image closer to her gaze. "So I went on Google and I looked up this Jax Diesel character, and imagine my surprise when I found a whole slew of his images. He even has a website. It's very professional. Very classy. Anyway, I clicked around, looked at all the pictures. Some of them were quite, um-"

"Mom," I stop her. I don't want to hear any more. "It's me. *I'm* Jax Diesel. I model for book covers, and that's how I've been making a living."

I can't look at her.

I don't *want* to look at her.

It's going to be a while before I can look her in the eyes after this.

Shit.

Fuck.

She's quiet. And I don't blame her. She just finished admitting she browsed hundreds of images of her near-naked grown adult son.

"I'm sorry," I say.

"For what? For making a career for yourself?" she asks.

I force myself to meet her gaze, though I'm still cringing hard on the inside. I'm half-tempted to add, "*At least I'm not making porn . . .*" but I bite my tongue. I'd rather end this conversation as soon as humanly possible.

"When are you leaving, *mio amore*?" she changes the subject, probably sensing my extreme discomfort in regards to this conversation, and places the book gently on my nightstand. I doubt she'll be reading it now. Would be a little awkward, I'd think.

"Tomorrow." I stare at the foot of the bed, my body rigid and frozen, like it couldn't relax even if it wanted to.

"Well, then, you'd better start packing."

Glancing up at my mother, she tosses me a wink, fights a smile, and shows herself out. I'm glad one of us finds humor in this situation because I sure as hell don't.

Chapter Twenty-Eight

Daphne

"Hey, hey," I tiptoe into Delilah's hospital room Sunday morning.

"Morning," she whispers with a smile. Her gaze goes from the baby to me and back again. He's cradled in her arms, wrapped in a white blanket as he sleeps.

"How was last night? You get any sleep?"

She blows a swift breath past her lips and softly laughs. "Maybe a few hours off and on? He eats like his daddy. Ravenous appetite."

"Where is everyone?"

"They ran out to get donuts. They were supposed to bring them this morning and they forgot. They got their coffee. Forgot the sustenance." Delilah rolls her eyes. "Men."

"Guess what?" I pull up a chair and scoot it closer to her bedside.

"What?"

"I got the job." I lift my fingers to my mouth, pretending to bite my nails as I grin ear-to-ear.

"What?!" Delilah's face lights. "Daph, that's so awesome! I'm so happy for you. When do you start?"

"Soon," I say. "They're flying me to Paris this week. I'm going to mentor with some professor for a couple weeks before the semester starts."

"This week?" She raises a brow. "That's insane."

"I know. They had to fill this spot as soon as possible. The professor who called me apologized for the last minute timing," I say. "I don't care though. I'm just excited to have a job."

"So you're moving to California." Delilah's mouth purses.

"Yeah. I'm moving to California."

"You're going to be so far away."

"Just a plane ride," I assure her. "You guys can visit any time."

"Did you know Weston's going to be a free agent?" Delilah catches me off guard with her left-field question.

My face pinches. "No. I didn't. And I'm not sure what you're getting at."

"Supposedly San Francisco's got their eye on him," she says. "At least that's what his agent says."

"O . . . kay. What's your point?"

Her mouth creeps up in one corner and her eyes glint. "I don't know. If you're going to be in California and he's going to be in California . . . maybe . . ."

"Delilah," I say, voice firm. "Stop forcing Weston on me. And besides, San Francisco is hundreds of miles away from Seaview anyway. Regardless, it's done. It's over. Let it go. I have. I never want to be with him again. Believe me when I say that."

"Okay, fine." She sits up straight, arms tight around Noah. "All I'm trying to say is that you loved him once, and he still loves you. Maybe it isn't over?"

"Trust me, it's over." I don't feel the need to explain to her all the reasons I refuse to play second fiddle or attach my heart to someone whose heart is still attached to someone else.

"For the longest time you weren't over him." It's like she refuses to understand what I'm trying to say, and if she weren't twenty-four-hours post-partum, I'd be a little less diplomatic with her. "Is there someone else? Oh, my god. Don't tell me it's the road trip guy."

Her gaze flicks over my shoulder and her expression makes my blood run cold.

We're not alone.

Glancing behind me, I see Weston standing in the doorway, a box of donuts in his arms. My dad and Zane flank his sides.

"Oh, hey guys," Delilah says, pretending like we weren't just having a conversation about my non-existent future with Weston. "Come on in."

Weston studies me as he walks in, and he places the box of donuts on a nearby counter.

"Daphne," he says. "Morning."

"Good morning." I force an awkward smile before shooting my sister a look. If Weston heard our conversation, I would feel horrible. Despite the fact that he hurt me, it wasn't intentional. And I would never want to hurt him intentionally either. He's a good man. He's just not the man for me.

"How's our boy, huh?" Zane makes a goofy face as he hovers over Delilah.

"Shh," she says. "Don't wake him."

Weston takes a seat in the corner of the room, and when I glance through the side of my eye, I catch him watching me. He rakes his hand along his smooth, angled jaw, and his brows are furrowed.

"I'm going to grab a coffee," I say, standing up. "I'll be back in a bit."

When I round the corner outside of Delilah's room, I bump into my oldest sister, Demi, and Royal.

"Hey," she says, wrapping her arms around me. "I feel like we keep missing each other. You came last night after we were gone, and when we came back, you were gone. Where you going now?"

"Just grabbing a coffee," I say. "I'll be back."

She studies my face. "Everything okay?"

I chuckle, though it feels as fake as the smile on my face. "Yeah. Why wouldn't it be?"

She pushes a breath through her nostrils and sizes me up. Demi knows me, and she doesn't buy this for one second.

"We'll talk later, okay?" I point toward Delilah's room. "Everyone's in there. I'll be back in a bit."

Royal squeezes my shoulder as he walks past and makes a funny face. Growing up, he was like an honorary big brother to us. He was my brother Derek's best friend, and he was over at our house all the time. That's how he and Demi started dating.

He's still as obnoxious as the day he first showed up at our doorstep, but I still love him just the same.

Heading toward the hospital coffee shop, I find a place in the long line and peruse the menu. A minute later, I grab my phone to pass the time. There's a white popup on my screen, telling me my voicemail is ninety-five percent full. Going through my messages, I delete some of the old ones. Most of them are Delilah, giving me pregnancy updates. Some are from my mother. I clear them out one-by-one, and when I get to the message I received this morning from that Ashley girl, I pull in a long, hard breath and hover my thumb above the delete button, holding it in limbo as I decide whether or not to listen to it one last time.

"Next," the barista calls.

Chapter Twenty-Nine

Daphne

"You need anything, babe?" Zane rises from the sofa Monday night. It's the de la Cruz family's first night at home. Mom, Dad, Demi, Royal, and Derek were here earlier, but they've since gone their separate ways.

"Maybe some more water? Pretty please?" Delilah blows Zane a kiss as baby Noah snuggles into her other arm. All this kid does is sleep, but my sister says that's what newborns do. I'm counting down the days until this kid is old enough to hold a paintbrush or charcoal pencil.

"I'm starving," Weston says from his chair on the other side of the living room.

"You guys want to order some pizza?" Delilah offers. "My cupboards are pretty bare. Didn't buy a ton of groceries since we're going back to Chicago next week. I'm sorry."

"I can pick some up," I offer. I still have that damn rental car and I'm paying a pretty penny for it, so I may as well get some more use out of it. Pulling my phone out, I call Giovanni's Pizzeria and order some pies.

"You're the best," Delilah grabs a bottle of water from Zane when he returns. "Daphne's going to grab some pizza for us."

Zane sinks into the seat beside his wife, new-father

exhaustion written all over his face. "Thanks, D. What would we do without you?"

Rising, I shove my phone in my back pocket. "They'll be ready in fifteen, so I'm going to head out now."

"I'll go with you," Weston volunteers.

"You don't have to . . ." I try to stop him, but the look on his face tells me his mind is made up. And he's only trying to be nice. In an instant, he's making his way across the baby-gear-littered living room and passing me, placing his hand on the small of my back as he squeezes between myself and a bassinette. I turn to my sister who winks because for the love of God, she won't give up this idea that the two of us are still meant to be. "Okay. Guess we'll be back in a bit."

***

It's snowing again. But it's a pretty snow; a dusting really. Giant snowflakes swirl and dance as I park my car in Giovanni's parking lot.

"I hope it's okay that I tagged along," Weston says as we climb out. He walks around the back of the car, his hands shoved in the pockets of his jeans and his eyes on mine. His cologne travels through the crisp January air, filling my lungs with the scent of clean musk and fresh snow.

"It's fine," I assure him. He was just trying to be helpful, and he's been staying at Zane and Delilah's the last few days, so I'm sure he was wanting some change of scenery. I can't blame him for that.

Dropping my keys in my purse, I'm startled when I look up. Weston's standing less than a foot away from me now. He's so close, the warmth of his presence radiates into my space.

"Oh, hi." I say, tittering. I'm not nervous – I'm just uncertain of what he's about to do. This isn't him. This isn't typical Weston behavior.

"Daphne." He says my name as he releases a held breath, and his eyes lock on mine once again. "Seeing you these last couple of days . . . you have no idea how hard it is . . . I look at you, and I just want to . . ."

His hand reaches for my face, cupping the side of my cheek. Weston licks his lips. I purse mine. Within seconds I feel his mouth graze mine, my heart pounding in my ears.

"Please stop," I say, pressing my hand against his chest and moving away.

"Daphne."

Placing my palm over my heart, I say, "I can't. I can't be with you."

"Why not?" His face is twisted in a way I've never seen before. My normally calm and collected Weston wears hurt and anguish, his features angled and dark.

"You're just not who I want to be with anymore." I deliver my line with as much care and gentleness as I can muster.

"I'm over Elle," he says. "If that's what this is about. You were right. I wasn't over her before. It was too soon. You and I happened so fast, and I hadn't had time to process anything. You knew I was still in love with Elle before I knew it."

My chest squeezes, and I glance away. I'll never forget the look on his face the first time he told me he still loved her. He apologized. Said he wished more than anything that he was over her, but he wasn't, and he couldn't go on pretending. This gentle giant held me as I wept in his arms. I wept for him, because he was hurting for me. I wept for myself, because I was so certain Weston was going to be that epic love I'd been waiting for. And I wept for us, because we could've been great together.

"It's not about Elle," I say, lifting my vision in time to watch his expression fall.

"Then what is it? Is it that road trip guy?" he asks, almost laughing because to him, it probably seems implausible.

"No," I say. "Not directly."

"Not directly?" He chuffs. "What does that mean?"

"I realized some things about myself this past week." Snowflakes land on my lashes and cheeks, melting upon contact. First cool, then warm, then gone. It may as well be a metaphor for my romantic life. "If I want love to find me, I have to stop looking for it."

He scratches the side of his head, and a lock of sandy blond hair falls in his eyes. "I'm not following."

"I need to do my own thing for a while," I say. "I need to live my life, chase my dreams, and focus on making myself happy. I have a really bad habit of falling fast for guys I hardly know. I put the cart before the horse. I get my hopes up. And I get hurt. Every. Single. Time."

"Daphne, I never meant to hurt you. I told you that. It kills me that I hurt you the way I did," he says, reaching for my hand. "But if you give me another chance – give *us* another chance – I promise I'll never hurt you again."

He cups my face with his hand, though this time I don't think he's going to kiss me. It's a sweet gesture. Loving. If we didn't have a history, we could be great friends.

Staring into his eyes, I offer a closed-mouth smile and pull myself away. "Pizza's probably ready."

He stands, sneakers in the snow, unmoving. The saddest man I've ever seen.

"Whoever loves you next," he says, shoving his hands in his front pockets, brows furrowed. "I hope he treats you the way you deserve to be treated, and I hope he never has to know what it feels like to lose you. It's a pain like you couldn't imagine."

Chapter Thirty

Cristiano

"*Ciao, Tomasso!*" I greet my cousin, Tommy, at his apartment in Florence late Monday night. He's from New York but is staying here on business all month. I called him up last night to reserve his couch for a few nights, and he was nothing short of ecstatic when he heard I was coming.

"Cuz, how's it going?" He throws his arm around my shoulder and pulls me in. Frank Sinatra's blasting on his speakers and an uncorked bottle of wine rests next to a plate of half-eaten cured meats and cheeses.

In the corner, a few girls and a couple of guys stop their conversation and turn their attention in my direction. The girls are beautiful, clothed in skintight dresses, their long, sleek hair dripping down their shoulders and reflecting off the city lights outside. Their red lips are slicked with red, glossed, and pulled up at the sides.

"Tommy," the woman on the left says in her thick Italian accent. She rises from her seat and sways my way, extending her hand after brushing her long, ebony hair off her shoulder. "Are you going to introduce me to your friend or what?"

"Cristiano, this is Luciana. She works with me at the agency." Tommy lifts his glass when he speaks. "Luci, this is my American cousin."

"Cristiano," she says, slipping her hand in mine and letting it linger. "Italian-American?"

I nod, pulling my hand back and moving toward the wine beside me. Pouring myself a glass, I say, "Born in Ohio. Raised in Jersey."

She lifts her long nails to her lips, giggling slightly. "I don't know those places. You'll have to show me on a map sometime."

"Yeah," I say to appease her. Sipping my wine, I glance at the rest of the party and turn to my cousin. "You always have people over this late on a work night?"

Tommy shrugs, jutting his bottom lip forward. "We landed a big client today. Thought we'd do some celebrating. We're going out tonight, by the way. Getting ready to leave soon. Freshen up, pretty boy. You're coming with."

I've been up since four this morning. I've spent hours in airports and almost nine hours in the sky. But I'll scrape every last piece of me off this wood floor if I have to. I didn't fly halfway around the world to sleep while the world spins madly on outside these walls.

"Yeah," I say. "Give me a bit. I'll be ready."

Tommy grins wide, his smile reminding me of Matteo's. Hell, people always thought the two of them were brothers growing up. Tommy, in a lot of ways, is more than a cousin. He's like a sixth Amato brother.

***

"So what brings you to Florence?" Luciana asks as we stand around a high top table at a club called Firenze.

"Visiting Tomasso for a couple days," I say. "then I'm making my way all over."

"Where are you going to see?" She lifts her brows, taking a sip from her dirty martini. "I apologize if my English is bad."

"I understand you just fine," I say. "I'm going everywhere I can. London, Paris, Amsterdam. No itinerary, really. Just going where the wind blows me."

"That is nice," she says, offering a smile. She's clung to me since the first moment she laid eyes on me. "I'm flying to New York next month. Do you live in that area?"

"I don't really live anywhere."

Her smile fades. I think she's confused.

"I travel. I don't stay anywhere for too long," I add.

"I see," she says, taking another sip. Someone pushes past us, bumping into Luciana and subsequently pushing her into me. Her body presses against mine in a flash of a second, and when she lifts her drink, it spills down her arm and onto my shirt. "*Dio mio*, that was rude."

She yells a slew of Italian words, flinging her hand into the air as she speaks, but her voice is drowned out by the pumping dance music blasting through the speakers behind us and her intended target is long gone.

"It's fine." I grab a cocktail napkin from a nearby table and offer it to her first. She dries her arm and then dabs at the damp spots on my shirt, just above my heart.

I feel nothing, which is strange considering this Italian beauty is all over me, touching me and smiling and acting as if I'm the most interesting creature she's ever laid eyes on. She's clearly down to fuck. She wants me. And looking at her and knowing how painfully obvious it is that she's offering herself to me on a shiny silver platter does absolutely nothing for me.

Yawning, I check my watch. We've only been here an hour, and already I wouldn't mind going back to Tommy's place and calling it a night. A couple of hours ago, I was all over the idea of going out. Not sure what changed, but for whatever reason, I'm not in the mood anymore.

"I think we're good here." I place my hand over Luciana's, taking the wet napkin from her and stepping back to gain some space.

She steps toward me, clearly not taking the hint, and I glance at Tommy, who's making his way back from the bar with a tray of *limoncello* shots. He shoots me a wink, his gaze moving from Luciana to me and back.

No.

I'm not screwing his co-worker tonight. I'm not screwing anyone tonight. I'm far too exhausted anyway, and if I'm being honest, the idea of screwing anyone who isn't Daphne anytime in the near future holds zero appeal.

Grabbing a shot off Tommy's tray, I wait for everyone else to take theirs before tossing mine back.

"Did you like?" Luciana asks, placing her palm on my forearm. She smiles, leaning in so close that her powerfully sweet perfume invades my air space.

I nod, but I don't make eye contact with her, hoping she'll get the hint. She lingers for a bit, and I feel her watching me, gauging my body language, and after a moment, she turns her attention to another one of Tommy's co-workers.

In the far corner of the club, a tall blonde woman stands with a wine glass in her hand, her back toward me. Her silky, flaxen strands are piled on top of her head, and the way her hips curve beneath her narrow waist reminds me of Daphne.

My fingertips burn with the memory of her flesh beneath them. My lips crave hers. There's a hardness in my cock when I think about how wet she was for me just a few nights ago.

What I wouldn't give to see her one more time. To *have* her one more time.

Glancing away from Daphne's doppelganger, I chuckle to myself. I need to snap the fuck out of this. Earlier today, at Newark airport, I could've sworn I saw her. And again on the plane. And at a little café I passed in the taxi on the way here.

So much for flying four thousand miles away to escape. She's everywhere I go. She's in everything I see. She occupies every thought I have, every recent memory. I can only hope it'll all blow over soon because missing someone who wants nothing to do with me is really going to put a cramp in my European tour.

Heading to the bar, I order myself a finger of Glenlivet and make a silent toast.

To Daphne. May she be happy and loved, wherever she is.

Chapter Thirty-One

Daphne

One Week Later . . .

". . . and that's how I came up with the Feather Touch charcoal technique. I'm working on a trademark now. And a textbook." Professor Halbrook lifts his wine goblet over our candlelit dinner at a restaurant overlooking the Eiffel Tower. This place is much too romantic for a professional dinner. Then again, so are most of the restaurants he's been taking me to since I landed last week. Time and again, I've insisted on eating alone. Grabbing something from a café and having dinner in the privacy of my hotel room, but he insists on spending every waking moment with me during my short tenure in Paris.

"Interesting," I take a sip of my water before scanning the room. There's a little bar in the corner that seems to be filling up by the minute. It's mostly younger people. They're laughing and having a good time, at least as far as I can tell. I'd hoped I'd meet some new friends while I was here. Maybe make some new connections. But Halbrook won't let me out of his sight for two seconds.

"*We don't have much time together, Daphne,*" he huffs whenever I try to sneak a free moment alone. "*We have to make every hour count.*"

The *maître d* at last night's restaurant thought I was Halbrook's younger lover, and Halbrook thought it was hilarious. He even casually suggested that we play along, placing his hand on the small of my back and invading my personal space until I moved away from him. I smiled politely and declined, feeling it wasn't necessary to point out that he was old enough to be my father, and even if I were into older men, I wouldn't be into pompous, arrogant, narcissistic artists.

Been there. Done that. No thank you.

Scanning the room, my gaze lands on the bar area once more. I've tuned Halbrook out for the most part, though I catch bits and pieces of what he's saying. He's talking about himself. Again. And I'm so bored I could gouge my eyes out with this shiny butter knife on my right.

"Would you excuse me for a moment?" I lift a finger to interrupt him before grabbing my purse and readying myself to prance off toward the ladies' room. Halbrook stares at me dumbfounded, his jaw hanging as if I've just committed a social faux pas by excusing myself in the middle of his story. But I don't care. I need to breathe. I need air. I need space.

He's probably wondering why I've had to go twice in the last half hour, but every minute away from this man is a godsend, and I'll feign a bladder issue as much as I need if it gets me some alone time.

Squeezing through the crowded bar section of the restaurant, I spot the line to the ladies' room and count at least six women ahead of me. Taking a spot in line, I grab my phone and check my texts. Delilah sends me daily updates on Noah, though I've yet to receive one for today. It's early afternoon in Chicago right now, but I know yesterday she said Noah was fussy and nobody was getting any sleep. They suspect colic, whatever that is. I just hope it's not serious. She'd tell me if it were. I kept meaning to Google it, but Halbrook has me so busy I keep forgetting.

I scroll through some old photos of baby Noah, smiling to myself. If I try hard enough, I can almost remember what he smells like, his sweet, powdery scent and the ultra gentle detergent Delilah uses to wash his super soft onesies. I can't wait to hold him again, breathe him in. I'm not much of a baby person, but already I love this little boy more than anything in the world.

The bathroom line moves ahead one spot, and I peer my head around the corner to check on Halbrook. His lips are pressed flat and he's scanning the room and checking his watch. He's annoyed that I ditched him, but I don't care.

Two women ahead of me are engaged in conversation, their faces animated. They're talking about a man. No. *Men*. Plural. French men versus American men.

"I love American men," the woman on the left declares to her friend, though she speaks in French. "They're so fast. I like it hot and heavy. I don't like to waste time. French men, they are too casual. Too laid back."

"But that's what I love about French men," the friend replies in her native language. "They're mellow. They don't rush you. American men try to rush everything. They sour the milk that way. French men take their time. They know how to do it right."

The women laugh, sipping their drinks and casually scanning the bar area.

The line moves ahead, and the women continue to compare and contrast. They're not wrong, at least in my experience. French men *are* laid back. They don't like to label things or rush the process. They're not in a hurry to make anything official. American men, at least the ones I've known, can be a bit intense. Then again, I can be a bit intense as well. I suppose it's just our "fast food" culture. We want things and we want them now. We don't like to wait, especially when we know the getting's going to be good.

A small crowd of people collect outside a window just past the bar, several of them smoking and talking, waving at passersby. There's a man with dark, ruffled hair, his back toward me. His height reminds me of Cristiano. His broad shoulders. His narrowed waist. His rounded biceps. The man is wearing a gray t-shirt and dark jeans, and he keeps his hands in his pockets while the two men beside him puff on thin cigarettes. My breath hitches for a moment, and I physically feel the tiniest piece of me long for that man to be him.

How funny it would be to run into him here. In another country. Thousands of miles from where we left off.

In that sliver of a second, I forget why it was I didn't call him back . . . why it was I chose to go my own way.

The bathroom line moves ahead another place, and I turn my gaze toward the chatting women ahead of me. When I glance back to the window, the three men are gone. My heart sinks more than I'd like it to, but I pull my shoulders back and pull in a deep breath and brush it off.

To my left, jingle bells rustle as the door to the bar side of the restaurant swings open. Two men step in first, one in pencil jeans and a striped Breton t-shirt, the other in a sweater vest and corduroy pants. I'm not certain, but I think they were the ones standing outside just a second ago. The door swings closed behind them. The third man, the Cristiano-lookalike, doesn't follow.

Exhaling hard, I tell myself this is getting ridiculous. I've been seeing him everywhere. Airports. Cafes. Shops. Places he couldn't possibly be. It's all in my head.

The bells jingle once more, and I can't help but turn my gaze in that direction.

But the second I do, my heart stops cold in my tight chest. The air is sucked from my lungs, making it impossible to so much as attempt to breathe.

There's. No. Way.

This isn't happening.

My mouth is dry, my face flushed. He's making his way across the bar, following his friends, but each step he takes brings him closer.

His associates grab some seats by the bar and then flag him down. He waves back at them, his mouth lifting at the side and revealing a hint of his bright white smile – the one that incinerates panties all over the world, I'm sure – and my heart pounds so hard I feel it in my eardrums. Nothing about this moment feels real.

My gaze is locked on him, and it's as if I'm certain he'll disappear into thin air if I look away once more. Watching him navigate through the crowded bar, I mentally calculate the distance between us and come up with the conclusion that he's no more than fifteen feet away now.

There's a thick, woolen scarf around his neck, and he yanks it down with one quick tug, letting it fall down his chest and shoulders. He seems happy, at least right now. And I wonder if any part of him misses me in any way. All things considered, we had a connection. And chemistry. And maybe we're not meant to be, but it doesn't change the fact that I've thought about him day in and day out since the day I left him in Scranton.

Licking my lips, I find myself completely entranced with Cristiano. He's seated between his friends now, saying something. I can't read lips, but I'm willing to guess he's speaking in French, and I'd give just about anything to know what he's saying. What he's been up to lately. If he's had any more "adventures" since I saw him last.

Cristiano eyes the bar, points quickly, and then leans closer to his friend to say something. A second later, he has left the table, headed even closer in my direction. His face scrunches as he reads the drink special hanging over several well-lit glass shelves holding polished bottles of top shelf liquor.

And then he looks away.

He scans the room.

My body freezes, well aware that any second now, we're going to lock eyes. He'll notice me. And he'll notice me noticing him.

And he'll look away, because that's what men like him do. They don't need to mess with girls like me, the ones who flee the moment they find some kind of red flag. He doesn't need to chase after me. He doesn't need to chase after anyone.

I'm just a small blip on his radar at this point. A girl he met once at an airport. A girl he drove nearly three thousand miles across the country with. A girl he knew for five short days of his long and winding life.

He'll forget me soon enough. Someday he may even forget my name. That's just how these things go.

I decide to look away. I don't want to know what his face looks like when it sees me – when it registers that we're standing in the same bar in the same restaurant in the same city four thousand miles from home. I don't want to know if he looks annoyed or indifferent or conflicted. I don't want to see.

The bathroom line moves forward once more, and the two girls ahead of me go in together. Fishing around in my purse, I pull my phone out in a desperate attempt to preoccupy myself with something else. I need a distraction, something that makes me forget how fast my heart is beating or how hot my ears are or how flushed my cheeks feel.

"Daphne." His familiar voice sends an electric shock through my entire body. I don't have to look up to feel his presence beside me. The warmth of his hand on my arm follows next.

Pulling in a deep breath, I look up at him. He's half-smiling, studying my face, equally as shocked as I was a moment ago. His dark eyes are lit under the dim bar lighting, and the space between us tightens.

"What are you doing here?" he asks.

My lower lip falls, but nothing comes out at first. I'm lost in his gaze for a second, trying to find my footing and pull myself together. I didn't think I'd see him ever again, and now he's standing in front of me, happy to see me, touching me, breathing me in just as much as I'm breathing him in.

"I'm here for work," I say.

His eyes search mine. "This is insane. I . . . I can't believe you're here. How long are you staying? You want to grab a drink with us?"

Just past his shoulders, I spot his friends. They're watching us, though they seem friendly enough.

"I can't," I say apologetically. "I'm only in the city a few more days, then I go home. I'm mentoring with this professor." I roll my eyes. "He's got my entire schedule on lockdown. Every free minute."

Cristiano chuffs, dragging his hand along his jaw. "Surely I can steal you away for an hour or two. I can't imagine being in the same city as you, halfway around the world, and-"

"I know, it's just hard to get away. Classes start in a week and a half, and I've got to make sure I'm prepared." I give him a bullshit excuse, though I think he's aware. I've taught before, back when I was in graduate school. I was a teacher's assistant, a studio assistant, and I taught two classes all on my own the summer after I graduated. This isn't my first rodeo.

"Where are you staying?" he asks, clearly not buying it.

"The Marmount. It's a tiny hole-in-the-wall place that has some kind of agreement with the college."

"I'm staying at the Four Seasons," he says. "Just up the street from you."

I nod, not sure what he's getting at. From the corner of my eye, I see the girls exit the bathroom. I don't have to go now. Honestly, I didn't have to go earlier either. Turning to the woman behind me, I tell her, in French, to go ahead.

"I want to see you tonight, Daphne," he says, squaring his shoulders with mine. Reaching for my hand, he slips it in his. "There's this little jazz club just around the corner from my hotel. Best trumpeter in the world is playing there tonight, and I know the bouncer. Come with me."

Glancing away, I begin to shake my head as I try to think up a legitimate excuse.

But I have none.

"Come on," he says, stepping closer, squeezing my hand. "How many times in your life are you going to be able to say you heard the legendary Stogie Williams play his heart out at the iconic Bleu Deaux Club?"

He has a point – despite the fact that I've never heard of that trumpeter or that club, I trust him when he says they're renowned. And this would, on all counts, be considered a priceless moment.

Smiling, I glance down at our hands, studying how intermingled they are, how naturally they fit. And then I find myself wondering if there's the tiniest possibility that I was wrong about him.

"Fine," I say, intentionally keeping my excitement subdued. "I'll go."

"Meet me outside your lobby at nine," he says, giving my hand another squeeze. He lingers for a moment, and then he lets me go, returning to his friends.

Flushed and strangely exhilarated, I return to my table-for-two, bracing myself for the wrath of Halbrook.

Taking my seat, I lift the metal cloche that covers my entrée and glance across the flickering candle to see that Halbrook is sawing off a chunk of his nearly finished filet mignon. He glances up at me over his thin wiry glasses, and pushes a hard breath past his nose, his double chin jiggling as he chews.

"I'm sorry," I say, taking my seat. "The line was really long."

"It isn't polite to keep a man waiting like that," he says.

My chest burns, like word vomit is churning, fighting its way out. Had he said "dinner guest" or any other like phrase, I'd have let this go. But I've had enough of his pompous, chauvinistic behavior.

Letting my fork hit my plate with an alarming clink, I scoot my chair away from the table and look him square in the eyes.

"Professor Halbrook." I say his name with a careful staccato. "I am *not* your date. I am *not* your girlfriend. I am certainly *not* some pretty little plaything sent here to hang on your arm and listen to you drone on and on about yourself as you charge extravagant dinners to the university."

The couple at the table beside us flicks their attention in our direction, stopping mid-chew to tune into the shit show about to go down.

"Daphne," he says my name with a brute cough, speaking to me as he would a misbehaving child. His beady eyes squint behind his frames and he sits up straight. "There's no need to cause a scene, young lady."

"Young lady?" I stand up, feeling the heat of dozens of stares as they land on me. I'm causing a scene, yes, but I don't fucking care. I've had enough of Halbrook's seedy behavior this week, and I won't tolerate another minute of it. "I am a twenty-six-year-old woman. I have a terminal degree. I am your *colleague.* And you will treat me with the same respect I have shown you."

All week, I'd convinced myself to stay cordial. To politely

rebuff his completely inappropriate advances. I'd been completely sure that if anything were to go down, he'd still be sitting pretty when it was all said and done, and I'd be blacklisted from every fine arts college in North America. After all, he had tenure and a whole pocketful of deans eating from the palm of his hand. Seaview College and its subsidiaries need Halbrook more than he needs them. And I'm just a nobody. They wouldn't believe anything I say anyway, and they certainly wouldn't admit to anything since that would set them up for a lawsuit.

I was dead set on not beginning my tenure at Seaview College of Fine Arts with a phone call to my lawyer.

But enough is enough.

"Daphne," he says, forcing a jostling chuckle in his tone as he looks around the restaurant, offering apologetic glances to our audience. "Come on now. Finish your meal so we can go."

"I'm not hungry anymore." I toss my napkin onto my plate and sling my purse over my shoulder.

Refusing to stand around and engage in conversation with Professor Caveman a second longer, I turn on my heel and show myself out, making a beeline toward my hotel so I can prep for my night on the town with Cristiano.

Flooded with nervous energy and a hint of excitement, I feel a smile crawl across my mouth when I pass the bar and glance inside. He's still sitting there, drinking with his friends. And in a fraction of a second, he turns to glance outside, spotting me.

His mouth pulls up in the corner, and he lifts his hand, his gaze holding strong on me until we disappear from each other's sight.

Chapter Thirty-two

Cristiano

My ears are ringing but my body is reeling as we leave Bleu Deaux. Strolling down the Avenue des Champs-Élysées, Daphne stays close, her arm brushing against mine as we take leisurely steps under a sprinkling of stars and city lights.

"What'd you think?" I ask.

"I loved it." Her face lights, and I believe her. She isn't just saying it to appease me. I watched her all night, noting how she leaned in, toward the music, watching her sing along when they played an old American Standard that she apparently knew by heart. Every once in a while she'd clap her hands, and sometimes she'd glance my way, meeting my stare with a smile that told me she was completely oblivious to the fact that I was sitting there completely entranced with her when I should've been watching old Stogie blow his horn.

He's getting up there in age. This may well have been one of his last shows on earth. But how many times will I get to have this moment? How many times will I get to be sitting in a jazz club with Daphne by my side, painted in genuine excitement, experiencing something so novel for the first time?

"I never knew you liked jazz," she says.

"There's a lot you don't know about me," he says. "They say a man's heart is as deep as the ocean."

259

She punches my arm. "Okay, little old lady from Titanic."

I smirk, meeting her gaze and loving the way her baby blues nearly glow under the night sky. Our shoes scuff along the pavement, and up ahead a busker plays Chopin on his violin. We walk beneath a canopy of trees, naked in their winter state, and a row of headlights whoosh past on the street, one by one.

Daphne shoves her hands in her pockets as the icy wind picks up, and I use the opportunity to wrap my arm around her shoulders and pull her closer against me.

"Why didn't you call me back?" I ask. I debated not bringing it up at all, but I have to know. And there's a very real chance that if I don't ask now, I'll never get my answer. This woman runs. She runs like I run. Shit gets hard, we're both gone in a flash. I'm not sure whether that makes us perfect for each other or exactly the opposite.

Her jaw falls for a second, her eyes widening. I caught her off guard, but I don't care. I need to know.

"It's complicated," she says. "A lot of reasons, really. None of which matter right now. We're having a nice time, can't we retire this conversation for another time?"

"No," I say, stopping beside her. I hook my arm into her elbow and pull her toward a park bench. Her hotel is just up ahead. A few more paces, and our night together will be over. "I need to know."

Lowering herself to the bench, she shoves her hands in her coat pockets and stares ahead, blowing a frosty breath past her rosebud lips.

"You never told me Joey was a girl," she says, monotone.

Furrowing my brow, I shake my head. "So?"

Daphne's gaze falls to the sidewalk. "When we were driving, every time we'd talk about that wedding you were going to, you'd act really irritated, and you'd mentioned you didn't want them to get married. You even said you'd stop it if you could. That they were all wrong for each other. I didn't think anything of it until I looked you up on Facebook." She rolls her eyes. "And I saw that Joey was a girl, and I realized that you didn't want her to get married because you had feelings for her."

"Why would you think that?"

"Why else would a man not want his friend to get married?"

Leaning back against the bench, I chuckle through my nose and angle my head toward her. "Daphne. If you only knew."

"What?"

"You have it all wrong."

"Okay? So, what do I have wrong?"

"I'm not in love with Joey," I say. "She was my best friend growing up. We've been through a lot together. I'm just protective, that's all."

My chest tightens the way it does when I think about what happened. I don't tell this story often, if ever, but if Daphne is so convinced I wanted to stop Joey's wedding because I'm in love with her, then I have to set her straight.

Pulling in a long, hard breath, I tell her, "A few years ago, Joey and I were driving across the country together. We thought we could make good time if we just drove straight through, no stops besides what was necessary. We were going to sleep in the car, race the sun, that sort of things."

She gives me her full attention.

"Anyway, by the second day, we were getting tired. Energy drinks and coffees were wearing off. We both needed to sleep, but she needed it more, so I told her I'd drive an extra couple hours so she could pass out in the back." I take a break from the story, let myself get a few good breaths going, and then resume. "Anyway, I passed out behind the wheel. Hit a guard rail. Flipped the car a few times."

Biting my lip, I look away. And then I feel her hand on my shoulder.

"Car landed on the passenger side," I say. "Crushed Joey."

I sit up, resting my elbows on my knees, and hang my head.

"I was a little disoriented at first, but when I saw her in the back, freaking out, I climbed over the seats and stabilized her neck, talked to her until she calmed down and stopped moving. Heard sirens shortly after that. Someone must've seen the accident and called 911."

"Cristiano . . ." Daphne rubs my back, inching closer. "I'm so sorry."

"Joey never walked again after that," I say. "For the first twenty-four hours, they thought she wasn't going to make it. She had a lot of internal bleeding. Lots of broken bones. They couldn't fix her spine."

Daphne covers her mouth with her hand, eyes glassy. "That's awful. I'm so sorry the two of you had to go through that."

Huffing, I roll my eyes. "It was all her. She's the one who went through hell and back. I was the coward who walked away with hardly a scratch and then ran away when it got too hard to look at her. Not because of the wheelchair or anything, but because seeing her so . . . changed . . . it was a constant reminder that *I* did that to her. *I* caused that. She said she forgave me, but I still wasn't able to forgive myself. So I ran. I got as far away as I possibly could. And while I was gone, she met someone."

She lets her hand fall down my back. "The guy she married? The one you said was all wrong for her?"

"Yeah," I say, hands folded. "Honestly, I don't know him that well. I know *of* him. I know things *about* him, but I don't know *him*. All I know is he lived at home until he was thirty. He has zero ambition. He's a bit of a wet blanket, especially when you compare him to Joey. She's so full of life. Even now. But she's on disability with her injury, and when I first heard about Trent, I was certain he was an opportunist. Never once considered that they might actually be in love with each other for reasons beyond the exterior."

"You were just being protective of her," Daphne says. "I see that now. It's really sweet, actually. She's lucky to have a friend like you."

"I'm sorry I didn't mention more about Joey." I turn to her. "I just figured you'd ask questions, and I didn't know you that well, and I didn't want to tell you about the accident...especially when we were road tripping across the country together . . ."

"It's fine." Daphne rises, returning her hands to her coat pockets. "I'm sorry I assumed . . . anyway . . . this explains a lot."

"Oh yeah?"

"Yeah, like why you were so insistent on coming with me. You didn't want me to go alone. You didn't know me, and yet you wanted to make sure I made it home safely. Says a lot about you, Amato." She winks, her pink lips lifting at the sides, and I rise, standing beside her.

Brushing my hands along her sides, I watch our breath evaporate into clouds as we breathe. I'm standing in one of the most beautiful cities in the entire world, but it's been relinquished to background noise because I can't take my eyes off the gorgeous woman standing before me.

"I was supposed to go catch the train to Amsterdam tomorrow," I say. "How long will you be in town?"

"I leave in three days," she says. "Two more nights."

"I'll cancel my ticket," I say.

"Cristiano."

"I don't want to be anywhere but here. With you."

Before she has the chance to respond, I crush her full lips with mine. Her lips part, our tongues catching, my hand lifting to the nape of her neck.

"I want to see you again," I say, lips grazing hers. I press my forehead against hers for a moment, and then pull myself away.

Glancing up at me through her lashes, she says, "I'm going to be working the next two days . . ."

"Then I'll see you after," I say. "Even if it's a half hour, right before bed, I want to see you, Daphne. I'll take what I can get. So how about tomorrow night? Same time?"

With a millisecond smirk and lit eyes, she steps away,

walking backward and giving me a wave.

I'll take that as a yes.

Chapter Thirty-three

Daphne

"So about dinner tonight." Halbrook's voice creeps up my spine, and I feel his weighty presence in the doorway of the studio where I finish today's Feather Touch Technique lesson.

It takes everything I have not to shudder in front of him, and when I spin around on my swivel stool, I'm immediately smacked in the face by the overwhelming scent of his cheap cologne.

"Yeah," I say. "About dinner tonight. Forgot to tell you I made plans."

He scoffs, arms folded. "You . . . made plans? With whom?"

"An old friend," I say. "They're in town a couple days, so we're having dinner. I won't be able to join you tonight."

I spin around and stifle the satisfied grin on my face.

"You'll have to cancel them," he says. "I made us reservations at a Michelin star restaurant on the Champs."

"You'll have to cancel the reservations, Halbrook. I'm not ditching my plans tonight." I drop my charcoal pencils into my carrying case and pull the zipper snug. Placing my drawings carefully into a portfolio, I scan the area for the rest of my things.

One. More. Day.

One more day studying under this narcissistic nut job and then I can hop on a plane, head home, and pack my bags for my big move.

"This is really quite rude, Daphne," he sputters as he watches me pack up, "to leave me hanging like this."

"I'm sorry, I was unaware we had a standing dinner date every single night of the week." I sling my bag over my shoulder and tuck my supplies under my opposite arm.

"I don't understand your hostility," he says, puffing his chest out. "I've been nothing but kind to you since you've been here. I didn't want you to have to spend your evenings alone. I was only trying to keep you company out of the goodness of my heart. And as for last night, I figured you were just . . . hormonal . . . I'm willing to forgive and forget, Daphne, but you need to work with me here."

He follows me around the room as I gather the last of my things, though he keeps a careful distance.

"I could have your job, you know," he says, sounding every bit like a desperate, lonely, pathetic old man.

Stopping, I turn to him slowly and say, "Really, Halbrook? You're blackmailing me into having dinner with you? You want to go there? Because think long and hard about what you're doing here. Hell, I could have *your* job."

His jaw falls, his jowls shaking as he struggles to form his response. "After everything I've done for you, young lady, this is quite the slap in the face."

Pushing myself past him, I stop and say, "Halbrook, if you

so much as demand I keep you company again or if I so much as catch you looking at my chest or ass one more time, then you'll have the privilege of knowing what a slap in the face truly feels like."

With that, I'm gone.

***

"I feel like we've come full circle," I say, perched on the edge of my hotel bed. Cristiano uncorks a bottle of red wine by the dresser, pouring two glasses.

He brings one to me and takes the spot beside me.

"A couple weeks ago, we shared a hotel room together for the first time," I say. "And now we're here, in some kind of twisted, fated, random coincidence."

"I don't believe in coincidence."

Wrinkling my nose, I say, "Really? After all of this?"

"I think we're always somehow exactly where we're supposed to be." He takes a sip and leans back, resting on his elbow and staring up at me. I'm not sure if his expression is dreamy or if he's simply exhausted, but it's late in the day, and it could very well be the latter.

"That night you kissed me in the hotel – after I'd come out of the bath," I confess, breathy. "I'd just made my New Year's resolution."

"Yeah? What was it?"

"I wanted to fill my life with priceless experiences; the kind money can't buy."

He glances up at the ceiling and then back to me. "Okay, we're a few weeks into the new year. How's that going?"

Fighting a smile, I lift my wine to my lips and say, "So far, so good."

Our eyes hold for a moment, and then I catch myself studying his lips, his hands, his shoulders, the rise and fall of his chest. I drag the spiced scent of his cologne into my lungs and silently will him to touch me again because there's a very vocal part of my ego that wants to feel his body on mine, and it's refusing to wait a moment longer.

Cristiano tosses back the rest of his wine, emptying the goblet, and then peels himself off the bed. There's a cool space that accompanies his vacancy, and I watch him move back to the dresser, pouring himself another glass.

"What's this?" he moves toward my portfolio, catching a hint of a drawing I did today and pulling it out.

My cheeks warm, and I sit up. "That's you."

Turning to face me, he glances at the charcoal drawing and then looks across the room at me. "You did this from memory?"

I nod, biting my lip.

"God, you're so fucking talented." He shakes his head, studying the portrait once more. "I kept that one you drew of me, from the hotel. Hell, might even get it framed, but that might be weird. Nowhere to put it. Don't want to hang it on a wall, but it's too good to be hidden away in some junk drawer."

Cristiano pours himself another glass and returns to the bed, the mattress sagging slightly beneath his weight. Reaching toward the nightstand, I place my glass on its wood top and stretch my body across my side of the bed. Rolling to my back a moment later, I massage the back of my neck, rubbing away the aches that accompany sitting on an artist's stool for eight straight hours.

Scooting closer, he takes my hand in his, pulling it away, and he gently rolls me onto my side. Brushing my hair from my neckline, he trails his fingers along my shoulders before pressing his thumb into the knotted muscles just past my nape.

Breathing a sigh, I close my eyes and revel in his careful, kneading touch. A moment later, the warm sensation of his lips against my bare flesh sends a quick jolt through me. Eyes open now, I fight a smile and try to quiet the pounding in my chest. Every nerve ending is wide awake, anxiously anticipating where he'll go next.

I listen to him breathe me in, steady and relaxed as he peppers kisses against my flesh. He's taking his time, savoring each endless second that drips between us. And I am too. I come alive in these seconds, and while his touches may be skin deep, I somehow feel them in my bones. In my soul. In my heart.

Rolling to my back, I catch his eye, lingering in a gaze that feels like delicious eternity, and I smile.

Because I like him.

I like him a lot.

And I don't want to think about tomorrow or the next day. I don't want to think about next week or next month.

I just want to be here. Now. With him.

I'll worry about everything else some other time.

"I want you, Daphne," he breathes, grazing his lips over

mine. The curtains on my hotel balcony are pulled wide, and the city lights sparkle beneath a star-lit sky.

"So what are you going to do about it?" I tease.

His full lips pull up at the sides, and he climbs over me, pinning me beneath him before his mouth crashes onto mine.

Chapter Thirty-Four

Cristiano

I'm addicted. The sweet taste of her tongue. The soft scent of her skin. The clean fragrance in her hair. The way her body melds to mine. The sound of her heart drumming in her chest and that barely audible sigh she doesn't know she's making half the time.

I want her. And I want all of her.

Lying over her, her curved body pinned beneath mine and her hands traveling the length of my sides, grabbing fistfuls of my shirt and pulling it over my head. I kiss her harder than I've ever kissed anyone before. My cock strains against the inside of my jeans, raging hard, impatiently waiting to feel her warmth. Gripping her waist, I roll to the side and guide her over my lap.

Her eyes are hungry, flickering with the same desire she finds in mine. She wants me just as much as I want her, though it's not a competition. This is survival. Two broken, damaged hearts seeking refuge.

Bending forward, Daphne lunges for my mouth, pressing her lips hard against mine until our tongues meet again. My hand cups her jaw, guiding her, keeping her near. Right now, I need her like the air I breathe, like the blood that courses through my body and keeps me alive.

Leaning up, Daphne still in my lap, I rip her blouse off her body, my fingers on fire against her cashmere-soft skin. Unhooking her bra, she smiles, dragging her fingers through my hair and tugging on the ends just enough that it hurts so good.

Cupping her full tits, I lower my mouth, taking a nipple between my teeth and pulling it taut. She sighs, giggling, and tosses her head back, and when she sits up once more, she presses her mouth against mine, exhaling as her hips grind against my hardness. She rocks back and forth, impatient for the inevitable.

When she sits up, she peers into my eyes, her lust-filled blue gaze searching mine, and I cup the underside of her delicate jaw. Raking my thumb across her full lower lip, she smiles, uncharacteristically vulnerable for all of a moment, and then she covers my hand with hers.

Biting her lower lip, she climbs off me, peeling her leggings off her long stems and tossing them to the floor before returning to bed. Her eyes travel to my lower half, her hand moving toward my belt as she flashes me a smile and an eyebrow raise as if to say it's my turn.

The floor to ceiling sliding glass doors to her balcony place us on full display, but judging by the electric heat between us, it's the last thing on our minds right now.

Working my belt buckle, her hands brush against my contained hardness, and I slide my wallet from my back pocket, grabbing a condom and tearing the packet between my teeth the moment she unleashes my rock hard cock. Preparing to sheathe myself, I pause when I catch her beautiful stare again, her pale eyes silently pleading for me to touch her.

Reaching behind, I click off the bedside lamp, wanting to see the way her naked body looks illuminated by the moon and stars and cityscape outside. She's glowing, radiant, her curves highlighted in warm light, her angles painted in darkness and begging to be explored.

She crawls toward me, my hands sliding down the outline of her hourglass curves before my thumbs land at the two dimples above her perfect, peach-shaped ass. Daphne's hips sway, and she lifts herself onto her knees as I grab a cupful of perfection behind her.

Her mouth curls into a curious grin as she slips a finger between her teeth, and her gaze moves from mine to my throbbing cock. Within seconds, her lips are pressed against the tip and her hand gently pumps my shaft. Grazing her tongue up and down my length, she takes the rest of me, her mouth warm and wet, her strokes hungry and desperate to please.

"Holy fuck," I say, exhaling. My hands lift behind my head as I fuck Daphne's bee stung pout. Those lips . . . they were made for my cock. I fucking knew it. I want this again and again. I could do this all night. Her tongue soft and wet on my cock. Her hand pumping in perfect rhythm. Her lips dragging against my hot flesh with just the right amount of pressure.

If she keeps this up, our night's going to end a whole lot sooner than I want it to.

Settling against the headboard behind me, I hook my hand under hers and pull her up. She wipes the corner of her mouth and flashes a naughty smile, and I fish around the sheets for the rubber I must've dropped. I grip the base of my cock and pull her closer, her legs parting as she straddles me. The scent of her arousal fills the air and I pull in a greedy lungful. Lowering herself onto my cock and carefully sliding down, a soft sigh leaves her lips and her head dips back. With her hands braced on my stomach, she rocks her body back and forth, circling her hips and bouncing on her knees, guiding my hands to her ass.

Daphne bites her lip, scrunches her eyes, and then relaxes her face each time she presses her body against mine. I'm not just inside her, I'm consuming every fiber of her, igniting her soul, filling a deeper part of her that perhaps she never knew was empty.

Leaning forward, her white-blonde waves spill across her chest, tickling my face, and she brings her lips to mine again. I pump myself into her, meeting her circling hips and pressing myself deeper and deeper.

But it's not enough.

I want more.

Grabbing her by the hips, I flip her onto her stomach and crawl over her. Gripping the base of my cock, I slide into her from behind, aided by her wetness, feeling the resistance of her sweet, tight pussy as our friction builds with every insertion.

Arching her back, Daphne mumbles and moans soft, sweet nothings. With her face buried into the pillow, she turns her face to the side to catch her breath, her hair sticking to her damp forehead and her lips gasping, breathlessly, for air.

A tightness builds at the base of my cock, and Daphne presses her hips back against mine every time I thrust deep inside her. Her sighs grow a little more desperate, a little more helpless with each passing second, and when she grabs a fistful of hotel sheets, I know she's close.

Her jaw falls and her face winces a minute later, and she screams into the pillow as I fuck her harder, faster, relentlessly, and when I blow my load, she fucks me back, harder than ever before, coaxing every last drop and draining me dry.

When I collapse over top of her, our skin sticky and sweet, I slide my hand beneath her jaw, angling her head to the side and searching for her lips in the dark. Every place our bodies touch is lit hot with flamed desire.

I burn for this woman.

My soul needs her.

She's the only girl who can make me forget about all the bullshit. All the shitty hands life deals.

She's the only girl who makes me want to think about the future, and that's something I haven't thought about in years.

***

"You should call in sick today." I watch Daphne gather her clothes off the floor the next morning, her body partially bathed in a pinkish early morning light. The rest of her is covered in a thin white bath towel, and her damp hair clings to her bare shoulders.

Brushing a strand of wet hair from her eyes, she stops, stooped over with an armful of clothes, and shoots me a grin. "Believe me, I'd much rather spend my last day in Paris with you, but this is my job. I can't."

Taking a seat on a nearby chaise, she dresses in front of me, slipping on her lace bra followed by matching pink panties, and it takes all the strength I have not to climb out of his bed and rip them off her and have my way with her all over again.

God, she's beautiful. So damn sexy. I could fuck this woman every single day for the rest of my life and it would never get old, of that much I'm certain.

My rock hard cock rubs against the comforter, a casual reminder that I'm completely naked under these covers. Last night, I made love to Daphne, and she fell asleep in my arms. I'm not a romantic guy, but I can't think of a better way to spend a night in the City of Light.

"What do you want to do tonight?" I ask. "One of my friends is in this play. He could get us tickets, backstage passes too. You want to go?"

Daphne pulls a blouse over her head. "Cool it, Romeo."

"What?"

"Just stop with all of this," she says, rising and stepping into a pair of skintight jeans that make me want to bite my fist. "We have fun together. We have amazing sex. But I don't want this to be a thing, you know? You don't need to take me on dates. You don't have to pretend that this is going somewhere when you and I both know it's not. Just spare me the formalities."

"Taking you out tonight is not a formality. I enjoy being with you. I have fun with you. It's not that complicated."

Stepping in front of her mirrored dresser, she pats some moisturizer into her skin and then slicks on a coat of pink lip gloss using the pad of her ring finger. Meeting my gaze in the mirror, she says, "The other night, at the restaurant, these women were talking about French men versus American men."

"Yeah?" I lift a single brow, not sure where she's going with this.

"Basically, they said that French men take their time. They don't rush things. And American men are intense. They want what they want, when they want it."

I nod. "I see nothing wrong with that."

"Yeah, well, in my experience, when people rush things, they tend to overpromise and under deliver." She clicks the lid to her lip gloss, spinning to face me. "And that's how people get hurt."

"I'm not going to hurt you, Daphne," I promise. "Now get to work, and I'll see you at seven. And stop acting like you're not excited."

Chapter Thirty-Five

Daphne

My body shivers so hard I can barely speak as I wait beneath the theatre awning. His friend's play just let out, and Cristiano's attempting to hail a cab, but the ones that have passed so far are either not in service or it's raining so hard they can't see us. Or they don't want to stop and have two rain-soaked passengers drench their backseat. I'm not quite sure, all I know is I've never had this hard of a time catching a lift in Manhattan.

I watch as he tries, in vain, to hail the tenth taxi of the night.

"It's okay," I yell out, though with the city traffic I doubt he can hear me.

He lifts his arm, watching another go past, and then he jams his hands in his pockets and runs back to me. January is the wettest month of the year in Paris. The coldest too.

"I'm sorry," he says, dragging his palms up and down my arms. "You're shivering. God, here. Take my coat."

"No, no. You need your coat." I refuse his gesture.

"We could always wait for the rain to stop."

"Could be hours," I say.

"I'm sure we can find a café or something. I could've

sworn there was an all night coffee shop just around the corner."

He takes my hand, pulling me behind him, and we run-walk to the next street corner, dashing over puddles and laughing as we dart through passersby and in between parked cars. This feels like a mad dash, a game of sorts, but before I'm aware of how long we've been running, we spot a well-lit café half a block ahead. From the outside, I spot the cozy glow of a fireplace and spot a gathering of soft furnishings beside it. Following Cristiano's lead, we make a run for it and enter the establishment looking soaked clear through to our bones.

My makeup is melted, my hair is sticking to my face, and my clothes are clinging to my shivering body, but damn if Cristiano doesn't look at me like I'm the most beautiful thing he's ever seen.

He pulls me aside, away from the draft of the door that threatens to freeze us on the spot with each patron's coming and going, and he wraps me in his arms. Peering down, I meet his gaze, losing myself temporarily, until he presses his mouth against mine. And in that moment, I find myself again. I'm ejected into the present moment. Here. With him.

But as beautiful and wonderful and magical as this moment is, deep down, I know it's only temporary. We're blinded by the romance of Paris. By the thrill of exploring an exciting city with a familiar face. By the promise of new love that we know will lose that 'new car smell' the second we set foot on home soil.

If it could always be this grand with him, I'd consider giving him another chance. Making it work. Seeing where this might lead. But the fact of the matter is, when we take the chemistry and the happenstance out of the equation, we're just a couple of lost souls floating in two entirely different directions.

This time next week, I'll be moving to California to start my teaching career, and he'll be . . . well, he'll be anywhere he chooses to be.

He's an adventurous soul. And I can't take that away from him. I can't clip his wings.

Cristiano slips his hand in mine, leading me to the bar where he orders us two piping hot drinks, and then we find a place by the fire, a cozy little loveseat. We remove our jackets and shoes, placing them by the glowing flames in hopes they'll be a little drier by the time the rain dies down and we have to prepare ourselves for the walk back to my hotel.

The sound of crackling wood and a rustic, smoky scent reminds me of home, of camping at our lake house as a young girl, and I find myself briefly fantasizing about what it would be like to bring him home and introduce him to my family. They'd love him, that much I know. He's charismatic and friendly. Wordly and interesting.

But I force myself to snap out of it. The present moment is where I need to be because there is no future for us.

And there could never be.

Chapter Thirty-six

Cristiano

It's two in the morning and I'm wide awake, listening to the sound of the rain slicking the hotel room windows, its gentle tapping a lullaby of sorts but not enough to lure me to sleep. Daphne lies on her side, one arm tucked beneath her and the other stretched across my chest.

Two hours ago, we burst into this room, tore off each other's rain-soaked clothes, and immediately proceeded to do what we do best. I fucked her against the wall. On the bed. Against the glass of the balcony. I could go again if she'd let me, but her warm body melted against mine is a sure sign that she's spent.

"I fly home tomorrow morning," she says with a sigh, trailing her fingernails softly down the center of my chest. "I'll leave tomorrow, spend a few days at home, and then pack up and head west."

"I was planning on spending next week in Amsterdam, but I'll come home a week early," I say. "I promised my mom I'd spend more time at home anyway."

She releases a breathy laugh. "Don't leave just because I'm leaving."

"I want to see you before you move." I tuck my hand beneath my head, staring up at the ceiling. "I came clean to my mom about law school and not graduating."

Daphne rolls to her stomach, sliding her hand under her chin and resting them on my chest. "Oh, yeah? How'd she take it?"

"Better than I expected."

"Did you tell her about Jax Diesel?"

Laughing and coughing at the same time, I say, "Yeah, about that. No, I didn't tell her. She stumbled across one of my books in the wild. Went to the Jax Diesel website because she couldn't get over the striking resemblance . . ."

Daphne giggles, covering her mouth with a cupped hand. "No she didn't."

Biting my bottom lip and cringing, I nod. "Yeah, that was a fun conversation."

"How'd she take it?"

"I don't know, honestly. I just wanted the conversation to end as soon as humanly possible. I think I blacked out that entire five minutes of my life."

"Aww," Daphne snorts through her nose. "Well at least it's over and done with. Anyway, can we be real for a minute?"

My gut sinks for a second. Nothing good ever follows a statement like that.

"Of course." I clear my throat, meeting her gaze.

"I'm moving to California. And you're always traveling. I don't think *this* is going to work," she says softly. "At least not for me. And I don't think we should kid ourselves. We're a little caught up in the moment right now, but after tomorrow, it's back to reality."

Sitting up, I lean my back against the headboard, my jaw tense. She rises to her knees, pulling the sheets around her naked body.

"Daphne," I say, "I don't know what I have to do to convince you that I'm serious about this. I want to make this work. I don't know how, but I know we can figure something out."

Her full lips purse. Whatever it is she's thinking about, she's keeping it to herself right now, and that's never a good sign.

"Do you want to meet my mom?" I blurt. "I haven't brought anyone home to meet her in years. And I'll catch a lot of shit for this from my brothers, but I'll do it. I'll let you meet my mom. That's how serious I am about you."

Her fingertips lightly graze her chest and she smirks. "You've known me since New Year's Eve . . . which means you barely know me. You're insane, you know that?"

"Maybe, but I don't fucking care." I pull her into my lap, letting the covers fall to her hips. She straddles me, and I run my hands up the small of her back as I crush her lips with a kiss. The sweet scent of her arousal fills my lungs, sending a throb to my cock. "You're addictive, Daphne. I'll do whatever I have to do to get my fix."

"Fine," she says between kisses. "But let's make one thing clear."

"What's that?"

"I'm not your girlfriend."

"Not yet. But you will be."

Chapter Thirty-seven

Daphne

"Need any help?" My mother stands in the doorway of my childhood room as I unpack from my return from Paris. A few loads of laundry and I'll be ready to start packing again for my move west. Fortunately I don't have to bring much since I'm renting a fully furnished apartment, and most of my things I can ship. I figured I'd bring two giant suitcases for the flight and FedEx the rest.

"I'm good," I say, offering a smile as I toss a wad of dirty clothes into a hamper across the room. "Thanks though."

"Oh, I almost forgot," Mom says, feet shuffling across the gray carpet. She moves to my nightstand, placing her hand on a small journal that I hadn't noticed until now. "Your father found this in the back of that rental car when he was returning it for you the other week. He brought it back, thinking it was yours, but I don't recognize the handwriting."

Cristiano's travel journal.

I remember it now.

I'd completely forgotten about it, and I'd only seen him writing in it once during our trip.

"Does it belong to your friend?" Mom lifts her brows.

"I think so. I'll make sure he gets it back," I say.

"Okay, well, anyway." She moves toward the hall, lingering in the doorway. "Demi and Royal are coming over for supper tonight. They should be here any minute now. I know we're all anxious to hear about your time in *gay Paree*."

My mouth pulls up on one side and I nod. "Of course. I'll be down in a bit. Just going to finish up here and grab a quick shower."

"All right, sweetheart."

The second Mom leaves, I abandon my half un-packed bags, close my door, and make a beeline for Cristiano's journal. We left things in a good place, and the last several days have been magical. He isn't coming home until tomorrow, and I'll be coming over the following day to meet his mom. Everything's happening so fast. Everything's kind of magical. But I can't help but feel like I'm waiting for the other shoe to drop.

They say when something's too good to be true, it usually is.

Cracking open his journal, I read the first entry and gasp.

July 3ʳᵈ

Cabo san Lucas, Mexico

I took a boat tour of Lands' End today, where the Sea of Cortez meets the Pacific Ocean. It was a sunrise tour, and I was in the company of mostly couples. Some honeymooners. Some thirty-fifth anniversary celebrators. I couldn't help but feel, in a strange way, that you were there with me, at least in spirit. And I really wish you were. You would've loved it. You always did love the sea. Anyway, the sunrise was beautiful. Streaks of pink and orange mixing with blue. Made me think of you.

August 12th

Brussels, Belgium

I met with my friend Anwar today in Brussels. Known him since my freshman year of college, when he was visiting on an exchange scholarship. Anyway, he showed me around. We went beer tasting and saw the Atomium sculpture park. You always loved art. Wish you could've been there. Tomorrow we're stopping by the Horta Museum and Parlamentarium.

I page ahead, flipping past date after date, country after country, and city after city. Each entry is written to someone. Someone he misses dearly. Someone he wishes could be with him during his travels.

Sinking into my bed, I close the journal, pressing it against my chest as I try to catch my breath. I don't know what this means, but it changes things. I feel the change in my bones, melting into a slight panic when I think about seeing Cristiano again in two days.

Flipping through the journal again, I look for a more recent date, my eyes unable to scan his writing fast enough when I find it.

December 31st

Seaview, California

Another New Year's without you. They just keep piling up, one after another it seems. And it never gets easier. Each new year always feels like a reminder that we should've been together, and that we'll never get the chance. Anyway, I'm flying home later today. Guess I'll see you soon.

I can't breathe for a moment. The oxygen has been sucked from my lungs and my chest burns hot.

All these entries . . . was he writing to Joey? And why would he do this? None of it makes sense. And he claimed he never loved her. That he was just protective of her.

The tromping of feet coming upstairs prompts me to shove the journal to the side. A few seconds later, my oldest sister Demi bursts into my room.

"Welcome baaaack!" she singsongs, hurling herself at me and wrapping her arms around me. I chuckle, and in an instant, I almost forget what I've just read. Climbing off me, Demi brushes her dark hair from her face, her smile fading. "You okay?"

"Yeah, yeah," I say, forcing a smile. "Just jet-lagged."

"Well, Mom's making lasagna and I think I hear the timer going off, so come on." She grabs me by the arm, yanking me off my bed. It's like we're kids again, though I don't mind. Life was a hell of a lot easier back then, that's for damn sure.

Heading downstairs, I promise myself not to let this little revelation ruin my time with my family. I'll think about it more, later, when I have a moment to myself. When I'm lying in bed, staring at the cracks in the ceiling. I need time to digest this journal, figure out what it means.

And I hope to God it doesn't mean he was lying to me.

Because I was finally starting to open up to the idea of maybe . . . just *maybe* . . . this thing we have going might actually be worth putting myself out there again.

Chapter Thirty-eight

Cristiano

"Hey, come in." I hold the door open for Daphne, watching as she takes a deep breath. She hasn't met my gaze once, and everything about this feels formal. She's dressed in black leggings and a white blouse, her hair piled into a neat bun on the crown of her head. Her bee-stung pout is slicked in bright red, a sign that she's not planning to kiss me, at least not anytime soon, and she keeps a careful distance from me.

She's nervous, that's it.

Cute.

Placing my hand on the small of her back, I usher her into the living room.

"Mom," I yell over my shoulder. "Daphne's here."

My mom appears a moment later, her white apron covered in blotches of red sauce. Wiping her hands down the front, she then quickly unties the knot behind her back and yanks it from around her neck.

"Hi, I'm Cristiano's mother, Valentina. So nice to meet you," she says, extending her hand.

"Wonderful to meet you as well," Daphne says, meeting her in the middle and smiling warmly.

My mom's going to love her, I'm one hundred percent certain. I dropped the bomb on her this morning, over breakfast, since I didn't really have a chance last night. I landed late, cabbed it home, and went straight to bed. It's going to be a while before I adjust to my new schedule, and right now, I'm tired as hell, but I'm excited for Daphne to meet my mother. She needs to know I meant what I said. I'm serious about her.

"Please sit. Stay a while," Mom says, pointing to the sofa. "Cristiano doesn't bring girls home to meet me. He doesn't bring anyone home, really. Heck, he hardly brings himself home."

Mom laughs, and Daphne glances at me, meeting my gaze for the first time since she arrived. She smiles, though I sense a bit of hesitancy behind her expression. I'm going to chalk it up to nerves, because the girl standing here is every bit as beautiful on the outside as the Daphne I know, but there's something off about her on the inside. I can tell.

"Cristiano tells me you met in California? That you're the young lady he drove across the country with?"

"Yes," Daphne says, sitting up stick straight. "He insisted on tagging along. I wasn't sure at first, but it worked out. It was nice to have someone to share the load with."

Her shoulders relax, but only slightly, and she glances my way again, this time looking as if she's studying me. I can't wait to get her alone so I can tell her to relax, assure her that my mom will be just as crazy about her as I am.

"I want to show you something," my mom announces to our guest before rising and moving across the living room.

"Mom, what are you doing?" I ask as I spot her digging through a pile of books behind the La-Z-Boy.

"Just looking for a photo album," she says, voice muffled from behind the chair. "Ah, yes. Here it is."

"No," I say. "No baby pictures."

Mom pouts her bottom lip. "But I had the cutest baby boys, and I never get the chance to show them off."

"I'd love to see Cristiano as a baby," Daphne says, smiling delicately, though I know she's only appeasing my mother.

The sound of crunching tires against our gravel driveway directs my attention to the front living room window, and I scratch at my temple when I see Joey's van pull up in our driveway. I wasn't expecting her.

"Who's here?" Mom peers up from her photo album, nose scrunched.

"Joey," I say, rising carefully. Turning to Daphne, I say, "Give me a minute, okay? I won't be long."

Stepping to the front porch, I make my way down the steps as Joey lowers herself from her van and wheels up the sidewalk. We don't have a ramp for Joey's chair, so we'll have to converse by the front stoop. It's been years since she's seen the inside of my childhood house, which was practically her second home growing up, and I'm not sure I'll ever get used to that.

"Hey, Jo," I say, shoving my hands in my pockets. "What's up?"

Squinting into the sun, she glances behind her, her gaze lingering on Daphne's car for a second too long before returning to me.

"I wanted to talk to you. You have a minute?" she asks.

"I've got company right now," I say. "But yeah, I have a minute. What's up? Everything okay?"

Pulling in a deep breath, Joey's lower lip trembles and she glances down and to the side.

"You were right about Trent," she says, her voice low. "I shouldn't have married him."

"Jesus, Joey. What happened?" I drag my hands through my hair, feeling my jaw tense. If he hurt her – physically or otherwise – he's a dead man.

"Nothing happened," she says. "I just . . . I think I married him for the wrong reasons, you know? After the accident, I didn't think I'd find someone. Someone to accept me exactly as I am. And then Trent came along. And yeah, he's not perfect. There are a lot of things I don't like about him."

She exhales, her shoulders falling.

"I settled, Cris," she says, looking up into my eyes. "I settled because I didn't think I had any other options, and it's been lonely these last few years. I don't get out. I don't go anywhere. People stop by, but they don't treat me the same. They act like they're visiting a sick friend. A shut-in. Or they treat me like a helpless baby. And Trent never did that. He treats me the way he treats everyone else."

"So what's the problem?"

Shaking her head, she smiles, and then her expression fades, bringing a tear to her eye. "When I was up there, saying my vows, I found myself wishing . . . Jesus, this is going to sound completely insane . . . I can't believe I'm even saying this . . . but I found myself wishing that it was you standing there instead."

"Joey." I bury my face in my palms for a moment. I can hardly look at her right now.

"When you came into the dressing room on my wedding day," she says. "a part of me hoped you'd be able to talk me out of marrying Trent. But then I saw the pain in your eyes. And I saw the way you looked at me. And when you said you always thought you'd be the one to take care of me, I knew you didn't mean it in a romantic way. And I'd never want to be a burden on you. So I convinced you everything was fine. I convinced myself too."

"I don't know what you're getting at here." I hook my hands on my hips.

Joey offers a pained smile, her eyes catching on mine. "I don't know what I'm getting at . . . I guess . . . I guess I'm coming to tell you that it's over between Trent and me. And I miss you. And I want you in my life again. I want you to forgive yourself so we can be us again. I just want things to go back to normal. And mostly . . . I came to tell you that I think I'm in love with you. And I think I've always been in love with you. But I don't think I realized it until now."

Her expression turns apologetic, and she chuckles, embarrassed. There's a pink flush to her cheeks, and her gaze falls to the ground.

"God, you have no idea how hard it was to say all that," she says, breathless.

"Joey." Taking a step toward her, I pull in a deep breath. "I don't know what to say."

Her smile fades, like I'm watching her heart break in real time.

"You know I'm always going to love you," I say. "But you

and me? Together? Now? I don't think that's in the cards for us."

"You met someone," Joey says, blinking away tears. She tucks a strand of chocolate brown hair behind her ears before crossing her hands in her motionless lap. "Ashley mentioned something . . . about the night of the wedding . . . you were trying to call some girl. I didn't think anything of it at first. She didn't give me any details. I guess I assumed it was one of those girls you call when you've had too much to drink. I laughed, actually, when Ashley told me because it seemed so typically Cristiano."

She glances down at her still hands pressed flat against her lap. Joey gets that way when she's upset. Her body tenses and she doesn't move. Even now, all the parts of her that are still capable of moving become as motionless as a statue.

"Yeah," I say softly, as if it could possibly cushion the blow. "I met someone."

"Okay, well." Joey looks up at me, forcing a bittersweet, close-lipped smile that sends an ache to my chest. I hate seeing her in pain. "Can I meet her sometime?"

Nodding, I say, "Of course."

"I should go." Joey chuffs through her nose, her cheeks pink. She's embarrassed I suppose. When she wheels her chair back to her van, she turns back to me with misting, smiling eyes. "Don't be a stranger, okay? Come see me more often, will you?"

Standing on the bottom step of my mother's front porch, I watch her load into her van. And then I watch her drive away, drying tears on the sleeve of her jacket.

Fuck.

Heading inside, I'm slightly dazed and still trying to wrap

my head around what just happened, but I force myself to snap out of it for Daphne's sake.

"Where'd Mom go?" I ask when I find her alone in the living room.

Daphne rises slowly, placing her bag over her shoulder and keeping her gaze fixed on the window by the front door.

"She's in the kitchen," she says. "A timer went off. She said she had to stir the sauce."

Yep. Sounds like Mom. I point to her bag, my brows lifted. "You leaving?"

"Yeah." Her gaze flicks from the living room window and rests unsteadily in mine. My entire conversation with Joey probably played out before her in real time. Doesn't help that these windows are as paper thin as these walls. You can hear everything through them.

Racking my brain, I try to play back my conversation with Joey, wondering if there was anything I said that may have given Daphne pause, but I can't think of a single thing. Joey admitted her feelings for me, but everything was one-sided.

Daphne moves toward the door.

"Daphne, wait." I follow her, placing my hand on the small of her back. "Where are you going? I thought you were staying for dinner?"

"I'm sorry," she says, reaching for the handle. "I can't do this. I thought I could, but I just . . . can't."

I follow her through the front door, half thinking this is a joke, half refusing to believe this is happening.

Letting the screen door slam against the house, I chase after her.

"Stop. What are you doing?" My shoes scuff the chipped and cracked sidewalk, every sound, every sensation from this moment magnified as if to offer proof that this is actually happening.

"Please, don't do this. Just let me go." Her voice is low as she glances over my shoulder. I follow the direction of her gaze and find my mother's next door neighbor, Fran Andrews, sitting on her front porch observing our exchange with watchful, unblinking eyes.

By the time I turn back to her, she's inside her car. Clearing my throat, I shove my hands in my pockets and walk casually to the driver's side window. I don't want to make a scene here, but I want to know what the fuck is going on.

Lowering myself, I say, "Daphne. Don't go."

She won't look at me. She only stares ahead. "Can we not make this a thing?"

"You made this a thing when you stormed out of my house for no apparent reason." I exhale hard. "Did my mom say something to you? Did she say something that upset you?"

"No. It's nothing," she says, her gaze meeting mine for a fraction of a second though long enough to confirm we both know she's lying. "It's nothing I want to talk about. Please just let me leave."

"Did something happen back home? Is everything okay with your sister?"

"Nothing happened back home." She starts the engine and

shifts into reverse, the car jutting backward in response as a soft clunk sounds from the engine. "I have to go."

"I'll call you," I say, stepping away and watching her go. Scratching my head, I make my way back toward the front porch, watching until her red taillights disappear over the hill.

What.

The fuck.

Was that?

Waiting until her taillights vanish over the hill, I slip my hands behind my head, give Fran Andrews a wave, and dip back inside.

"Where'd she go?" Mom stands in the middle of the living room, a wooden spoon coated in thick red sauce in her left hand.

Shrugging, I release a held breath and plop into one of the easy chairs. Resting my elbows on my knees, I stare ahead at the blank TV screen.

Mom frowns, taking a seat on the sofa beside me, her free hand cupped beneath the dripping spoon. "Did you say something to upset her? I thought things were going well. I really liked her. I could tell you really liked her too."

I shake my head. "I thought she seemed a little different when she walked in. Just thought she was nervous. Maybe something had been bothering her. I don't know." Leaning back in the seat, I blow a hard breath between my lips and add, "I'll call her later. She just needs some time to cool off. I'm sure once we talk . . ."

I don't finish my thought. Truth is, I'm not sure of

anything. Maybe she's back with her ex? The football player? Maybe she came here to break things off for good? Maybe she knew from the second she stepped foot in here, that she'd be leaving soon enough?

But that doesn't make sense.

If that were the case, she could've blown me off altogether. A lot easier to no-show than to drive a couple of hours to meet someone's mom.

"Cristiano," my mother says sweetly, reaching over to place her hand over mine. "Everything will work out the way its supposed to, that much I can promise. But in the meantime, if you really care about this young woman, and I can tell that you do, I suggest you fight like hell to get her back before she's gone forever." Rising slowly, she extends her hand. "Now come help me in the kitchen. The table needs setting."

Snorting through my nose, I take my mother's hand and follow her into the next room. Tonight I'll call Daphne, and if she doesn't answer, I'll call her tomorrow.

And the next day.

The day after that, too.

I'll keep calling until I get through . . . until I can get her to talk to me.

It'd be easy to hop on a plane again. Fly somewhere exotic. Leave this bullshit behind. But if I do what I've always done, I'll end up where I've always ended up: alone and convincing myself that I'm living the kind of Bachelor-in-paradise lifestyle most guys only dream of.

But it's not what I want anymore. Because *she's* what I

want.

And now I'm going to fight like hell.

Chapter Thirty-Nine

Daphne

I pull into my parents' driveway four hours later. I don't remember leaving Cristiano's. I don't remember the drive here. The radio is silent. The engine calms to nothingness as I pull the keys from the ignition.

I'm in a daze.

I'm numb.

I feel everything and nothing all at once.

I didn't hear his entire conversation with Joey, but I heard enough to know she still loves him. She wants to be with him. And I heard him tell her he'll always love her.

If that journal means anything, and if those words he wrote were true, he still loves her. And up until December 31st, he was still writing those entries to her.

It all makes sense. He traveled the world, wishing she was by his side, only he knew she couldn't be because she was with someone else.

But now she doesn't want to be with that someone else – she wants him.

Once again, I'm someone's consolation prize.

And I can't.

I can't do it.

***

Four Days Later . . .

"It's for the best, really," Delilah says into my ear. My phone is cradled on my shoulder as I hang clothes in the closet of my rental apartment in Seaview's Campus Town section. "Given your history with Weston and how much that nearly destroyed you, I can understand why you wouldn't want to get involved with someone who's still hung up on a past love. Nobody wants to be second place. Nobody wants to live in the shadow of the one who came before her. You did the right thing. I know it's hard, but it's for the best."

"He's been calling me all week. And texting." I hang up the last of my clothes and collapse on the lumpy bed in the center of my room. "Do I owe him an explanation?"

Delilah scoffs, and I hear baby Noah rustling awake in the background. "You don't owe him an explanation, sweets. You knew him for what, two, three weeks? It's not like he was your boyfriend. You didn't even break up. You just went your own way."

Earlier, I told Delilah all about the journal. About Paris. About Joey and the accident. She knows it all, and she's one of the most objective people I know, so having her in my corner should be reassuring, but there's still a part of me that feels somewhat unsettled about my decision. But it's probably the very same part of me that got my hopes up, that spent the last part of her Paris trip in a state of denial and optimism.

I wanted us to work out. As much as I hate to admit it, as much as I had to wrangle my excitement into submission until it was nearly undetectable, I really wanted us to work.

"Anyway, I should let you go. I've got to run to campus and print out my syllabi and drop some things off in my new office," I say with an exhausted sigh.

"You nervous?"

"Not really," I say.

"What are you teaching again?"

"Studio Drawing I and Introduction to Charcoal," I say. "Easy peasy."

"All right, well, keep me posted. Call if you need anything." Her voice is temporarily muffled, followed by the squeaky whimpers of Noah beginning to fuss in the background.

"Come visit soon," I say.

"I will."

Hanging up with my sister, I head to the shower, but first taking a second to clear off some old text messages. But in the midst of sending back a couple of quick replies, I pause when it hits me that for the first time all week, I don't have any missed calls or texts from Cristiano.

My chest tightens. I didn't think 'the end' of us would feel so . . . heavy. So dark. I thought cutting ties would be easier than this. But this is how it has to be. This is for the best. As life has demonstrated to me time and again, some things are momentarily wonderful and sometimes those wonderful things aren't meant to last.

Stripping out of my clothes, I twist the shower knob and step inside. The water is cold at first, covering my skin in gooseflesh, but I hardly feel a thing. I'm head-to-toe numb, inside and out.

And I miss him already.

I miss the prospect of us. The promise of something neon-electric intense. Everything we could've had. Everything we'll never know. Everything that wasn't meant to be.

Chapter Forty

Daphne

"Professor Rosewood," my teacher's assistant, Alexandria, taps my shoulder shortly before Studio Drawing I Wednesday afternoon.

"Yes?"

"Our female live model canceled," she says, her red brows arched as she bites the tip of her pencil. "Betty said she found a replacement, but since it was such short notice, she could only get a male. Is that okay? She said he's a professional model. Should I send him in?"

Taking a deep breath, I make an executive decision. It's only my third day teaching and so far it's been smooth sailing. This hiccup is only minor and definitely not worth getting my panties in a bunch.

"Yeah, it's fine," I tell her. "We're learning to draw the human form. Gender doesn't matter so much right now."

Alexandria's face lights and she nods. "Okay. I'll go get him."

Taking my spot at my desk, I log into my university-issued computer as the rest of the students file in and head to their stations. Checking my school email quickly before class starts, I send off some quick replies and clear my inbox. When I glance up, I see Alexandria strutting back into the room, a robed gentleman following behind. Glancing toward the classroom, I see all eyes are on him, though I don't see his face yet. This is nothing new. A lot of live models are very comfortable in their skin and many of them model for a living, thus many of them are attractive.

My students need to stare and gawk and get it out of their system, because they're going to see a lot of naked bodies this semester. By the time they're done with my class, they're never going to want to see another penis or vagina again. At least not anytime in the near future.

"All right, everyone," I say. "Settle in. Let's get started. We only have fifty-five minutes and a lot to cover today."

Alexandria steps aside, and the gentleman appears. He's looking at me – and only me.

That bronze skin. That shaggy dark hair. Those familiar, deep brown eyes. That charming smirk.

Holy shit.

Summoning every ounce of professionalism I have, I clear my throat and pull my shoulders back.

"He looks really familiar," a student whispers a few feet away.

"Is that . . . is that Jax Diesel?" her friend says, whipping out her phone and tapping her nails quickly against the screen.

"Please disrobe," I say to Cristiano, my gaze quickly averting. "You can stand up here, on this platform. Face the students and select a pose that will be comfortable for you." Turning to the rest of the class, I say, "Please get started. I'll be back in a moment."

Rushing to the hall, I drag in deep breath after deep breath, trying to compose myself before I go back in.

Was. Not. Expecting. That.

Chapter Forty-one

Cristiano

The rustle of paper and notebooks and book bags signals the end of today's class period. Relaxing my pose, I step down from the platform and slip my robe over my shoulders. Daphne is seated at her desk in the front, her stare concentrated on her computer screen.

One by one, her students flee the classroom, and I notice her glancing up for a millisecond, our gazes catching.

"Daphne." I casually approach her desk like it's no big deal that I flew clear across the country, slipped the administrative assistant in her department a couple Benjamins, and finagled my way into becoming her class's nude model.

She closes her laptop with force before crossing her arms and peering up at me.

"What the hell are you doing here? Are you insane?" She rises, stepping around her desk. "This is where I work. This is my job. You can't just . . . do you know how this looks?!"

Reaching toward her, my hand hooks her waist and I pull her against me. "Daphne, Daphne. Shh."

She stops berating me for a second, her baby blues locked on mine.

"All my life," I say, "I've run when things got too hard.

Things get uncomfortable for me? Boom. I'm out of there. But something changed these last few weeks, and you're the common denominator. That part of me that always wanted to run off? It's not as strong anymore. I don't want an escape anymore, Daphne. I just want you."

She looks away, exhaling.

"And you want me too," I say. "You're just too scared to admit it. You're too scared to give up control of your heart to someone else."

Daphne's eyes flick to mine.

"The men you've given it to in the past have thrown it away. They've taken it for granted," I say. "But I won't do that, Daphne. I promise you."

Cupping her chin in my hand, I breathe the sweet scent of her exotic perfume and it transports me back to Paris in a single fleeting moment.

"We both have issues," I say. "But if we can put our pasts behind us . . . if I can stop running and if you can trust someone with your heart again . . . we could have a life together. The kind we've been searching for our whole lives."

"I read your travel journal." Her voice is monotone. She doesn't blink.

Releasing a held breath, I take a step back, dragging my hand over the side of my head before massaging my temple.

"You're obviously still in love with Joey," she says. "And I don't want to be your consolation prize."

"Daphne, what are you talking about?"

"I heard Joey tell you she still loved you," she says. "Last week, at your mother's house. I heard your conversation. And your journal entries . . . they were all written to her. You wrote nearly every single day that you missed her, you wanted her to be there with you. Cristiano, you can't tell me you're over her because you're clearly not."

Pinching the bridge of my nose, I fight a smirk.

She has it *all* wrong.

"Daphne . . ." I begin to say.

"Please. Go," she says, stepping away.

Voices waft in from outside in the hall, and the sound of shuffling feet grow nearer until the doorknob twists and students for the next class begin filing in.

Daphne shoots me a look, gathers her computer and her bag, and navigates toward the hall, squeezing through the sea of students filling the space.

"Oh, I bet that's our model," a red-haired student says to her friend as they pass me by, their gazes zeroed in on me, enormous smiles on their faces. "Good lord. I could sketch that man for hours."

Tightening my robe, I show myself out.

I've got to fix this.

I've got to get her back.

Chapter Forty-two

Daphne

"Betty, do you know who put this here?" I stand outside the faculty mailboxes the following afternoon, holding a small leather-bound journal I found in mine. "I think it was put in my box by mistake."

I place it on the edge of her desk, hoist my bag over my shoulder, and eye the doorway.

"No, no," she says placing her hand over its chocolate-brown cover. "It's for you all right."

Arching an eyebrow, I glance at Betty then to the book. She pushes it across her desk, urging me to take it with me on my way out. Sliding it off her desk, I tuck it under my arm and head out of the administrative office. My next class starts in five minutes, but curiosity overtakes me. Stopping beside the drinking fountains down the hall, I flip the book to the first page, which is dated for yesterday – the day Cristiano showed up at my classroom. I kicked him out as the next class filed in, and I kept an eye on my phone the rest of the night, fully expecting him to call or text or even show up at the door of my apartment. But he went radio silent.

Until now.

My eyes scan the page, recognizing his handwriting in an instant.

January 18^{*th*}

Seaview, California

You're probably wondering why I haven't written in a few weeks, but once I tell you about the girl I met, I think you'll understand. I think you'll be happy for me too. I met her in an airport of all places, which feels fitting in a lot of ways, and I think you'd agree. We spent almost an entire week together, traveling across the country in a laughably tiny economy car. She was trying to get home to see her sister who was having a baby any minute, and I was trying to get to Joey's wedding. Anyway, this girl likes to talk. She may even be chattier than you were. And she likes to ask questions. She's curious – like you always were. And she got me to open up in a way that I haven't been able to since . . . well, since you know when. Anyway, it turns out this girl is into traveling and adventure, and there's this genuine quality about her that I've yet to find in anyone else since you. I don't want to compare the two of you. That wouldn't be fair. And you're both night and day from each other in every other aspect. But I think you should know that I'm falling for this girl.

It's time for me to move on.

I didn't think I could love anyone else after you.

But now I have hope.

And her name is Daphne.

While I'll cherish the time we had together and the love we once shared, it's time I let you go.

And it's time I let myself live.

Yours,

Cristiano

I don't know exactly what this means, but I now know the girl he was writing to . . . it wasn't Joey.

Flipping the journal to the next page, I'm desperate to read more. But there's nothing but blank, unwritten pages. With a pounding heart and a racing mind, I grab a cold drink of water from the fountain beside me, take a deep breath, and compose myself before heading into my classroom.

***

Ambling back to my apartment after my last class of the day, I stop at the corner and press the 'walk' button. Traffic is robust at this hour, most people just having left work for the day, and it looks like I'll be waiting a while for a green light.

Sticking my hand into my pocket, my fingertips graze the cool glass of my phone's screen, and there's a tightness in my chest and an electric swirl in my middle that accompanies the thought of calling Cristiano.

I don't know if he's still in town or how he got the journal into my mailbox today, but I can't imagine he'd come all this way just to leave again.

Pulling my phone out, I thumb through my contacts until I

find his name. I press the green button and lift the phone to my ear, my heart running wild and my mouth dry.

"Daphne," he answers on the third ring, his voice a low vibrato against my eardrum.

"The journal in my mailbox . . ." I say. ". . . we need to talk. You still in town?"

"I am. Here until tomorrow."

"Come over. I'll text you the address."

***

I pace my apartment, re-reading his journal entry over and over, trying to figure out what it means despite the fact that I'll soon have my answers.

A swift knock on my door nearly sends my heart into a dizzying freefall, and I lunge for the door, pulling it open with a clean jerk. I want to get this over with. I can't stand another minute of not knowing who he was writing to or why he left that journal in my mailbox.

Cristiano stands on the other side, a pale gray t-shirt wrapping his muscled torso and his hands shoved into the pockets of his jeans.

"Come in," I say, stepping away and then closing the door behind him. He stands in the middle of my apartment, eyeing the closed journal resting in the middle of my coffee table. Arms folded, I keep a careful distance. "You want to explain what that was doing in my mailbox today?"

He smirks, like this is some kind of funny to him, and his dark eyes hold on mine.

"Daphne," he says my name in one slow exhale, and then he looks down for a second. "My travel journal, it's not what you think. And what you read? I wasn't writing to Joey. I never was."

Taking a step back, I lift a brow, my arms crossed as I impatiently await his explanation.

"Three years ago, my girlfriend passed away in an accident," he says. "I never got to say goodbye. I was in Oregon, with Joey, and when we found out Amanda had died, we were rushing to get back home for the funeral. That's when our accident happened, and, clearly, I never had the chance to say goodbye."

My arms unlock, falling limp at my sides, my hardened exterior melting in real time.

"After the accident, and after losing Amanda, I guess I wasn't handling things well. I wasn't eating or sleeping. I was drinking too much. I was behaving recklessly." He shakes his head, eyes squinting as if he's recalling a dark time. "One of my friends convinced me to go to talk to someone. A professional. He suggested I keep a journal and write letters to her. I thought it was a stupid idea, but it was supposed to make me feel connected to her, I guess. It was a way to get closure. And he said I'd know when the time was right to 'say goodbye,' and I could do it pen to paper."

I want to move toward him, but I stand, frozen, glued to his every word, my heart in my throat.

"So I traveled, and I wrote letters to her. When I came home, I'd stop by her grave, leave a filled notebook and move on, starting another one. I must've filled at least half a dozen over the years," he chuffs, glancing away.

"Cristiano . . ." My jaw falls. I don't know what to say, but I'm sure it lies between an apology for his loss and some sort of words of comfort that could never be enough.

"I don't blame you, Daphne, for assuming it was Joey." He rakes his hand along his five o'clock shadow. "I thought about it some more, and I'd have come up with the same conclusion. You didn't know." He takes a deep breath. "But now you do."

"I'm so sorry." My hand splays across my heart, my body humming with a kaleidoscope of emotion.

Without thinking, I go to him. I throw my arms over his shoulders, and I bury myself against his chest. He doesn't move at first, and then his hands rest on my hips. The warmth of his breath skims the top of my head, and I shut my eyes, listening to the steady thrum of his heart.

"I was wrong about you," I say, my words breathless against his chest.

His hands slide up my sides, pulling me tight against him. I glance up, meeting his soulful gaze, my lips parted slightly. I want him to kiss me. I want a sign that all is not lost despite the rollercoaster ride we've been stuck on these past few weeks.

"Daphne," he says, brushing a strand of hair from my eyes. "I'm crazy about you. Since the moment you came into my life, you've flipped it completely upside down. You're the part that I never knew was missing, and chasing after you? It's been nothing short of an epic adventure."

My lips curl in the corners, and I rise on my toes, pressing my lips into his, melting into him when his soft lips take command of mine.

"I'm crazy about you too," I say. It feels good to own my feelings. To blurt them out loud. To give them life and not try to deny their presence. "More than you could ever know."

He hoists me up, wrapping my legs around his waist, his face buried in my neck, leaving a trail of fiery kisses along my collarbone. My arms rest on his shoulders, my head tossed back, and he carries me to the kitchen, depositing me on the counter and situating himself between my spread thighs.

"I can't believe I'm about to say this . . ." his voice trails softly as his mouth curls upward with a nervous smirk. "But I'm falling in love with you, Daphne." He takes a moment. "I . . . I love you."

My heart swells in my chest, and I press my mouth against his. The words linger, caught in my throat, bursting with a threat to spill out the second we come up for air. My whole life, I've been the girl who falls fast and hard and gets burned in the process. I didn't want to be her anymore, but being here, next to him, looking into his warm brown gaze, I feel it.

I couldn't deny it if I tried.

Cupping my hands around his shoulders, I pull myself away and whisper, "I love you too."

Running my fingers through his hair, there's a pulsing warmth between my thighs that quivers in anticipation, my heart rapid-firing as his fingers work the button of my jeans.

"I love you. But right now I need you, Daphne," he breathes, impatiently tugging on my zipper. His lips press against my collarbone, and I feel him softly inhale against my flesh. "I have to have you."

PRICELESS

Chapter Forty-three

Daphne

"You know, if you were any other guy, I'd be extremely creeped out by what you pulled off yesterday. Today too." I nuzzle my cheek against his bare chest as we lay in my bed that night, tangled in sheets. We started in the kitchen, made a detour to the living room, and finished in my bed. "I still don't know how you pulled those off."

He grins, his fingertips grazing the backside of my arms.

"Who did you bribe?" I ask, half teasing. He doesn't answer. "Oh, my god. You bribed someone. Was it Betty?"

Shrugging, he settles into the pile of pillows behind him, tucking his free hand behind his head and staring at the ceiling. He's glowing. I am too. I feel it. There's a slick heat between my thighs, and my sex still pulses with tiny aftershocks of pleasure.

"Regardless, that was a bold, bold move, Amato," I say. "But promise me something, will you?"

"Sure."

"Since I work here, please don't bribe any more administrative professionals. Given your track record, I'd say you have a knack for it, but I kind of want to keep my job, so . . ."

"You got it."

Cristiano rolls to his side, scooping me in his arms and pulling my body against his. I love his warmth and the way my body molds perfectly to his.

"You sure this is what you want?" I ask, wincing, knowing he's going to be annoyed with my question. Clearly, given his grand gestures and all, this is what he wants. *I* am what he wants. But I don't think he's examining the big picture here. "I only ask because I'm planting roots here, and you're a free bird, and I don't want to be the one to clip your wings."

"Ridiculous metaphors aside, I told you, we'll make this work."

"Okay, but how? I can't exactly pack my bags on a Wednesday and fly to Belize on a whim as much as I would absolutely love to."

"You get spring break, right? And summer vacation. Fall break. Thanksgiving. Christmas. President's Day? Labor Day?"

"Yeah, something like that."

"Okay, then. We'll do our local getaways on the weekends. We'll travel nationally during extended breaks, and we'll do our big travels in the summer." He kisses the top of my head. "So, I'll have to stick to a schedule for once in my life. Big deal."

Burying my smile into the curve of his neck, I breathe him in and slip my hand beneath his arm.

I love this man.

But I don't want to rush this. I want to savor it. I want to make it last. And if that means taking my time, then so be it. But something tells me he won't be going anywhere for a while. He'll be right here beside me patiently waiting for the day I'm ready to hand over my heart in it's stitched-and-taped-together entirety.

"Promise me something, Daphne," he whispers into my ear. The glow of the California sunset outside my windows has faded, and darkness falls around us.

"Sure."

"From here on out, when life gets really fucking hard – when this relationship gets hard, because those kinds of things are inevitable - we run to each other," he says. "Can you promise me that?"

Exhaling, I nod. "Yes."

"You know, for the first time in years, I've found myself thinking about the future," he says, his voice holding a wistful quality. "I hadn't thought about it for a long time. It was too painful. Almost as painful as thinking about the past. You think you have your life planned, you think you know who you're going to spend it with, and when that doesn't happen, it takes the joy out of wondering what's next."

"True."

"But you changed that for me," he says. "I can't predict the future. Hell, I can't *control* the future. But I hope you're in mine. I want you to be in mine."

Turning to face him, I smirk. "Remember that fortune teller in Colorado?"

He glances to the side before lifting a brow. "Yeah? What about her?"

"She said I'd already met my soulmate," I tease him because I know he doesn't believe in that stuff. "I'm sure she tells everyone that. I meant to tell you that you were probably right. There was nothing she said to me that gave me any kind of definitive proof that she was the real deal. She knew I was the baby of the family, but that could've been a lucky guess. Wait. She knew I was an artist too. I don't know . . . maybe . . ."

Cristiano's quiet for a second, and then he pushes a hard breath past his lips.

"What'd she say to you, anyway? You ran off that night, and I never asked because you were in a mood," I say, studying his face.

He rolls to his back, running his hand through his hair and looking straight up at the ceiling.

"She said my father apologized for not being the man we needed him to be. That he was proud of us. All of us. And that he watches us," he says.

Chills run the length of my spine, and my arms are covered in gooseflesh. "Wow. That's . . . that's pretty powerful. I mean, how would she know just by looking at you that your father had passed on?"

He's silent.

"So maybe she *was* the real deal?" I shrug.

"Maybe," he says. "But it doesn't really matter in the end. We're not supposed to know what comes next, at least I don't think we are. That's the whole point. Life's one big adventure. Nothing's promised. Nothing's guaranteed. There's an up for every down. And if we're lucky enough, the good stuff will outweigh the bad. And if we're even luckier, we get to know what real love feels like."

Cristiano rolls over on top of me, pinning me against the mattress. His hand tenderly lifts to my jaw, guiding my mouth toward his.

"I don't want to know what happens tomorrow or the next day or the day after that," he whispers, his lips grazing mine. "I just want to know you're going to be there."

EPILOGUE

Daphne

Ten Years Later

"We're here!" I call out as we step into the foyer of my parents' home in Rixton Falls. Cristiano dusts snow off his shoulders, and I shake it from his hair.

It's New Year's Eve: the tenth anniversary of the day we met and our seventh wedding anniversary. It's been eight years since he proposed outside a four-hundred-year-old castle in Tipperary. It's been six years since we embarked on a belated honeymoon to Bangkok. Five years since we had our first near-catastrophic fight in Sydney. Four years since we rode camels in Egypt, toured the pyramids after hours, and almost got caught. Three years since we were held up in customs in Moscow and lived to tell the tale. Two years since we stumbled upon a little orphanage in Costa Rica that opened our hearts - and minds - to the kind of adventure neither one of us ever imagined was on the horizon . . .

"Aunt Daphne! Aunt Daphne!" Our five-year-old nephew, Nolan, tromps down the hallway, arms open wide, and he jumps into my arms, wrapping his legs around my waist.

"Hey, buddy," Cristiano grins at Nolan. "How's it going? I heard Santa stopped by your house last week. You must've been a good boy this year, yeah?"

"I was so good, Uncle Cris! I was better than Noah!" he says. I stifle a laugh because I know it's true. Noah's been quite the handful lately from what we hear. "I was so good, Santa brought me Optimus Prime *and* a little brother!"

"*Mamá?*" A sweet little voice beckons me with a tug on the back of my jacket. It's the strangest thing having someone call me that, and while we're still in the getting-to-know-you phase, I've never been more sure of anything in my life. I don't know her favorite foods yet. Or cartoons. Or Disney princesses. I don't know her favorite color (mostly because it changes every time I ask her). I don't know how long it's going to take for her to adjust to this strange new world we've brought her to. I don't know any of that. But I do know one thing.

I am her mother. From now until the end of time.

"Yes, sweetheart?" I place my hand on her shoulder and gently guide her around. Her wide, deep-set brown eyes take in the sweeping foyer of my parents' house before settling on her new cousin.

"Who is this?" Nolan points.

"This is Lidia," I say, brushing soft, chocolate-brown hair from her forehead. "She's your new cousin. She's five. Like you. And she's really looking forward to getting to know you."

Lidia brushes against me, stuck like glue. She's been this way since we stepped off the plane from Costa Rica last week, but I don't blame her. I can't imagine this is easy for her, and at times, I imagine it's been terrifying, but Cristiano and I have devoted every waking moment to ensuring she's comfortable and happy and has everything she could possibly need to make this a smooth transition for her.

"*Lee-dee-ah*," Nolan says her name slowly, correctly. I'm impressed. He slides down my side standing close to his cousin. Probably too close. But he wears an expression of sincere fascination, and something tells me they're going to be fast friends.

Lidia nods, chewing her lower lip and tucking her chin against her chest. She's a little shy, and we knew that from the instant we met her at the orphanage in San Vicente. We first visited two summers ago, passing by the *Ciudad de la Esperanza* orphanage and stopping inside as we followed a trail of children's laughter. We spent the rest of our trip volunteering there, mostly building maintenance and doing chores like cleaning and laundry. Every once in a while, they'd let us interact with the children, but they needed to get to know us better, and they needed references and background checks to clear, understandable. A few months after that, we returned. And every chance we got over the months that followed, we went back.

Lidia arrived at the orphanage during our visit last summer. She had dirt on her face, dark circles under her eyes, and wore tattered pajamas. She was malnourished, frightened, and shy. And for whatever reason, she would only allow Cristiano to come anywhere near her.

It was an unusual bond at first, but the more time we spent around her, and the more I saw the two of them interact, the more we began to feel an undeniable attachment, and the more we began to realize that imagining a future without this little girl in it felt sort of . . . empty . . . in a way it hadn't before.

We talked it over, our discussions ranging from casual to

in-depth. But it wasn't until last January, when we were knee-deep in our usual routine, when we realized it was Lidia's birthday, and that she wouldn't be sharing it with a mother or father. We both wanted to be there, celebrating with her, showering her with love and confetti and balloons. We missed her smile. Her laugh. The way her tiny arms felt wrapped around our shoulders.

So we made some phone calls. We returned, yet again, to the *Ciudad de la Esperanza*. And we set the wheels in motion to make this little girl ours.

Delilah pads lightly from around the corner, a baby swaddled in a blue blanket sleeping soundly in her arms, and oversized house slippers covering her feet. There's a contented peacefulness in her exhausted expression.

"Look who's here-" she begins to say, stopping in her tracks when she sees my sweet little dark-haired angel. Her eyes widen before glistening, and she lifts her hand to her lips, sucking in a startled breath. "Daphne . . ."

I glance at Cristiano who wears a proud beam as he rests his hand on Lidia's shoulder. Lidia reaches up and slips her tiny fingers into his palm, smiling when he gives it a reassuring squeeze.

"This is our new daughter, Lidia," I introduce them. "Lidia, this is your aunt, Delilah. My sister."

"One of your aunts," Cristiano corrects me. "You have several."

"That's right," I add. "Lots of aunts and uncles and cousins. *Gran familia*."

She turns to Cristiano, burying her face against his wool coat. Scooping her up in his arms, she wraps her hands around his neck.

"It's a lot to take in, I know." I say, rubbing comforting circles into her back.

Delilah steps closer, her gaze flicking between Cristiano's and mine. "I had *no* idea . . ."

"No one knew," I say with a soft grin. "The adoption process was lengthy and complex, and there were no guarantees. We didn't want to get anyone's hopes up."

"So this is why you're on sabbatical?" Delilah says with a smirk. "I should've known you were up to something."

"Nobody knows then?" Delilah asks, giving me side eye. "Not even Mom and Dad?"

"Not a soul," I say, grinning.

Lidia turns her attention to Delilah, peering over her arm and clinging to Cristiano like her life depends on it.

Delilah steps closer, one hand cradling her baby and the other reaching toward my new daughter, then pausing as if she knows to take things slow. I know my sister, and deep down, she's dying to wrap her arms around this child and give her a warm, Rosewood welcome, but the licensed therapist in her knows it's best to wait until Lidia's comfortable with her.

"Aren't you the sweetest thing," Delilah says softly. "I can't wait to get to know you, Lidia. And I can't wait for you to meet the rest of the family. Your grandma and grandpa are going to swallow you whole."

Lidia's wide gaze latches onto mine, suggesting Delilah's message got lost in translation. I whisper words of comfort and she exhales softly.

"English is her second language," I say to my sister with a wink.

Glancing down at sleeping Nico, I pull the mink-y blanket away from his face and take a closer look. "Hello again, sweet baby." I was fortunate enough to be there three weeks ago when he was born. I was there when Nolan came into this world too. "I can't believe how much he's changed already!"

Delilah wears a tired smile, her eyes half drooping. "Yeah. He really has. Nico takes after the Rosewood side I think. Noah's all de la Cruz and Nolan's a fifty-fifty blend. But Nico, he's got a lot of us in him."

Baby Nico stirs awake, his eyes fluttering softly when he hears his mother's voice.

"Uncle Cris, I wanna show you my new toys. Lidia, you can come too!" Nolan slips his little hand into Cristiano's, pulling them all toward the family room.

"He sure loves his Uncle Cris," Delilah says, watching them disappear around the corner. "I told you about the framed picture right? The one he keeps on his nightstand? Every night, we have to say, 'Goodnight, Uncle Cris!' before we turn out the light."

"That's adorable." I chuckle, wrinkling my nose. "Where is everyone?"

"Derek, Serena, and their girls are in the kitchen with Mom and Dad. Demi, Royal, Beckett, and Campbell are on their way. Zane and Noah are in the basement playing video games last I knew." Delilah situates Nico, moving him to her other arm. "Did Cristiano bring his camera?"

I nod. "Yep."

Over the past several years, Cristiano's taken up photography, turning it into a full-blown career. He's officially retired his "Jax Diesel" persona, opting to be on the other end of the camera, only he doesn't just photograph cover models, he captures weddings, engagements, babies, and families. His photos are creamy and dreamy, using all natural light and candid moments. He truly has a knack for capturing all of life's priceless moments on film.

"Awesome," Delilah says. "I'm going to have him snap a few of Nico and his brothers together. Would be nice to get a few of all the cousins together too."

"He'd be honored," I say, following her into the kitchen. Peering to my right, we pass by the family room, and I watch as Cristiano sits cross-legged on the floor between Nolan and Lidia, surrounded by an army of action figures and little toy cars. The children are playing hard and giggling at something Cristiano just said, and I'm willing to bet their little imaginations are running wild.

Leaning against the wall that separates the family room from the kitchen, I spot Cristiano glancing up at me from across the room.

"Everything okay?" he asks, his dark eyes reflecting off the twinkling Christmas lights covering the blue spruce tree beside him.

Smiling, I nod toward the man who owns my heart and soul. I love watching him as a father. He's so good with Lidia. So patient and sweet. So doting and protective. He looks at her like she's the greatest thing he's ever seen in his entire life. I couldn't ask for a better partner as we embark on this thrilling, and at times challenging, new chapter in our lives.

"Yes. Everything's fine," I assure him.

In a few minutes, I'll bring my parents and the rest of my family in here to meet Lidia, and the day after tomorrow, we'll head to Jersey so she can meet the other half of her family. All four of Cristiano's brothers are in town with their families, and Valentina's cooking up a world glass, traditional Italian dinner. None of them know about Lidia either, and I know Cris is dying to introduce them.

While the anticipation of what's to come in the immediate future sends tingles and butterflies zipping through me, it's the great unknown that excites me the most. When we return home in a few days, to Seaview, it'll be the three of us. Me, Cristiano, and our Lidia: the three Amatos. And I have a feeling that whatever lies beyond that, are the most priceless adventures this trio will ever know.

THE END

Dream Cast

Daphne – Claire Holt

Cristiano – Joseph Cannata

Weston – Wyatt Russell

Joey – Nicola Peltz

Delilah – Nina Dobrev

Zane – Mario Casas

Bliss – Blythe Danner

Robert – Tom Selleck

Demi – Mila Kunis

Royal – Zayn Malik

Derek – Jamie Dornan

Serena – Jessica Chastain

Fabrizio – Julian Casablancas

Valentina – Isabella Rossellini

ABOUT THE AUTHOR

Wall Street Journal and #1 Amazon bestselling author Winter Renshaw is a bona fide daydream believer. She lives somewhere in the middle of the USA and can rarely be seen without her trusty Mead notebook and ultra portable laptop. When she's not writing, she's living the American Dream with her husband, three kids, and the laziest puggle this side of the Mississippi.

Connect here: www.facebook.com/authorwinterrenshaw

WINTER RENSHAW

Made in the USA
Lexington, KY
30 January 2017